To keep up with Lorraine Bradner's latest life updates, books, merch and exclusive release details, please visit her website and subscribe to her newsletter at **lorrainebradner.myshopify.com**. It's the only place you'll get an inside look at her life, collabs and a peek inside the crevices of her mind.

Make sure to follow her socials to interact with her and her amazing community:

TikTok: @lorraine.bradner

Instagram: authorlorrainebradner

Youtube: Lorraine Bradner

Editor: Mallory Day (MalloryDay.Editing)

Cover Designer: Len DeMar (lendemarllc)

Featured Biker Collaborators: Roaming.Gambit, YG_ressless and Yamacho.R6 (all bikers can be found by these tags on their social media accounts).

Trigger Warnings

Your mental health matters. Please review the following trigger warnings and make sure you're in a good head space before reading.

The trigger warnings in this book include but are not limited to:

Explicit sex scenes, violence, self-pleasure, virginity loss, sexual harassment, traumatic crash, medical episode, interfamily conflict.

You exist for a reason:

Suicide and Crisis Lifeline: 988

DEDICATION

For my social media babes who love faceless bikers:

Leave that comment.

Send that DM.

Because you never know who might be watching.

And I promise you… you'll never regret trying more than doing nothing.

What's the worse that could happen? They don't answer?

But what if they do?

Shoot your shot.

To listen to the playlist, please open your camera and click the QR code

Or you can type in Beneath the Helmet on Spotify and Click the Playlist by Lorraine Bradner

Chapter One.

"Charlotte! Charlotte Rose, hurry up or you're going to be late for school!"

"*Ughhh,*" I groan on my bed, staring at the ceiling.

I didn't oversleep. I've already been fully dressed, with make-up on, what little I wear anyway, for the last half hour. I just don't feel like going to school today. Senior year has been *a lot,* to say the least, and I'm ready for it to be over with.

Last year, I couldn't wait to be a senior. I had my college choices picked out for months, knew where I was going to apply, had my major pinned down, and started applying for scholarships to help cover tuition. I had it under control, like I always do. Everything was in order; everything was in my control, just how I liked it.

Then I became a senior and all my imaginary control flew out the window. Rejection after rejection flooded both my virtual and physical inboxes, each one a heavier blow than the last. Now, with the end of April fast approaching, time is running out for me to be a socially accepted human instead of a societal disappointment.

The only two schools I haven't heard back from are Wyvern University and Charle's College, but since everyone else has gotten their acceptance letters from them both already, I figure it's unlikely I got into those either.

I don't know what I'm doing wrong on the college applications. Is it because my family is too well off? I haven't been through anything that could be considered a hardship in my life so that already puts me at a disadvantage to stand out.

I've never had to go to the ER or been extremely ill. No one I've ever been close with has died or experienced anything significantly life changing.

Who would've guessed having an easy life was a bad thing? Turns out, colleges only want people with trauma. Not average people who were dealt the lucky hand.

Maybe that's too harsh... but bitterness has consumed me, gnawing its way into every crevice of my mind day and night, leaving me with a sour personality as of late.

Plus, all my so-called friends at school have already been accepted somewhere, whether it be an elite school or a standard university, except me. Even Julia, a B-average student, who barely slides in above their standard GPA acceptance rate, and has never volunteered for anything in her life, got into Wyvern University down the road. How did she get accepted into college, you ask? She had bone cancer when she was seven.

Now I don't want to sound heartless, because I'm not... I'm just frustrated right now. I mean, come on. How am I supposed to compete with that?

I've volunteered for the local dance academy, set up props during school plays, lead the theatre's operations team through an entire play from start to finish, have a 3.0 grade point average and run in track and cross-country... and yet, it still isn't good enough. What else am I supposed to do?

Ben was accepted into Oaklen, the elite school across the country, but he chose to go to Wyvern around here instead for a reason he won't tell me. He slacks off but he still, to my confusion, has a 4.0 grade point average. The kid was born a genius.

Sudden heat sears my cheeks involuntarily at the thought of Ben. My fingertips gently brush against my skin where they burn from the heat radiating through the pores.

Anytime my body produces a reaction, I have to investigate. I'm basically a curious hypochondriac without the fear component. My mother's constantly yelling at me for poking and prodding at bruises, swellings or anything that hurts on my body. Sometimes I'll even poke something so often it causes more pain because I'm attempting to uncover what the cause is by seeing if it still hurts when I poke it again for the millionth time. When I tell her it hurts worse, she always retorts, "That's because you keep poking at yourself. Stop messing with it and it'll heal."

"True," I'd say, doing my standard shrug and tilt of the head in agreement, finally moving on, having had my fill of my investigation.

Because of the nitty-gritty, curious nature of my brain, I've decided the best career for me to pursue is forensics. It'd be fascinating to cut open bodies to explore how bodily trauma affected the organs and cells and find the exact nature of death. The tiniest, most unexpected things can result in sickness, or the most minute chain reactions can cause our unexpected, untimely end. The whole process exhilarates me.

A knock breaks me out of my thoughts. My mother stands in the doorway, staring at me with a warm smile. Ugh, why is my family so nice all the time?

"Charlotte, what's wrong, honey? You've seemed down lately. Is it because you haven't gotten into any colleges yet? You still haven't heard from Wyvern and Charle's! Keep your head up, sweetie. As a matter of fact, keep your head up along with your body and your torso and the rest of ya, because you gotta leave now or else you'll be late for school. We can't have that tardy on your record after you've gone this far without one!"

"Ayyeee, zinger!" my father yells, peeking his head in from behind her with a wide grin slapped on. I roll my eyes, but a reciprocal grin appears, nonetheless. I can't help but laugh at their goofiness. I swear those two were a match made in heaven. Anytime there's an opening for a pun or a dad joke, they both pounce on it, never failing to make each other laugh.

"Shouldn't you two be getting to work as well?" I ask, hoping it saves me from enduring another dad joke.

I grab my phone off my desk to check the time but instead get distracted by the mountain of texts coming in from my usual person, *Benny Boy*. My lips curl, yet again, involuntarily upwards. A motorcycle engine roars by, causing the heat to resurface on my cheeks.

"See, even Benjamin is going to beat you to school, and you don't want that, now do you?" Mom shoots me a mischievous grin.

There she goes again. She's always joking that Ben and I should be dating but that'd be weird. He's never seen me that way, nor I him. And I don't really know what love or crushes feel like, but I imagine I'd know if I had one on him, right?

Avoiding her obvious implication, I change the subject.

"Yeah, yeah. Aren't you guys late for work now too? Make sure to drive safe." My arm sarcastically motions toward the end of the hallway.

"It *is* a rather long commute. I better jump on the train and get going." With a wave, she jumps on my dad's back and rides him into their office down the hall, shutting the door behind them to hide the rest of their giggles.

Chuckling, I shake my head at them, grab my bag and dart down the stairs.

My parents, both best-selling authors, write in practically half the genres that exist. Mom tends to write romance and horror while my dad strays more toward thrillers and non-fictional history. Although, she's written more books than him. He has a social life and takes more breaks than she does. She doesn't have much of a social life unless it's hanging out with me, doing press tours or marketing her books. That's most likely where I get my personality from.

I love that their successful careers allow them to work from home and make their own schedules because it's enabled them to be available for every sports meet, parent-teacher conference and important event of my entire life. So even though they make me nauseous with their sappy love and happiness most days, I'm extremely grateful for them and hope I find a love like theirs someday.

My phone vibrates, rattling my car's cup holder.

"You have a text from Benny Boy," the Bluetooth in my blue Prius announces as I pull into the school parking lot.

"Read," I instruct it, keeping my hands on the wheel.

"Yo girl, you about here? I saved you a seat, but you better hurry before Greta the troll takes it. She's been chomping at the bit to get a bite out of me, if you know what I mean. Hurry up and come save me before it's too late."

I burst out laughing as I throw my car in park. Benjamin Beltre never fails to make me laugh.

He's been my best friend since we were little. We met because our parents both used the same babysitter, although we didn't become friends until the day Cooper, the nastiest little boy, tried forcing me to eat dry dog food because he thought it was funny. Laughing, he shoved a handful of it in my face and tried to pry my mouth open to eat it, but Ben stepped in and saved me.

He pushed me out of the way, snatched the dog food out of Cooper's hand and shoved it into Cooper's mouth instead. We've been inseparable ever since. Well... mostly.

As soon as I walk into class, Ben enthusiastically waves at me and mouths the word "hi". I approach him with a smile and study him for a second, treasuring our born-again friendship and being back to normal.

He's such a rare breed of human. And by that, I mean he's a contradictory sociable loner who spends most of his time in the gym lifting weights by himself or riding his motorcycle which he's been riding since he was practically a toddler. His parents literally gifted him a mini motorcycle when he was four years old.

And he knows everybody, and I mean *everybody,* and they all love to know him. I guess I see the appeal... he's athletically fit with a six pack and a V-cut who's ridden his motorcycle to school ever since he got his official license.

He can't walk anywhere without someone stopping him to say hi. I always try to stand off to the side, but he pulls me in to make me feel included.

Well, when he's allowed to be near me that is.

Curious as to why there's the need for a restriction for him to be near me? One word.

Tree.

His on and off girlfriend. *Ugh*.

She's popular, a nationally ranked soccer player with abs of gold and calves for days, her dark brown skin seems to glisten any time she sweats, and her curly hair always looks perfect. If only her personality was as beautiful as her looks.

She and her friends have always been secretly cruel, bullying people quietly enough to keep it hidden from the adults, but public enough that everyone knows not to mess with them. I've personally only talked to her on a few occasions and none of them were pleasant. I'm not bitter about it, but I also wouldn't have minded if she fell down a storm drain and never resurfaced.

Anyways, when they're together, I'm blocked, and he's forbidden to speak to me. In the beginning of their relationship, it didn't matter. He would always find a way around it to see me in private for a quick chat to reassure me we were okay. After a month, the chats fizzled but he would still sneak away and give me a high five in between classes or stop by the computer lab to say hi when he could. That stopped abruptly once Tree found out.

Currently, they're broken up again, but I figure they'll be back together before graduation. So, I'm just enjoying the time we have together in the meantime. Even though the thought of losing him again twists my stomach in knots.

"Hurry!" Ben yells, patting the seat next to him, pulling me out of my daze.

"Good thing I got here when I did. I see it was a close call," I chuckle, trailing my gaze across the barren area of the classroom.

"You didn't see it, Char! She was circling me like a shark. It was only a matter of time."

As soon as I sit, he pats me on the back, *hard*, knocking me forward in my seat before turning around to his computer. I smack him on the back of the head lightly in retaliation.

Yeah, I don't think if you had a crush on someone, you'd pat their back. He definitely doesn't see me that way...

Mrs. Coxe rushes into class with her lab coat hanging halfway off her arms, revealing a shiny blue pant suit and purple high heels, and tosses it on the chair. When she doesn't have her lab coat on, she's always dressed to the nines, sporting high heels and a colorful business suit. I admire her style, but I don't know if I could ever pull something like that off. My style can only be described as "tomboy", rotating between jeans and a t-shirt or sweatshirt year-round. I can't even remember the last time I wore a dress.

Mrs. Coxe drops her phone in her hurry, accidentally yeeting half the papers off her desk when attempting to catch it from falling to the floor. The chaotic woman is always running late. In her defense, she's spread pretty thin due to how many subjects she teaches here. Computer class, chemistry, and calculus. Not to mention helping run the research laboratory at Wyvern.

"Hello, hello, hello, class. How is everyone this morning? Sorry I was a little late. You know how it goes. Please take out your textbooks and run through the exercises in Chapters 10-15. If you have any questions, let me know!" she says, rounding up the last of the papers from the floor and sitting at her desk to organize the mess she made.

Since we're seniors, and this is a fluff course we all took to earn an easy credit, we usually work through the exercises independently while she works on items for other classes.

Typically, I finish them within forty-five minutes, leaving me another thirty to do whatever I want. Lately, I use my extra time to peruse forensic articles, scour college sites or check on my outstanding college applications. Benjamin, on the other hand, always chooses to distract and mess with me the whole time. Much less productive, but that's okay. It's helped pull me from the loud thoughts parading through my brain telling me I'm a failure and not getting into college anywhere.

He buries his nose in the textbook and his black hair settles on his face, barely covering his brown eyes. He has the same haircut most of the popular guys have around here—a skin taper fade. It's shaved from the neck up to mid-way on the sides, with long hair on the top that he either gels back or leaves relaxed where it can be played with.

It's a popular haircut choice because the guys think it makes them appear "sexy" when they play with their own hair. Plus, the girls in this school seem to love it, which doesn't help the façade. All it does for me is trigger eye rolls.

I catch Ben watching me from his peripherals. He reaches his left hand out, the silver rings on it shining in the fluorescent lighting, and gently nudges my head toward my own textbook. He always wears a silver ring on his index finger with a cross cut out of it, and two plain silver rings on his middle finger and pinky that are linked by a chain. A tingling warmth returns to my cheeks and my stomach leaps into my chest at his hand in my hair. I'm going to miss that once he's away at college.

The corners of my lips fight turning up as I wander over the page, not absorbing any real information as I attempt to focus on anything other than his touch.

Chapter Two.

The rest of the day blurred by. I completely checked out in every other class because I couldn't get out of my head. Each person squealing with excitement at their acceptance letters further fueled the anger and self-loathing bubbling under the surface, fighting to get out.

Unfortunately, those seem to be the only emotions I'm in touch with anymore. Growing up as an emotionless zombie never bugged me, until recently. I've only cried five times in my life, and Ben witnessed two of them, one of them being in public. Crying at a junior high dance when no one would dance with me was a low point, but Ben was kind enough to leave his date to slow dance with me a couple times and made sure I was okay before he went back to her.

But right now, hearing everyone talk about what major they're going to pursue, how stoked they are to go to college, who they're going to room with, and their big plans for the summer make me want to stab someone.

Next week is May. No one *ever* hears of anyone getting acceptance letters in May, which means this weekend is my last chance to hear from any colleges. If I don't get in, I have no idea what I'm going to do, let alone how I'm going to show my face in public.

I pull open locker twenty-three and pretend to get dressed for track practice, sifting through my gym bag and all the crap crammed in it. Per usual, I wait until everyone leaves before changing.

Being shy about my body isn't anything new. I developed over the summer of my junior year, but my flat abs, small chest and thin legs just can't compare to what God gave the other girls my age around here. Tossing my small frame out in front of the other girls' voluptuous bodies wasn't something that enticed me.

I change into my sports bra and athletic shorts and stare at myself in the mirror in a futile attempt at some confidence building. Well, I guess having a B-cup is better than nothing. I turn to the side and stare at my small waist, six pack and petite butt.

My mother says my petite figure is "cute". I disagree. *I* think it keeps me looking like a little girl which can't possibly be attractive to guys. I brush off the thought and pull my long brunette hair into a high ponytail, taking a deep breath to clear my ruminations before going to the track field.

Ben typically stays around after school to either watch me practice or lift weights but a quick scan around the stadium and behind the bleachers tells me he isn't here.

Is he with Tree?

I sigh at the intrusive assumption.

Their relationship has become a spectacle everyone's invested in. The question as of late? Will they get back together before graduation or finally break up for good this time? Thankfully she was accepted into Patron University which is five hours away from here so the odds are in my favor.

I hope beyond hope they're done. He's completely miserable when he's with her so I don't know why he keeps going back. He tells me each time he dates her again that he wishes he wouldn't, but it's like she has a death grip on him. I once joked she invoked some witch curse on him, but then I heard the truth and realized it was nothing so nefarious. It was sex. And since sex forms not only a physical bond, but an emotional one that's hard to break... leaving someone behind who you did it with can be challenging. Something in how our brain chemistry works or whatever. Or maybe he's just weak, I don't know.

Regardless of the reality of it, I *loathed* to my core that he wasted his first time on her.

I walk over to a group of my teammates who're standing in a tight circle on the grass in the middle of the track field with their heads bowed down. Shirley turns around and smiles at me when I try to peek over her shoulder.

"Hey, Charlie!"

"Hey. What's everyone looking at?"

She motions me into the group and points at Kate's phone.

Ahhh. Him.

Kate restarts the video on her Xypher social media app right when I lean forward to see better. Last month, this guy randomly appeared on social media, taking the school by storm. And when I say *took the school by storm*, I mean took the *girls* at this school by storm. Their obsession with him is beyond unhealthy.

The video plays on repeat as an insanely hot guy, from what I can tell, dances seductively in a motorcycle helmet. He keeps his identity a secret—no one can figure out who he is, how old he is, or if he's even in school. His anonymity is the only thing that keeps him hot... or it could be the tight black shirt and grey sweatpants he wears in most of his vids.

Thus far, I've avoided creating an account on the app, so the only time I've watched him is when other girls show him to me on their phones.

"Isn't he *so* hot? I mean his biceps practically rip his T-shirt sleeves every time he flexes, and you can *totally* tell he's got a six pack under there! Ugh, and his tan skin? *So.* Fucking. Hot," Shirley gushes with a girlish squeal.

I roll my eyes in response. "Sure, Shirl."

Weaving my way out of the circle, I step back far enough so I can speak to the entire team.

"Are we gonna get started or what? Let's go!" I yell at the girls, beginning our warm-ups with high knees down the field.

Coach named me team captain, which means I lead warm-ups on the days he runs late. People call me a goody-goody for it, but I don't care. In fact, I secretly love it. Being a teacher's pet makes me unpopular with my peers, but I'm the one who gains the perk of getting out of study halls and boring classes to hang out with whatever teacher I want. No one else has ever gotten to do that before.

All the girls groan, angrily throwing their phones in the grass, but they comply and file in behind me, nonetheless. They think I'm annoying but keep it to themselves when I'm right in front of them, although their hushed words behind my back do reach my ears at times. Their typical favorite criticisms are, "know-it-all, goody-two-shoes, weirdo"—you know, nothing original.

I've never had the courage to confront any of them about it. Plus, what good would it do anyways? We graduate in a month, which means I'll hopefully never see these people again. I just have to put a brave face on and get through it.

Coach Lukas jogs up to the track, hands on his knees, panting dramatically.

"Made it!"

He flings his head up, revealing a grin that moves the long stubble on his face upwards. We've never seen him fully clean shaven but that's probably for the best. If we did, we might assume he was a student. He graduated college a few years ago, but they hired him as our coach this year because he was a nationally ranked runner during his time here. Not to mention they couldn't find anyone else to do the job.

He catches his breath enough to blow the whistle and round us up. It took less than one minute for him to recover, already breathing normally after literally running five miles from work to here. That's how much of a beast this guy is.

I don't understand why he chose to be a coach here instead of trying out for the Olympics. The rumor circulating is that when he married his wife during college, they decided not to pursue it, choosing to have a family and travel together instead. Sadly, it didn't work out for them. They can barely afford to go anywhere on their salary with their family of four, even sharing one car. On Tuesdays and Fridays, she has the car, which results in him running here after work. His situation sounds sad to me, but he's always positive and happy. I'll never understand it. I would never give up on my goals or dreams for a relationship, but that's just me.

"Alright, ladies. Huddle-up! Today we're starting with four rounds of 40-meter resistance sprints. Partner up and make three rows. After that, we're doing four rounds of 50-meter unresisted sprints. These will be timed. If you break your past record time, then you don't have to do the extra weightlifting homework for the weekend." He briefly glances over in my direction before shouting, "Charlotte and Shirley, grab the resistance equipment, please!"

More groaning fills the air as the girls line up into rows while Shirley and I make our way to the equipment barn.

Our past coaches never required us to weightlift, but he mandates it, even making us do it on the weekends.

I shouldn't complain, our team *is* better than it was last year, but the underclassmen are the ones who'll benefit from this program. There's not enough time for it to benefit the seniors. Cross-country's more my sport anyways, but that season already ended, and I never made a stir or broke any records.

Average like always.

My shoulders slump forward in self-pity.

I walk in silence next to Shirley who continues to talk my ear off about the biker boy and how hot our coach is. It's not much of a change from her usual topic—hot actors. She's never had a boyfriend, but she's had her first kiss and messed around with a couple of guys at some parties.

I wouldn't call her experienced, but she's definitely not innocent. She should be more careful about who she lends her body to or she's going to be the next teenage pregnancy statistic.

The rest of practice dragged on. I didn't beat any past records, but Kate and Laure did. They're two of our freshmen who contain enormous amounts of potential. I guarantee they're going to make state and be nationally ranked by the time they're my age. Jealousy surges deep within, but I remind my brain I can never be them so why stress over it?

When practice ends, I search for Ben one last time, but his bike isn't here. Hopefully he just went home already. He lives in the country on a farm about ten minutes away from my house and twenty minutes from school.

Ben's independent, even more than me. Between never being in trouble, getting good grades and how focused his parents are on farm work and their side business endeavors, they pretty much leave him to his own devices. His parents own a local butcher shop in town where everyone buys their antibiotic-free meat and another small store where they sell fresh homemade ice cream, butter and milk. It's great food but it takes up a lot of their time. They don't make him a lower priority out of ignorance or not caring for him, but he gets put to the wayside more than a kid should. Sometimes I feel bad for him, but he's never told me their actions bug him. He's an only child so he likes being a loner, or so he says. Who am I to question that?

I can't relate to him in the slightest, in that regard. My parents are my best friends and never miss anything, always showing up for me no matter how big or small the moment. They're the most supportive parents in the world. That's probably another reason why I'm okay not having anyone else close in my life besides Ben. Who I have is enough for me. Why complicate it?

I pull into the driveway and park in the garage. My parents always leave a space for me so I don't get rained on if the weather's crap. Living in Washington, we're always prepared for pop up rain showers. Although, my hometown, Roslyn, is one of the drier towns in this state, we still get thirty percent more rain than the rest of the United States.

On cue, a roll of thunder claps overhead.

Sigh.

At least the rain waited until *after* practice this time. I hate running in wet shorts. Even though I'm slender, my thighs still chaff so much when I run, it's unreal. I can't imagine being one of the girls with thick thighs who deal with it on a regular basis. That would suck.

Huh, Dad isn't home.

It's unusual his car's gone at this hour but maybe he had a late meeting today. He's usually in the kitchen waiting to greet me first thing as I walk in the door so we can start the weekend off celebrating, but to be honest, it's a relief he's not home right now. I'm in no mood to celebrate the weekend being here. I'm in no mood to celebrate anything, actually. I just want to lay on my bed and waste the days away until I figure out what I'm going to do with my life.

I jiggle the door handle for the house, but it doesn't budge. Locked. Mom must be with him too. They both must've had a meeting with their agents or something.

Oh well.

This will make it easier for me to wallow in self-pity which I'm oddly looking forward to. I rarely get opportunities like this without them trying to cheer me up. Sometimes I just want to feel sad, you know?

My keys *chink* against the metal doorknob, a sharp *click* confirming the lock releases. I drop my keys on the kitchen island along with my backpack and spot a stack of envelopes and folders on the kitchen table.

Rain pounds on the window glass accompanied by constant deep rumbles of thunder. Lightning strikes dramatically, lighting up the papers like a scene out of a horror movie.

Was this our mail for the day or were these materials for their books?

Do I dare hope? Maybe this is it. This could be what I've been waiting for.

My shallow breaths mismatch my long strides toward the table, my heart thudding painfully against my ribcage. I inhale a deep breath to steady my shaking hands and grab the stack of mail. I sift through it slowly, tears welling up from overwhelming disappointment as each unremarkable folder and envelope drag me further from my dream.

About to lose hope, I shuffle through them faster until I reach the last one, a large manilla folder with a return address to Charle's College. All the other rejections were small letters or short emails. Dare I dream? Did I get accepted into Charle's?

My feet pound up the staircase in a hurry so I can be alone in case my parents walk in. I want this moment to myself so I can process the outcome in my own way.

I sit at my computer desk, intently studying the folder in my hand. The rough wavy edges reveal it was caught in the rain more than a few times, drying over and over again.

My shaking index finger slides under the folder's opening on the left side and slowly drags it to the right to avoid a paper cut. The stack of white papers idly waits for me to make my move since no words yet show my fate.

Deep breath. Either way it's going to be okay. I'll be okay.

If only I could believe myself...

My fingertips clasp onto the paper's top edges and pull.

Congratulations Charlotte Windsor,

You have been accepted to Charle's College for the academic class of 2030.

Welcome!

I didn't even bother reading the rest before screaming, "YES!" My arms swing and my knees practically hit my chest as I jump up and down, unable to contain the excitement while the papers, still in my grasp, flail wildly.

A sigh of relief escapes.

I'm not a failure. Thank God.

I immediately grab my phone and text Ben.

ME

Guess who got into Charle's College!

Coming to a standstill, I try to catch my breath as I watch three little dots appear in the text message chain.

BENNY BOY

Hell yeah, Char! I KNEW you'd get in somewhere! Congratulations. Let's celebrate this weekend :). Do you want to go out somewhere or just hang out on the farm?

Eek!

I press the phone close to my chest and close my eyes, rolling my lips in to contain the overwhelming emotions pouring out of me.

Yes. This is worth celebrating. I rarely make a big deal out of things, but he's right to remind me that I deserve to celebrate this. This is huge. And now it's confirmed Ben and I won't be going to college too far away from each other so we can still hang out and have future celebrations. Charle's is only thirty minutes away from Wyvern.

Before I can text back what I intended to, something else came out of its' own free will. Something I've never dared ask him straight out.

ME

Are you back with Tree?

Oh God. What did I just do?

My breath hitches, my eyes widening at the words on the screen. I hurl my phone on the bed like a hot potato and back away in horror.

Why did I send that? Why did I type that? I've never asked him straightforward questions about his relationship. Why do I suddenly care right now?

My phone landed face down, inhibiting me from seeing if he was typing back. With one arm crossing around my waist, holding my other's elbow, my teeth nervously scrape against my thumbnail. But the bounce in my feet and sharp bite against my nail is doing nothing to starve off this awkward, nervous energy.

Gah! It's like the phone's calling to me, telling me to pick it up. I want to look but I also don't want to look.

Should I go downstairs to distract myself and then lie to him by saying my parents came home so that's why I didn't respond for a while? That way I completely avoid an entire conversation about his relationship?

The front door shuts downstairs and my parents' voices travel up the staircase. I guess it wouldn't be a complete lie...

Yet, as I turn to walk out my bedroom door, my body once again does something of its' own accord, conspiring against me.

I quietly shut the door for privacy instead of going downstairs, wander over to my bed and lay down on my stomach, resting on my elbows with my feet hanging off the edge. I flip the phone over to reveal one unread text from Benny Boy.

My heartbeat picks up like the gun just sounded at the start of a race. Breathless, I tap his text.

BENNY BOY

I don't know, really. We still hook-up sometimes, but I wouldn't say we're together, together or anything. Why? You've never asked me anything like that before. Are you jealous or something? :).

Sharp pin pricks gather under my skin and spread throughout every inch of me. Good God, did they turn the heat on? What is this feeling? Jealousy? Embarrassment? Maybe it's both.

Seeing him confirm they still hook up even after being broken up sets a heaviness in my chest that anchors down into my stomach. I didn't realize he did that sort of thing.

I always viewed him as more of the innocent type. I mean, I heard he had sex, but that was from rumors around school and gossip in the girl's locker room. Hearing it from him directly made it more real, more devastating. I don't know how to feel about it. How do I even respond to him now?

A knock pulls me from my racing thoughts.

"Charlotte, you here?" Mom says softly, sticking her head in through the small crack she made in the doorframe. "I see we got some more mail. Any luck?"

I place my phone face down, covering it with a blanket to hide the embarrassing conversation. Not like my parents ever go through my phone, but still… I don't want her accidentally seeing it and asking uncomfortable questions.

With the phone safely hidden, I shoot up and grab the papers, holding them up to show her with a wide grin on my face. Without saying anything, she rushes over and embraces me in a comforting, tight hug.

"I knew it was only a matter of time, honey. I'm so proud of you."

I bury my face in her hair, my nerves and adrenaline relaxing instantly from breathing in the smell of her lavender shampoo. Man, I needed this hug. She always holds the longest, never letting go first.

When I finally let go and lean back, an expression of pure joy is on her face.

"Thanks, Momma. It's been tough lately but hearing I finally got in somewhere is going to pull me out of this slump. I just know it."

Her warm palm lingers on my cheek as she takes me in, analyzing me. I stare back into her glasslike blue eyes, wondering what she's searching for. They water like she's about to cry so I graze my thumb under them to wipe away any wetness that may fall.

"Oh, look at me being a big baby," she sniffles, standing up straight and pulling herself together. "Do you want to come downstairs and tell your father? You know he's going to make a huge fuss about it." She winks.

I nod; beaming as I follow her down the stairs. We run into him halfway, giving me the opportunity to dramatically whip the papers out from behind my back to hold them in front of my face, waggling my eyebrows for extra effect. His eyes widen right before he throws his fist up in celebration.

"You did it! I knew there was a school out there for you who would see how incredible you are! Woohoo!"

He grabs the papers and throws them in the air, letting them fall like money while taking hold of my hands at the same time, making me jump up and down with him. I'm *so* incredibly happy. This moment feels like the last scene in a movie before it cuts to credits.

"How do you want to celebrate, honey? Ice Cream? Pizza? Whatever you want for food tonight, you got it. *And* it's a Friday, so you know what that means? I get to kick your butt in some games." He places his fists on his hips, confidently standing in a superman pose, gazing off into the distance.

My lips are going to rip at the seams if I smile any wider. Relief washes the doubt away, calming every wired nerve in validation that I'm not a failure. I'm going to have an opportunity to better myself and get the kind of education I want. I haven't felt this relaxed or excited in months. God, it feels good.

"Let's order in Greek from Dolph's, pick up ice cream from Rosco's Gas Station and play card games!"

"You got it!" he says, checking the time on his watch. "Let's order the grub and get this party started!"

He rotates his hips in a circle, fists still on his waist with his tongue out and eyes crossed, earning loud laughs from Mom and me.

My phone and conversation with Ben now laying forgotten in the back of my mind, I follow my parents down the rest of the stairs to enjoy our night of celebration.

The muscles in my abs and cheeks hurt from laughing so much over the next few hours. We stuffed ourselves full of gyros before walking off what we could on our way to Rosco's to grab three pints of my favorite flavor of ice cream, Chocolate Oreo.

We dug into the ice cream, finishing a pint each, back at home while playing cards the rest of the night. It wasn't until midnight that my parents called it quits, giving me hugs and kisses and trudging off to bed mumbling about their old bones needing rest after such a rowdy night.

I sit at the kitchen table, now alone, listening to the crickets chirping through the open bay view window, enjoying the slight breeze and crisp smell of the rain from earlier. My eyes close, completely immersing myself in the peaceful melody floating in from outside. Echoes of laughter from the evening mix in, making me feel content and light as a feather. Smiling, I open my eyes, letting them land right on the dishes from the night's meals still sitting in the sink, yet to be cleaned.

Another thing I love about my family? We don't fuss about the messes. Sure, we keep our house clean, but we prioritize the moments that really matter, like spending time together, and save the things like dishes and chores until the next day so the night has no stress attached to it.

I put my arms up and stretch while kicking my legs out to relieve their muscle pain as well.

I'm not tired yet, but I should probably try to sleep. Maybe I'll go running tomorrow after I lift. Might as well take advantage if I'm in the mood for it since I haven't run for fun in a long time.

Closing up for the night, I lock the house doors, shut the windows and go upstairs to my bedroom where I poorly navigate the dark, tripping over myself trying to feel around for my bedside lamp. The small chain fumbles into my grasp and with a *click*, a low yellow light floods the small space by my bed, giving me just enough light to change into my matching white silk tank top and shorts.

My cool silk bedsheets whisper on my skin as I crawl under the covers, but the shadow of an object flying in the air onto the floor catches my attention.

Shoot! My phone. I completely forgot about it.

Reaching my arm out, I pause, my fingertips hovering right above it.

Oh, right.

The previous conversation with Ben floods my brain, sending butterflies into my chest.

Inhaling a deep breath for courage, I quickly flip it over. My notifications show three unread texts from Benny Boy and a missed call.

Small bouts of guilt for ignoring him and forgetting about the conversation surface until I remember he's done the same thing to me before. In fact, he's done it way more to me than I've ever done to him. The guilt subsides at my epiphany.

Yeah, he can deal with it like I've had to in the past. He'll live.

I swipe up and tap his messages, curious about what he said.

8:43 PM BENNY BOY

Sorry if that was weird when I asked if you were jealous. I was just jokin'.

9:30 PM BENNY BOY

So, what did you want to do this weekend to celebrate? Want to hang out tomorrow night? We can go to the movies or just hang out on the farm.

11:00 PM BENNY BOY

Are you mad at me? Listen, I didn't mean to make anything weird. I'm sorry. Can we talk, please?

11:55 PM *Missed Call from* BENNY BOY

The top corner of my phone shows 12:30 AM. Is he still awake? Do I text him or call him back? Would that be weird this late?

Ugh.

What is happening? Why's my brain doing this?

Calm down brain, this is not that big of a deal, get a grip.

Expelling a breath, I lay flat and pull the covers up, keeping my elbows outside the blanket to tuck me in. I stare at my phone clutched in my hands hovering over me, wondering what to do and knowing that the longer I wait, the more likely he won't answer because he'll be asleep. Would I even want him to answer?

I hate this feeling. Whatever this feeling is. It's so unbelievably uncomfortable. The debate in my brain continues as my eyelids get heavy and my hands lower. Guess my body decided for me.

Chapter Three.

"Char!"

"*Ahh!* What the heck?"

I fling the covers up to my mouth because I refuse to believe who stands in front of me.

"Ben, what the *heck* are you doing here this early? Let alone in my room?" I shyly mumble under the blankets.

"What's wrong? I've been in your room before." He winks with a sly grin, looking like he just opened his favorite Christmas present.

Oh God, did my boobs slip out of my top in my sleep? Did he see them?

I whip the covers all the way over my head and exhale in relief seeing that my top is still on and straight. Was it like that when he walked in, though? My face heats in anticipatory embarrassment, unsure of how to feel about him possibly seeing part of me naked.

My bed dips on the left side, rolling me to lean that way.

His hands gently and slowly land on the blanket right over my torso and settle on each side of me. Without further hesitation, he tickles me aggressively, keeping me pinned down with his arms.

I squirm, squealing in between giggles, "*Stop*! Ben, please! I'm gonna pee!"

"You gonna stop hiding from me?"

His biceps press harder into my sides to keep me still while he continues his assault. Dang, I knew he was in shape, but I never *really* paid attention to *how* in shape...

Unable to breathe nor bear the pain of how fiercely his tickles dig into my skin, I cave.

"Yes, yes! I'll stop hiding. Just stop!"

Defeated, I lay there panting, dying from lack of air under the blanket and peek my head out of the covers as a white flag to show he wins the battle. Resituating myself upright, I tuck the blanket under my arms and around my body enough to cover my boobs. He removes his hands and sets them on his lap while he stares at me with those magnetic dark brown eyes.

"There you are!"

"Hi," I say bashfully.

"Hi," he chuckles.

His smile fades, as a long pause settles between us, neither of us knowing what to say next as his strong leather and mint cologne wraps its tendrils around me. Last night's unanswered texts hang in the unspoken silence and my brain draws a blank on any other topic.

"You didn't text me back last night. I was worried. You didn't even answer when I tried calling you...and you always answer when I call..."

His expression is serious as his eyes search mine for answers, the intensity making my heart flutter.

"I'm sorry. Right after I texted you, my parents got home and, *of course*, they were thrilled about me getting into Charle's and wanted to celebrate, so I got distracted. By the time I got back upstairs to my bedroom and saw that you called and texted me, I figured it was too late to get back to you."

His gaze softens upon hearing my excuse.

"I was still up, you know. Plus, I don't care if you wake me up. I've never cared about that, so call me back next time." He shoves my shoulder playfully.

I keep quiet, unsure of what to say back. A new tension, something heated and unfamiliar, settles between us, setting my nerves on edge.

"You know...that way I don't go to sleep worrying you got murdered or went insane from how seriously you take everything." His elbow nudges my leg in a joking manner to break the silence.

And just like that, the tension disappears, bringing us back to our normal selves. I roll my eyes and give him a swift kick in the side. Well, as much as I could from that angle.

"Well, as you can see, I'm fine. Now get out of my room, perv, so I can change."

I stick my tongue out at him. Complying, he stands, chuckles, and walks out the door.

My body immediately relaxes when the door closes. Wow, I didn't realize how raised my shoulders were during that whole encounter. Bending my neck from side to side to stretch it, I throw my sheets off and stand up to change.

A noise catches my attention behind me making me whip my head around.

Was that a door click? Was he peeking in to watch me change? What the heck is going on with him right now?

If I'm being honest with myself, I'm flattered, but still...

People suspect correctly that I've never had a kiss, or even held hands with a boy, but I've never admitted it out loud.

My first crush was in the eighth grade on an extremely shy and intelligent, beautiful dark-skinned boy named Julius. By that time, most of the other girls already had their first kisses out of the way, but not me. So, with the junior high dance coming up, I was hoping Julius would ask me to go with him so I could get my first kiss too. Instead, he asked me to ask Shirley to go with him. Of course, she said yes.

They shared their first kiss together at that dance. I was unlucky enough to catch it from the back of the gymnasium where I sat on the bleachers alone, my stomach twisting in knots and moisture clouding my vision.

I went home from the dance early and cried the whole way to my mom, making it a point to avoid dances after that. I'd rather study or hang out with my parents than ever feel that pain again. Not to mention, no one's ever asked me to go with them to a dance before, not even Ben.

Now Ben's never had any trouble getting dates. Nine times out of ten, girls are the ones asking him out. And he always says yes rather enthusiastically, like he expects it to happen. I confronted him about it once, but he denied it, leading me to believe his ego wouldn't let him admit that he liked all the attention.

The door whips open, pulling me out of my reverie and causing me to jerk my head violently.

"Char, what the hell is the hold-up?"

"Ben, I could've been naked! Who goes around whipping doors open like that?"

"It's been like fifteen minutes. If you were still naked, I'd consider you an elderly lady who would've needed my assistance to get dressed anyways because you were taking so long."

Help me get dressed? He'd be ok seeing me naked?

"Oh, really?" I chuckle. "I was totally zoned out, sorry. I'll hurry up."

"Oh, yeah? Zoned out about what?" he inquires curiously, tilting his head and leaning on the now open doorway with his arms crossed.

"Uhhh..." I utter, trying to think of an excuse other than what was truly going through my mind.

"So, me, huh?" he says slyly, the corners of his mouth tilting up.

"Pfft, no," I forcefully exhale at the *ridiculous* assumption.

"Then why are your cheeks turning so red, huh?" He winks.

Crap, they're on fire. Leave it to my cheeks to give me away.

"The only thing I was thinking about was what will happen when we go away to college. So yes, I admit, I thought about you in relation to that," I stumble out, praying he can't see through the lie.

His confident façade drops immediately as his brows furrow and he begins to chew on the inside of his bottom lip. Is he sad we're going to different colleges too?

"What, no sass, Mr. Ben?" I say, trying to pick the banter back up along with the mood in the room.

He awkwardly chuckles and pulls out his phone instead of answering me.

My stomach drops.

Is it her?

He stands in the doorway looking conflicted and continues typing on his phone like I'm not even in the room.

Are they back together?

A familiar tug deep in my gut resurfaces bringing me back to how it felt junior year when him and Tree started dating.

The soccer girls, who'd just finished training on the track, were all staring and giggling at Ben who was just leaning on his motorcycle with his leather pants and jacket on, minding his own business. Long story short, the girls made a bet and Tree won. So, without saying anything, she grabbed him by the jacket and kissed him.

It was the first time I'd witnessed him being physical with someone. The stabbing pain in my chest at the visual was not something I enjoyed, but it never crossed my mind that things would change between us because with all his other flings, it didn't.

But that's probably because he didn't lose his virginity with anyone else. It was after homecoming when he lost it to her. I found out the news that Monday in the locker room after overhearing some of the other girls talking about it. The information hit me like a train, pulling all the air from lungs from the weight of it. We were about to head out for cross-country practice but instead, I ripped my locker door open to hide because it felt like I was having a heart attack. Tears spilled out of my eyes as I fought for breath bent over. White-knuckled and gripping my shirt to loosen the crushing weight on my chest that wasn't really there, I panicked and almost reached the point of hyperventilation. By far, those were the five scariest minutes of my life.

After it passed, I got the heck out of doge and raced home. I didn't want anyone asking me questions about why I was upset because I literally didn't know what to tell them. If I didn't know what was going on, how could I explain it to them?

Little did I know while I was sobbing to my mother that night over what happened, Ben had already blocked my phone number.

Fear of losing him again from the memories waved over me until enough courage surfaces to ask the burning question on my tongue.

"Is that Tree?"

Ben, too engrossed in his phone, didn't respond.

When I got to school the next day, I texted him in the morning before class, but it wouldn't go through. Then in class, he completely ignored me and wouldn't sit near me or acknowledge my existence.

Clueless as to what was going on, I was heartbroken. I didn't know how to survive without Ben, nor did I want to and there was nothing I could do to get him to speak to me.

It wasn't until the weekend when his mom talked to mine that I discovered what was going on. Tree made him block all the girls he talked to and demanded he no longer have any other friends of the opposite sex. The fact that he went along with her demands shocked and angered me. It was all out of my control, leaving me feeling completely helpless about the situation and I hated it.

But the rule ended sooner than expected when she dumped him a month later because he talked back to her. He was heartbroken and broke his silence, reaching out to me for support. I picked up the phone to him immediately apologizing for blocking me and sniffling out that they broke up. I knew I shouldn't have forgiven him so quickly, but I missed him so much I didn't care.

After that night, we were back to our old selves for a few weeks...until they got back together. I had texted him before class, per our usual routine, and the message never went through, immediately confirming my underlying fears that I was blocked again.

Round two didn't last long either though. He broke up with her after two weeks because he was sick of her bossing him around.

And so repeated the cycle.

Each time he came back to me, I accepted him with open arms, but the pain of being repeatedly abandoned by him for her was making me numb. Therefore, it became an unspoken agreement between us not to ask questions about relationships or anything regarding the opposite sex to stave off that repeated uncomfortable conversation. Until now apparently.

"Ben? Is that Tree?" I repeat softly, afraid of the answer.

"Huh?" He looks up from his phone confused. "Oh, no, no, but I uh... gotta go. I'll talk to you later, ok?"

He shoves his phone into his pocket, fakes a quick smile, and walks off, leaving me alone in my bedroom with a crushing silence.

Chapter Four.

I spend the entire rest of the day in a dazed state of confusion, starting off with burning my breakfast omelet to bits because I can't stop replaying our morning together.

Why the heck did Ben charge in and seemingly flirt with me? What was he doing on his phone if he wasn't texting Tree? Was he lying to me?

My parents' conversations flow in one ear and out the other because I'm so lost in the fog of hypothetical scenarios about our entire encounter and what each touch, each word and each deep stare meant.

The rest of the day is spent obsessively checking my phone in the hopes he'll text me to restart the conversation we were having this morning. The flirty banter, the touching... but he didn't.

Multiple times I typed out "hey" only to delete it seconds later, too afraid I'd be blocked again.

After a stressful day of overthinking, I call it a night and plug my phone into the charger on my desk so it's far enough away from me that I can't reach it from bed. I can't sit here staring at it anymore, wondering if he was just being flirty for fun or if it meant something deeper...or worse he didn't mean anything by it at all.

My head slams into my pillow and a forceful exhale blows my hair out of my face in frustration.

Ugh, I'm going insane.

In all our years of friendship, we've never been in a spot like this. A territory possibly borderline from a point of no return. But maybe I'm just kidding myself and it's not the reality of the situation at all.

Throughout the night, uncertain ghosts of truths whisper in my ears, always coming back to one question: *What is this new thing between us?*

I wake up the next morning with dread in the pit of my stomach at the reality I may not have a text from Ben. So instead, I go downstairs, leaving my phone on my desk and out of sight, to see my parents already awake and making breakfast.

"Going to church with us today, honey?" My dad grins and shows me his pan filled with an egg and bacon smiley face.

I didn't really want to go, but I know once I'm at college, I won't be able to go with them as often, so I say yes.

We finish our breakfast, throwing small food fights, laughing and joking around and then all change out of our PJs for church.

Mom and Dad went with jeans and T-shirts but I chose to wear my loose long-sleeved, floor-length black dress paired with low black heels. I don't know why a dress sounds appealing to wear, but I'm going with it. Plus, it's long enough to prevent my thighs from sticking to the pews which is a major bonus.

I leer at my phone like it's challenging me to a staring contest.

Nope, I'm not taking it with me. I don't need it at church.

And with that, I stick my nose up defiantly at it like I just won some mind battle and leave it on the desk in my room.

The church sermon's a bit awkward. The pastor decides to try something new and preach to the congregation about dating.

I uncomfortably sit next to my parents, forcibly listening to the purity speech while flashbacks of the horrific sex talk they gave me years ago resurfaces in my brain. It involved a slideshow of graphic pictures, a how-to video on YouTube which was then followed by a demonstration involving a banana, a condom and a cream-filled donut.

I shudder at the memory.

Luckily for them, my parents have it easy. I've never dated, and I don't really see myself dealing with it at this point. It just doesn't seem to be in the cards for me. I'd rather focus on my upcoming successful forensics career anyways.

Ben's face flashes brightly through my mind before another thought replaces it… *At least dead bodies can't hurt you, either.*

The pastor drones on in the background about how important it is to have the man lead and how to date as a Christian, while I zone out, observing the aesthetics around me instead.

I've always loved the vibes of churches. Ours is one of the smaller ones in town. It was built in the early 1900s, bearing the typical old-school stained-glass windows flaunting multitudes of reds, blues, yellows and greens, depicting pictures of the bird of peace, angels, children, Jesus and a huge blue cross. The stained-glass needs to be redone though because a lot of the color's peeling off.

More sunlight peeks through the breaks in color than it should, leaving some people blinded in their pews from the sunlight reflecting so brightly on them.

I made the mistake once of sitting in a pew in its line of fire. My back was killing me by the end because I had to have my chin resting on my arms that settled on the pew in front of me for two hours without moving, otherwise the sun would've blinded me. Dad made fun of how I hobbled to the car afterwards which was extremely unhelpful.

My dad hits me playfully on the back of the head with the church pamphlet that details the sermon and agenda for the service, pulling me out of my stupor. I smirk at him. He returns it with a wink and silently mouths "pay attention". I silently mouth back "I am" and sarcastically roll my eyes. He scratches my head to acknowledge the joke and turns forward to pay attention to the pastor. Luckily, the pastor begins the closing message and prayer, so I'm spared the act of fake listening any longer.

"Amen," I say with the congregation after the closing prayer. I stand up and follow my parents around, awkwardly smiling at all the older folks and listening to the small talk they make on the way to the exit.

Sadly, this church won't be around much longer. The congregation only consists of individuals over sixty and their children rarely come to the service. Meanwhile, the pastor looks like he'll turn to dust if he gets caught in the wind.

Dad stops to chat with a few people he's known since he was a kid while I walk to the car with Mom. She's more like me, social to a point but also hates small talk. Plus, she didn't grow up here like he did. She grew up traveling the world with her own father who was in the military.

Before she settled down with my dad, she was living in Barcelona—fresh out of college and doing research for her first horror novel when they met.

Dad was in Barcelona on a group trip with his high school buddies at the time. He said he and his friends were walking around and checking out the local bars when he spotted her under one of the patio lights. She was at the edge of the bar away from all the loud fuss of the drunks, sitting with her laptop open like no one else in the world existed but her.

Instantly captivated by her aura, he confidently walked up to her and said in a low voice, "Hey pretty girl, I like your style." She responded by faking like she was going to hit him in the balls and then laughed hysterically when he fell over out of surprise, until he pulled her down with him and planted a big kiss on her.

They had the typical romantic night of talking until dawn and then spent the next seven days together. After that, it was history. They got married the week after and started their life together.

Every time he tells me the story of how they met, a goofy, sappy expression takes over like he's watching his favorite movie. I love it.

The car door slams shut, making me jump out of my seat.

Man, I'm out of it today.

Wow, he's back already? It only took him twenty minutes to make his rounds and talk to everyone instead of forty. He officially beat his personal record. His previous all-time record was thirty minutes so we're making progress.

Mom cracks a joke about his record like she read my mind.

"Don't jinx it," he chuckles.

Dad starts the car and takes us to Pop's Pizza Bar for our typical Sunday ritual; Church, pizza, then home where they work on their books, while I either do homework, workout, watch TV or hang out with Ben.

Oh. Ben… I forgot about Ben for a minute.

Has he texted or called me today? Now I wish we weren't going to Pop's Pizza so I could check my phone.

"Wow, I've rarely seen you eat so fast," Dad exclaims as I shove down my third slice of a large extra cheese pizza. In retaliation, I smile with my mouth full of food to be silly and get a joking smack on my head from my mom which is her fun way of telling me to be polite.

As I heave another huge bite down my throat so we can hurry up and go home, a familiar voice reaches my ears from behind me. I turn around, my cheeks filled with pizza like a chipmunk and leftover sauce splattered on my chin from eating so fast, and about choke.

It's Ben. He's shaking hands with Duke, the owner of the shop, and Tree stands right behind him.

Pulling a speedy evasive maneuver, I duck down in the booth to hide and sink under it until just my head is left, resting on the cracked, red leather seat. A ball of pizza bobs in my throat, threatening to come back up at the sight of them together. I finish chewing what's in my mouth and hard swallow to get the rest of it all the way down.

If they're here together then they must be back together which also means he blocked me again. Which also means there's no way he texted me. And why would he bring her here anyways? She seems way too stuck up to eat at a place like this.

My stomach violently twists into knots. This sucks. This all just sucks so much. Why does he have to be so obsessed with her? Does that mean the flirting yesterday really meant nothing? I rest my head on the leather of the booth and let the coolness of it settle on my skin.

"Um, sweetie? What are you doing?" Mom asks, bending over and peeking below the table, wearing a know-it-all smirk. She already knows why I'm hiding but doesn't want to tell my dad to save me from possible embarrassment. I put my finger up to my mouth, signaling for her to be quiet.

It didn't work. Dad chimes in...and *not* quietly. As loud as a car horn, he yells, "Charlotte! How many times have we told you *not* to eat the crumbs off the floor! We can afford to have food on the table now that you've started working here!" He peeks down at me and starts laughing.

Completely mortified, I throw my face into my hands to hide. I want to die. I guarantee Ben could hear him. He knows my dad's voice, and it was *not* a quiet joke. Maybe since he's with Tree he won't come over here. A girl can hope.

"Heyyyy Mr. and Mrs. Windsor, how are ya?" Ben spouts happily.

My stomach drops like I just fell thirty floors, my breath catching in my throat. His usual black and white sneakers appear right in front of our booth with black heels following closely behind.

It's them. I can't believe he stopped by to say hi while Tree's with him.

Oh God, please don't check down here.

My palm presses into my mouth hard to stifle my breathing, unable to come up with anything else to do at the moment.

"Oh, you know our names, come off it with that," Mom chuckles back.

They always do this. Ben gets a kick out of calling them that, because he says our last name sounds like something spies or secret agents have. Plus, it makes my parents uncomfortable. He takes pleasure from the oddest things.

"I know. I just like seeing you squirm. How ya doing Sarah and Brady?"

"Well, we were doing good until just recently." Oh no, Dad's got that mischievous tone in his voice. He's going to give me away. I just know it.

No one speaks for a minute as the sounds of the restaurant and my hard, nervous breaths on my skin fill my ears.

My eyes widen in horror as Ben's dark jeans crease, each inch showing more and more of his legs.

Oh, God. He's bending down to check under here. How the heck do I escape this situation?

But my panic's meaningless. There's no way out.

Thick black hair strands appear just under the table's edge first. He gelled his hair for her...

It must be a real date then because he rarely does that unless there's a special event. Another punch to the gut threatens to send me reeling.

Next his forehead, bushy brows and caramel brown eyes come into view. I've been caught. He waggles his eyebrows up and down in his usual joking manner, his smile revealing itself as he fully bends down. I'm surprised he's approaching me like this in front of her.

Oh God, what do I do?

"Whatcha doing down there?"

With no other option, I fake an awkward smile and force out a laugh to break the tension. I didn't think this through.

How do I gracefully get out from under the table?

I arch my back as much as possible to try and create space to slink back up into the booth but misjudge the space between the booth and the table. The salt and pepper shakers and plates *clink* as the table shakes from where my head hits it.

"Ouch," I whisper, finally clearing the table and avoiding everyone's gaze while I rub the top of my scalp, attempting to lessen the sting.

I can feel Ben staring me down, waiting for me to look at him.

Deep breath. You can do this.

Clenching my jaw, I dare a peek. Yet, instead of seeing him, my gaze meets right with Tree's.

Crap.

Her grey eyes are almost black, sucking me in like an animal caught in a tar pit. I open my mouth to speak but freeze under her death glare. Is she a witch? This intimidation is of supernatural levels.

Ben catches onto my discomfort because he interrupts the stare down.

"Well, hey, we're gonna go sit down. I'm starving, but I'll see you all later, alright?" he says confidently, turning away toward a booth in the back of the restaurant.

Tree gives me one last glare that would scare any person in their right mind and then follows behind him pompously with her shoulders back and breasts pushed out. She reaches to grab his hand, but he nonchalantly shakes it off.

Maybe he's not back with her after all? All the signs would point to no, but they're together alone, so I don't know. Plus, he talked to me with her here and he's never done that before...

Do I dare text him when I get home and ask him? What if he's still with her when I do?

Oh, God, no. I can't. I won't. I'm not going to get tangled in that

"*Oooohh*, who's that girl he's with?" Dad says in his high-pitched gossipy voice.

"That's his or was his girlfriend. I'm not really sure if they're still dating or not," I whisper, leaning over the table.

"There's no way. She's not *nearly* as pretty or smart as you." He winks.

"DAD! Stop." I attempt to hide my face to save myself the embarrassment he's putting me through, but my mother removes my hands, forcing me to participate in this conversation. "It's not like that. You know Ben and I are just friends. There's nothing there. He's like my brother."

But the words felt wrong as they left my lips. He definitely doesn't *feel* like a brother anymore. Once again, my brain defaults back to the "what is this" question.

I dare a glance over at Ben and Tree but all I can see is their heads leaning toward each other over the top of the table with their hands intertwined.

My stomach plummets again. I feel sick. This emotional turbulence mixed with stuffing my face too quickly is not a great mix. Turning away, my nose and mouth crinkles from the nausea. I can't watch them anymore.

"You okay, Charlotte? You look a little pale." Mom's gaze bores into me so deeply it's like she's peering into my soul. She pauses before glancing over her shoulder at them and then turning back to me.

"Uh, yeah. Can we go, please? I need to go home and lay down."

"Sure, sweetie. Did you want to go say bye to Ben first before we head home?" Dad says, pointing over to their table the exact moment I catch them stealing a kiss.

Kill me.

"No." I force out a small chuckle to hide the pain. "I don't think they want to be disturbed." Wetness clouds my vision as I bite my trembling bottom lip, focusing on my fingers twiddling nervously with each other in my lap.

Mom lightly punches Dad in the shoulder, making him retort, "What? What'd I say?"

On the way to the door, I pretend my eyes itch and rub all the wetness out of them to prevent any trace of unwanted tears. All I want is to go home, go to bed and not think about anything.

The drive home was quiet, an awkward tension hanging in the air. So many new uncomfortable emotions surfaced this week.

Is this going to be a new normal?

God, I hope not.

The second the car pulls into the garage I'm out, kicking my shoes off at the door and speeding upstairs to my room to check my phone and see if he texted me at all, knowing I'm glutton for punishment.

My heart flutters as I softly close my door and stare at the phone sitting face down on my desk. I want to see if he texted me, but I also dread checking because if he didn't, I won't be able to hold back these tears that I've been fighting back since we left the restaurant.

I whisper some encouragement to myself, willing myself to believe it. "This doesn't matter. I'll be fine either way. So what if he didn't text you? I've been through this before with him."

Okay, deep breath and... I flip my phone over quick like it's on fire.

Nothing. The screen is still black. I click the side button to wake it up and nothing. Really? After all that I can't even check it? How is my battery dead? I had it plugged in all night.

Squishing myself in between my desk and the wall, I spot my charger laying on the floor, unplugged. *Ugh.* I reach back and plug it in so my phone will charge. Maybe this is the universe sparing my feelings.

Sighing deeply, I stand in the middle of my room, looking around like a lost duckling. What do I do with myself now? It's only three o'clock.

Well, I could go on a run to try and clear my head, but if someone tries to kidnap me, I'm toast, so I guess that's out.

Hm...I could see if I have any paperwork to do for college admissions now that I'm accepted somewhere, but then I'd have to sit at my desk where I'm sure I'd just stare at my phone the whole time.

Mandatory weightlifting for track, it is. At least I'll be out of the house and away from my phone for that.

But when I reach for my car keys off the hanger above my desk, my phone lights up, now charged just enough to show life.

My breath catches in my throat, heart skipping a beat. A text from Ben!

I snatch my phone up and sit staring at it, debating whether I should swipe up and read it now or wait. The high of seeing he reached out could sustain me the rest of the afternoon, but what if I waited too long and got my hopes up for nothing? What if this isn't a good text? Slinking down in my chair, the internal battle consumes me.

I've never intentionally explored my feelings about Ben before.

What I've been feeling lately can only be described as jealousy toward Tree. Not jealous because of who she is but because of what she's gained. Him. His body. His mind. Knowing him in a way I never have and becoming a completely intimate part of him.

The real question is...am I only jealous in a friendly way? Because of the way she knows him, and I don't? Is it possessiveness over our friendship?

Yesterday popped into my mind, reminding me that wasn't it. How I felt when he was most likely flirting with me was definitely a want for *him*, and not just as a friend. And it wasn't embarrassment that he might see my almost naked body, but anticipation. I was nervous about his touch, but I wanted him to be there with me, to explore and touch me in a new way.

How did I never realize it before? I've always looked for his motorcycle everywhere. In town, at his house, at school... I'm always checking to see if he's around. Does he do the same for me?

He monopolizes my mind often before bed. Ruminations churn on what we'd talk about, if I'd get the chance to see him, what it'd be like to be back to normal when he's with Tree, what he'd be wearing to school, his hair, how he looks when he rides his bike...what it would feel like to be on the back of his bike, especially since he's never let anyone ride it with him, even me.

I've been so blind. This is a crush. I have a crush on Ben!

An obvious epiphany, but an epiphany, nonetheless. Guess my parents were always right about Ben and me, at least on my side. I do like him, and I want him to want me and not Tree. To be with me and not her. But maybe it's too late for that. Maybe he just thinks of me as a sister and nothing more. Will I ever find out?

My phone almost slips out of my hands, making me jump-catch it. It's no use. Knowing what I know now, I won't be able to get any lifting done if I don't read it before I go.

With bated breath, I turn the phone over and swipe up on his message.

BENNY BOY

Your cheeks were as red as my favorite leather motorcycle jacket when I caught you hiding under the table. Am I right in thinking you were jealous this time?

I scoff. The *nerve*.

Is he just wanting attention? Like, what is this obsession he has with making me jealous this weekend?

I refuse to admit to him that I *was* in fact jealous so instead I text back the only thing I can come up with.

ME

I don't know...

Yeah, Charlotte, that'll do it. I roll my eyes. A few bubbles pop up showing he's typing back before disappearing and then reappearing over and over again.

What seemed like the longest few minutes of my life went by with no reply. Was my response too cold? This is so uncomfortable. I've never had a conversation like this with a boy before. How am I supposed to navigate this?

Screw it. I'm breaking this barrier between us.

ME

To be honest, I don't know what's going on with me. You know I've never really had crushes... I'm not sure if what I'm feeling is jealousy or not.

Anxiety rises through me as I tap send. The bubbles quickly pop up again.

BENNY BOY

I can't tell you, Char. You're the one that's going to have to tell me.

At my wits end, I throw my arms up in awkward aggravation. What the heck? He makes it sound like this should be *so* easy. If he has something he wants to admit then he should. Why am I the one that has to admit it first and possibly be rejected?

Yeah. I don't *have* to tell him anything. They're *my* feelings. It's *my* choice.

My only child personality quickly resurfaces. The bratty part of my brain and I agreed. Nope. I don't owe him an actual answer if I don't have it or want it.

ME

Luckily for me, I don't have to tell you anything if I don't want to. You'll just have to guess.

Grinning from ear to ear, I shoot the text off. Let's see what he has to say to *that*.

BENNY BOY

I see Miss Stubborn-Ass has entered the chat :). If you tell me your true feelings, I'll tell you a secret :).

My lips curl up, my entire body prickling with heat after re-reading his text repeatedly.

I love this feeling, although I only just figured out I probably have a crush on him like five minutes ago. I'm not going to tell him anything unless I'm one hundred percent sure. Plus, he's the guy, shouldn't he tell me his feelings first?

Actually... speaking of feelings...

ME

So, since we're on the subject of feelings... Are you back with Tree then? I saw you guys kissing at the restaurant. And if you are back together, does that mean you're going to block me soon? Are you even allowed to talk to me right now?

The unsent message shakes in my hand from my knee bouncing so violently, my nail occupying a space in my teeth. Drawing a deep breath to gather up the nerve, I fast tap on the send icon. Bubbles appear and disappear over the next couple of minutes. Either he's texting me a whole book, or he's typing and erasing what he's trying to say. I stare at the bubbles reappearing and disappearing for way too long.

This is driving me mad. Why won't he just send me what he's so obviously typing? I give up.

Disappointed, I toss my phone on my bed, grab my keys and go to the school gym to do my lifts. This should keep me busy the rest of the evening. In fact, maybe I won't reply to him at all even after he texts me back.

Yeah. Then I'll have all the power.

Let's see how you like that, Benny Boy.

An hour later, after the fastest and probably sloppiest lifting session of my life, I'm back home in a continued staring contest with my phone. It was all I could think about at the gym.

No. I need to have some self-restraint. He deserves to wait for a message.

Sighing in defeat, I sit at my laptop to work on my college acceptance paperwork and dorm preferences. But as soon as I open it, a ping sounds on the school's instant messaging website, Trolley from Shirley.

SHIRLEY

Hey, Charlie! Please tell me you've finally taken the plunge and downloaded Xypher? BikerBB64 literally just posted like 5 new videos, and they are SO hot.

ME

BikerBB64?

SHIRLEY

Girl, do you even listen when I talk to you?

Not really, I think to myself.

SHIRLEY

Shirley has sent you a link. Click *here* to open it.

SHIRLEY

Charlotte, click on the link I just sent you. You won't regret it! :) I'll be testing you tomorrow at school on the footage so you better study up.

A low ding sounds, signaling she signed off.

Sigh.

She's so pushy. I hate feeling pressured to do these things...but I'll admit I have been curious. The one video I saw of him at practice made me feel something interesting. Something different and new but appealing.

What the heck. I'm eighteen. I can watch stuff like this now. I'm about to go to college where I'll likely see stuff like this more often anyways.

I slowly roll the mouse over her message and click the link. A website with black and blue stripes pops up with light blue coding designs integrated within to make it appear high tech. The top of the website in large bold letters states, "Welcome to Xypher" with Log in or Register next to it. Exiting out, I return to her instant message and click the link again only to be directed to the same thing. Looks like I can't view the video unless I sign up for an account.

Everyone I know gets addicted to this site so I was hoping I could view it without creating a permanent account.

But I'm smart enough not to get addicted... I think.

I bet everyone at college will have this, and I do want to try to fit in more there. Plus, maybe this is a way to keep in touch with Ben once we're apart. It'll be another way for us to connect.

Screw it. I'm signing up.

I click Register and fill out all the applicable information. The last step is username. Hm...

My fingers move along the keyboard involuntarily, picking out the username. Unknown99. Good enough, I guess.

Bypassing the profile picture section to keep anonymity, I click create, then exit to go back to her IM, hoping her link works now. Finally, the mysterious biker boy's profile pops up...or should I say *man* by the looks of it. My eyes widen as I take in his whole page. Videos upon videos of him dancing shirtless with a helmet on fly upwards, mixed with even sexier videos of his abs, wet grey sweatpants...many, many things that make my body burn from the inside out.

My God, his abs.

The videos where he's dancing in the rain are *so* incredibly hot. The one the girls showed me before was just of him dancing fully clothed in a motorcycle helmet in an old parking lot. I had no idea that behind that video were others that were way more intense, way more...sensual.

An unfamiliar tingling sensation develops, increasing in intensity as I continue watching his videos. It's a pleasing sensation that I don't know what to do with as it spreads outward, igniting the burn to a tingling fire throughout my body.

From what I can see, he began to make these sexier seduction themes in the last month. There are so many thirst traps posted in that timeframe that it's overwhelming me to get through them all. What prompted the change to make him go this route? Not like I'm complaining...

A hint of shame paired with excitement spreads through me as I continue watching and scrolling, unable to take my eyes off the screen.

Is this wrong? Should I not be doing this?

I get out of the chair and pace, unsure of what to do with this unfamiliar energy buzzing inside me. How do I deal with this new feeling? How do I release this sensation? Do I tell Mom?

Ick, no.

The thought of telling my mother about what I'm doing and feeling right now disgusts me. It feels... dirty and forbidden, but I secretly like it. Do I explore this? *Should* I explore this?

Eight o'clock...hmm. I know what I'll do. I'll think about what to do while I get ready for bed. Yeah. That way I'm not making any rash decisions.

My normal nightly routine is spent in a daze, the motions autonomous as my brain fixates on the biker instead of what I'm doing in the present. Just the few seconds of intro that the videos showed me play on repeat in my head, making that sensation in the nether regions constant.

The shower doesn't help. If anything, the warm water makes it worse.

I slip into an oversized white T-shirt and stare at myself curiously in the mirror. My shirt sticks to me in a half-wet state because I never have enough patience to dry myself off fully, leaving my black cotton panties and hard nipples clearly visible. Their light pink coloring pushes through the T-shirt's cotton while my long brown hair sits soaking the shoulders and back of the shirt.

I've never been a skinny, skinny girl, but I've never had much to me either. There's some shape there but only enough to be considered small and not petite. I secretly hope once I stop running that I'll get more shape to me.

Turning around, I focus on my backside.

Tree has a bubble butt that sticks out like a freakin' table, but mine's way more subtle. Definitely nothing to wow at like hers is.

"Hm….," I say aloud, analyzing my body. It's hopeless to dream of ever looking like Tree with her perfectly slim waist, plumps lips, a v-cut in her abs and thick butt. She was naturally born with a beautiful body and long black curly hair. I had no chance.

The tingle quickly fades from all the thoughts about Tree and how my body can't compare. I turn away from the mirror, disappointed, and sit on my bed, feeling discouraged and vulnerable, especially as I check my phone and see no further communication from Ben after asking if he was back with Tree.

Chapter Five.

The last few weeks of school go by in a blur, everything feeling the same yet different, like what I've always known is slowly fading and the school no longer feels like a place I belong.

With graduation next week, the buzz through our senior class is electric, albeit mixed with hesitation about the new world we're about to enter into.

Rumors flow around the school that Ben and Tree aren't officially dating, but they've been seen together randomly, acting like they're a couple anyways. I don't understand it but at least Ben and I are friends again, regardless of his situation with her. Turns out, he never texted me back that night because his phone died, dispelling my fears that I'd been blocked.

It took two weeks, but I finally mustered up the courage to re-ask him in person what his relationship with Tree was and he answered the question without all the jealousy jokes.

"We're not officially dating because I'm sick of her boundaries...but we are friends with benefits." Then, he awkwardly shrugged his shoulders and walked away. I had no idea what that meant until I ran into Shirley after school, and she told me what friends with benefits entails. It really upset me that he's not even dating her but continues to sleep with her. I don't understand the point. Why mess around with someone if you don't intend on being with them? There's no way a situation like that ends well, and Shirley agreed with me.

She also said Ben's a typical guy and just wants to satisfy his sexual cravings, but I can't see him like that. He's always been my sweet, caring guy friend who would never need something like that.

We've been back to our old selves besides these few random incidents that made me question how I felt about him. He's flirted more openly with me on a few occasions, as well as other girls around school. I don't know if I like this new side of him. His constant flirting shows he's changed. Ben seems to be two different people. I rarely know which one I'll encounter each day.

I know he always has women after him, but he's never played into that playboy type until lately. Tree, on multiple occasions, has threatened the other girls he's flirted with. Not with anything crazy, but with empty threats such as, "look at him again and I'll cut your eyes out with the scissors in my backpack", or my personal favorite, "if you talk to him again, you won't make it to graduation".

She hasn't pointed any threats at me so far, but I'm assuming it's because she knows if she does it'll risk any chance she has at fully getting back together with Ben. Although that doesn't dissuade her from staring daggers at me any time I enter her line of sight.

We never all hang out together, but if I'm sitting with Ben at lunch or in class, her lips will tense into a thin line and her eyes will blacken from anger in the distance. It's quite off-putting.

I don't egg her on, but I definitely don't hide from her anymore either. She's never followed through on any of her threats on any of the random girls he's flirted with, so I assume I'm safe. If she actually does do something to someone one of these days, then I'll reassess, and tell Ben.

"Hey, Charlotte!"

I turn around in the parking lot to see Jared, one of the relay runners on our track team, running up to me.

"Oh, hey Jared. What's up?"

His long blonde hair is in a tied-up bun, the sides stuck to his tan, clean shaven face from sweat. He's still training because he's going to Jenkins University after graduation, the school notorious for pumping out pro-athletes for Track and Field. You can always find him at the track after school.

"Nothing much! I wanted to give you this while I was thinking about it," he beams brightly handing me his graduation party invite.

"Oh! Thanks Jared, that's so nice of you. I'll try to stop by."

"Is that an actual I'll try to stop by, or an 'I'm just being polite Charlotte' response where you don't show up," he confidently states, giving me a wink.

My neck twitches back, taken aback by his upfront honesty, especially since we've barely talked over the years. He was right though; I've been invited to track and cross-country parties each year since the seventh grade but never went because I didn't want to and my automatic response when invited has always been "I'll try to stop by".

"Sorry, Jared. I promise I'll be there," I chuckle awkwardly, shifting on my feet with my previous true intentions hanging in the air.

Guess it won't kill me to go. Plus, I'll likely never see him again after his party anyways, and he's always been an all-around nice guy. What could it hurt?

"Good! Are you having a graduation party or anything? I'd love to come!"

My shoulders turtle up. No one's asked me if I was going to have one let alone if they could come.

"Um, no I'm not, actually," I awkwardly mumble, staring down at my feet.

"Why not? I mean, I know you're not a partier, but this is a once in a lifetime thing to celebrate with people. You should totally have one."

Avoiding his gaze, I now focus on my fingers fiddling with my car keys.

"Well, uh, I don't really have any family that I'd invite other than my parents, and I'm not super close with tons of people so I just figured I'd go to other people's parties and that'd be good enough."

His smile falters, his voice switching into a warmer, more compassionate tone.

"Oh, I'm sorry. I didn't mean to offend. I was only curious. Well, you had better go to everyone's parties who've invited you. You'll never have this chance again, and who knows when we'll all see each other next. Plus, being social is important."

He playfully fist bumps my arm, pulling a small twitch of my lips upwards.

The only grad party I initially planned on going to was Ben's since he's my best friend. I've been invited to five others, well six including Jared's, but now I feel more pressured to go.

Ugh.

"Hey," Ben says walking up to us.

Jared's smile drops instantly into a tight line.

Huh, that's weird. Does he not like Ben?

Regardless, I'm relieved to see him. Hopefully he can get me out of this conversation.

"Hey, Ben, what's up?" I say brightly.

"Hey," Jared replies shortly to Ben before quickly turning to me, ignoring Ben and resuming his bright demeanor.

"I gotta get back to training, but Charlotte, I'll see you next weekend, okay?"

He waves goodbye at the same time he runs off toward the track. I wave back with a smile and turn back to Ben who furiously stares Jared down.

"You, okay? You seem upset."

"What did *he* want?" he retorts in an unnecessarily aggressive manner, brows furrowed and mouth downturned.

"Jared? He's on the track team with me, remember? He was inviting me to his graduation party."

Ben continues to stare daggers at the track where Jared's working out.

"Are you sure you're okay?" I playfully touch him on the arm to see how he responds.

His face relaxes at my touch. "Oh, right, right. Yeah, I'm fine. I was just wondering what you two were talking about." He pauses for a minute then grins. "So, you're coming to mine too, right?" He winks.

Aaand I see we're back to Ben's flirty side. I roll my eyes, shoulder bumping him lightly.

"Of course, I am. Duh. You're my best friend."

He smiles, brushing my arm with his hand. A quick burning prickle instantly creeps up the back of my neck and into my cheeks at his touch, making me move away from him out of instinct. His brows furrow again as he catches me distancing myself from his touch, his smile dropping.

I instinctively clutch my left elbow in embarrassment at the awkward situation my body made by moving away on its' own. He's touched my arm plenty of times throughout our friendship, including hugs and play fighting, but we've changed since then. It's...different now.

Is this what happens when you move into adulthood? I suppose it's inevitable we'd change if I ever thought realistically about it. It just never occurred to me it would change like *this*.

He kindly backs away a step to give me some space and plasters on a strained smile. Yawning, he stretches his arms, pulling his shirt up with them and tightening his white shirt on the rest of his torso. Now given a front row view of his deep v-cut that dips into his leather pants, my mouth waters and my tongue and teeth scrape the inside of my cheek as I fixate on his now exposed olive skin. That tingling sensation below fiercely returns, giving me an aggressive urge to run my fingers over his abs. His shirt, in seemingly slow motion, ruffles back down, covering his stomach fully again.

"Eyes up here, Char," he whispers, winking.

Oh my God, I want to die.

He caught me staring? What is wrong with me?

"Don't flatter yourself. I was stuck in a stare and your abs just happened to be there," I retort, playfully sticking out my tongue.

It's the best excuse I can come up with. I hope he buys it, but since my cheeks are on fire, I'm guessing he won't. The last time they felt this hot was when I accidentally walked in on two girls hooking up in our locker room last year and ran into the door because I tried to escape with my eyes shut while profusely shouting "sorry!".

At least his smile is back and a calmness settles between us instead of the previous tension there seconds before.

The v-cut into his leather jeans emerges in my head again. If only I had an internal AC system to cool my cheeks and hide my true reactions. Being so easy to read is super inconvenient.

My skin tightens and that familiar tingling sensation runs rampant in my shorts like the first night I saw that biker on Xypher. Another urge hits me, this time a magnetic pull drawing me toward him, his mouth. I zone out on his lips, forgetting he can see everything I'm looking at. They're plump for a boy and moist from the Chapstick he must've put on before he came over here.

Moist, pink and so, so inviting.

Without thinking, I step forward, my eyes still locked in, my teeth instinctively biting my bottom lip. Ben chuckles softly and steps toward me. He slowly licks his lips, knocking me out of the trance I'm in.

I stutter step back. What the heck is wrong with me?

I want to leave and sit in a bubble where no one can see me until I figure out what all this is.

Do I truly want to be with Ben or am I just attracted to him? *Or*, am I finally hitting that lustful stage of being a teenager right before I'm shipped off to college where it's easy to have orgies?

Trying to make sense of everything, I shake my head and stroke my fingers through my hair, pulling it away from my face. I'm aware of his stare, but I avoid his gaze.

The heat in my cheeks and below are unbearable. I need to get him out of my sight and cool down before he figures out my body's current reaction to him.

"Char?"

"I gotta go. I'll talk to you later, okay?" I spurt out way too loudly as I spin around and book it to my car.

"Char!"

His shout rings in my ears but I pretend I can't hear him. If I stay near him, I'm going to ruin our friendship. I *have* to clear my head. My body *has* to calm down.

The rest of my name yelled from across the parking lot cuts off mid-way when I slam my car door shut. The rush of the AC blasting drowns out any other noises as I bolt out of the lot before he can get to my car.

All I want to do is kiss him, feel him against me in some way, skin to skin...and the thoughts of him doing those things to me aches my body, igniting it all on fire.

"Ahhhh!" I scream into the empty car, trying to alleviate everything I'm feeling, gripping my steering wheel so tightly I can't feel my fingers anymore. It isn't working. Nothing is working. Not even the AC is able to cool me down and pull me out of this internal inferno.

The drive home goes fast, either from speeding or from zoning out, my mind stuck in the gutter.

Images flash on an endless loop, whiplashing my emotions. Images of his abs, mixed with a longing for him... images of him rejecting me, and losing our friendship forever...

Now home, I slam my car door shut and escape to my room, throwing my bookbag on the floor. Thank God, my phone shows no messages from Ben questioning my reaction. With relief from avoiding another awkward conversation, I throw it down on the bed so it's out of my sight. I sit at my computer with my head in my hands and let my hair fall over my face, cascading down to cover the keyboard of my laptop.

In the quick moment of silence between thoughts, an idea occurs to me. I check the clock to see how much time I'll have alone. Four o'clock. Okay, my parents are at their publisher meeting and won't be home until at least six. I have plenty of time.

Without wasting another moment, I turn the lights off, close the blinds, put my hair up and open my laptop. Other girls talk about doing this, but I've never had the urge to try it myself until now. Nervous energy rushes through me even though it's ridiculous. It's my body after all. I shouldn't feel uncomfortable… exploring it.

With my browser already open to Xypher's website, I go straight to BikerBB64's page and scroll through a few of his videos until I find the one that makes me feel how I did with Ben today.

Dancing seductively in the pouring rain in a white t-shirt, grey sweatpants and a waist pack?

Yes, please.

His drenched shirt rests in the grooves of his muscles, clearly outlining his abs and v-cut while his biceps push against the sleeves causing them to tighten every time he moves. The video is only twenty seconds long, but it replays automatically. This is going to be the one I use.

I pause it and mentally prep myself. How do I begin?

Guess I'll just have to experiment. Sucking in a lungful of air to strengthen my resolve, I slowly move the mouse over and click play on the video. Music blasts out of my computer speakers, signaling the beginning of his sensual dance in the rain with his motorcycle in the background.

My right hand gently caresses the back of my neck before slowly dragging down my front, grazing my shirt over my breasts and resting on my stomach.

This feels wrong, but I can't pinpoint why. I'm not doing anything illegal, so it has to feel wrong only because it's new and exciting, right? I do my best to convince myself and push past the feeling, shutting my eyes in the hopes it helps with the slight embarrassment creeping up.

His movements clearly play in my mind, feeling even more real than the video now. He's dancing just for me, motioning for me to come to him as his hips sway back and forth.

My left hand rests tentatively on my chair while my right slides underneath the waistband of my loose grey shorts. Ever so lightly, I trace circles just under, gaining the courage to enter myself.

He lifts his shirt at the same time he pulls me into him, our wet skin making contact with each other. His hips sway against mine, his hands tightly gripping my backside. Lightning and adrenaline burst through my entire body as I take the plunge.

Oh my God, this feels amazing.

One finger stays in me, pulsating with the flow of the music, while my left hand grips the cushion on the chair, forcing me to bend over, my body tensing naturally as I continue. I flatten my right palm and enter a second finger in. A whispered moan escapes my lips, encouraging me to quicken the pace.

Sweet pleasure I've never known existed builds and settles in my chest. My skin tightens. I'm going to explode. This build-up is too much.

Heavy breaths and moans mix with the music from his video.

My toes curl as my breath hitches and I experience a release that sends chills and alarming pleasure into every corner and crevice of my soul. It pulses in my fingers as an addicting thrill completely fills me up from head to toe.

Still panting, I lean back in my chair and exit myself, the realization of the power I have to make myself feel this way whenever I want settling in.

Wow. Just *wow*.

No wonder other girls rave about this. Is this what sex feels like? God, I can only imagine.

The pleasure consumes me completely, my mind devoid of everything else but feeling this over and over and over again. I want to feel it again. *My God*, did I want to feel that again. Can I do this twice in a row? Does the body allow it?

The music continues echoing into the now steamy air. Sweat trickles down my spine, tickling me as my heightened senses pick up on every small sensation occurring on my skin.

I lean forward and take my shirt off, throwing it on the floor, then stand up, figuring I might as well take my shorts off too. They drop to the floor and with a kick of my foot, land in my laundry basket.

Taking in the new me, my gaze slowly wanders up and down myself in the floor-length mirror, studying it like a map that leads to a destination that's never been uncovered before. My ab lines cut down to my hips, glistening in the low light of the laptop with sweat. Splotchy red spots trail down from my cheeks onto my chest and all over my back and neck. Is that normal?

The music stops, tossing me violently into a loud silence. Then darkness surrounds me fully as my laptop goes to sleep. Without the music and light seductively keeping me on the high, exhaustion hits me like a truck.

Curiosity gets the better of me though, as I wake my computer to see if my body will let me go again. I exit out of the current video and scroll for a new one, waiting to feel that same sensation. It didn't take long.

The corner of my lip curls up as wetness pools, confirming I can go another round. Excitement and anticipation build quickly this time.

I stop at a new video where he's slowly lifting his baggy black t-shirt to reveal a six pack and v-cut, pulling down his biker pants just enough to almost see where he dwells beneath them. This is one hundred percent the one I'm going to use.

Maximizing it to full screen, I sit back down and watch him dance to the music, envisioning that he's seducing me privately. Ready for more, I reach down to my wet essence, flatten my palm and idly draw circles with my fingers right over the top.

Another enticing idea surfaces. My left hand works its way under my bra, squeezing and caressing my breast to the music mindlessly. On their own, my hips start moving, grinding to the music and against my fingers, begging them to go in. I obey and push two in. Fast, immediate tightening signals their acceptance.

I knead my breast harder, pushing into it, leaning my head back in bliss. Lightning and energy well up inside me, pulsing throughout my entire body. It's not as strong as the first time but *God*, it still feels amazing.

My heavy pants and groans come faster, louder this time, intertwining with the music and making the fantasy more real. He grabs me, pulling me into his chest, the warmth of his skin on mine and his tight grip on my arms... that's all it took this time.

I squeeze my breast hard and grip myself tightly as I pulse to a final finish. Out of breath, I remove my bra and stand to observe myself in the mirror again. My entire face is red along with every single part of my body. My abs flex from how hard I pant, the muscles still tense from the release, my own scent dripping down my leg.

I feel so empowered. Hot. Different. I want more. I can't get enough.

But before I get the chance to go again, I'm snapped out of my reverie by the front door shutting downstairs. I've never been disappointed to have them home but all I wanted now was to be alone with myself, my thoughts, my body, and the biker on Xypher.

"Charlotte!" Dad calls up the stairs. "We brought dinner. Come and get it!"

Upon hearing my father's voice, another unexpected emotion hits me. Shame. Guilt.

A pit opens in my stomach. If my parents ever find out that I've pleasured myself, they'll see me differently. Not that I expect to ever tell them this, but I always tell them everything. I've never kept anything from them.

But this... This is something I can't share. It'll completely shatter their impression of their innocent daughter if I do.

Was this wrong of me to explore? Should I not have done this?

Thoughts race through my mind as I frantically grab new clothes out of my dresser and gather the courage to face my parents. The mirror shows small splotchy red marks are still visible on my exposed skin, but it's better than it was five minutes ago.

"Charlie! What're you doing up there? The food's getting cold!"

"Coming!" I yell down in a higher pitched voice than normal. Crap. Will they catch onto that? Will they suspect what I've done?

No. No way. I'm being *way* too paranoid right now.

The high I previously experienced fully dissipates, leaving me with only an empty feeling and burning questions.

Jogging down the stairs, I throw a fake smile on and hug them. They beam at me with their usual shining faces. Good. They don't suspect anything. At least now I know I can keep a secret from them. Well, so far that is. I mentally facepalm myself. That *cannot* be a good thing.

We eat and joke around during dinner, talking about what fun things we could do during our last summer together. But the forced smile feels unnatural, and I can already tell that this secret's going to be hard to keep, especially from my mother. My mother, who's always been my best friend and confidant.

But I can't tell her this. I can't ruin her image of me.

They suggest we watch a movie together after dinner, but I decline, unable to fake being okay anymore. Therefore, I lied and said I was tired and just wanted to shower, finish some last minute to-do items for college and read a book.

A small flare of concern popped up on their faces, but I plastered that fake smile on once more which eased their expressions slightly.

Once in the shower, I turn the knob as cold as it can go to shock my nervous system and get rid of this edged feeling, letting the water roll off my hair and down my back. Goosebumps cover my trembling chilled skin, but I stay, embracing the clarity coming from it, the emotional turmoil slowly falling away.

Once the shivering becomes unbearable, I grab a towel and go to my room, wrapping my hair up to keep it off my skin.

Avoiding the mirror, I pull out my favorite blue silk pajamas from my dresser and get dressed. I lay on my bed with my phone on my chest, trying to keep myself distracted from looking at my laptop.

Shame hits me in waves each time I glance at the place where I touched myself.

Rolling on my side away from my laptop, I face my bedroom wall and unlock my phone.

Oh, Ben called me.

Oohhh, Ben called me during *that* time. Subtle heat burns dully underneath the surface again. The thought of him calling me while I touched myself seems too close. Like he'll know what I was doing during that time if I reach out to him now.

But that's ridiculous. Right? He didn't leave me a message or voicemail which is rare for him if I miss his call so I should call him back in case something happened. It's not until after I hear the ringing on the other side of the phone that I remember how I left him in the parking lot.

Oh, God. What if he's calling to ask about that? The other side picks up. Too late.

"Hey, you."

"Hey. What's up? I saw you called me."

"Yeah. Why didn't you answer?"

Crap, I knew he was going to ask me that. Think. Think. Think.

"Oh, sorry. I was filling out college stuff on my computer and my phone was on my bed on silent mode, so I didn't hear it when you rang."

"Sure, you were." His deep chuckle playfully echoes through the phone. "So, do you wanna hang out? I feel like it's been forever since you've come to the farm, and we've just relaxed and talked."

"That's because it has been. Tree wouldn't let us hang out, remember?" I spit with an unintentional bite.

He pauses on the other end of the line, a silent tension pulling taught between us.

"Well, she's out of the picture now, and I miss my best friend. So, how 'bout it? My parents are still out in the field. We can play video games in my room, or we can hang out in the back pasture and star gaze on the wood pallets by the barn?"

One of my favorite pastimes with Ben has always been gazing at the stars in the field until late at night; especially in the fall when it gets cold. He always gives me his sweater, so I stay warm too. Then I insist that he take it back when he starts shivering and he always swears he isn't cold even though I see the goosebumps.

Hm…That does sound nice but ugh, I'm already showered and in bed.

"That *does* sound great. It's been way too long since we've hung out together doing our favorite things, buuuuttt, I'm already in my PJs and showered, so I don't know if I feel like getting dressed and driving over. How much would you hate me if we hung out another night instead?"

His calm breaths resound through the line. "Are you avoiding me, Char?"

My head jerks back in surprise at the forward question. "No? Why on earth would you think that?"

Oh, probably because you ran away from him in the parking lot like a crazy person, Charlotte. Duh.

"You haven't asked me to hang out in forever. Normally after Tree and I break up, you're the first one to reach out and ask for a hang out like old times. Now lately you don't even text me back half the time-"

"Because I forget!" I interrupt quickly.

"You never used to forget. Then today you completely avoided me after school. Was it because of Jared? Was I interrupting something between you two when I walked over?"

"Wha...no! What are you talking about? Jared and I are just friends. Just like you and me are. I don't understand where this is coming from. If anyone has been acting strange lately, it's you.

He huffs out a harsh breath over the phone.

"What, Ben? What's the problem here?"

"Char, I..." he stops mid-sentence.

Anger bubbles underneath the surface, stemming from confusion and the constant mixed signals he's been giving me lately. What is this? Is he playing games with me, or what?

"We *are* friends. I'm sorry, I've just been going through it lately, and I haven't really had anyone to talk to about it."

My anger softens. Is that pain in his voice? His parents are typically busy on the farm and they're not the "let's talk about our feelings" type of folks. Why didn't he talk to Tree or call me if he needed to talk that badly prior to this conversation?

"I'm sorry that it feels like I haven't been there for you. That wasn't my intention. But with you and Tree being practically back together, I figured if I asked you to hang out outside of school, you wouldn't want to or be allowed to." My stomach sinks as the image of them kissing resurfaces. I freakin' hate this.

"We're not together," he replies quickly.

"Bu-"

"We're not together. We haven't been together for a while. I told you that already," he says fiercely, cutting me off.

"You did, but your actions say otherwise. I don't understand it. Like, why'd you kiss at Pop's pizza or even bring her there on what looked like a date if you weren't together or considering getting back together? You said you were friends with benefits so I assumed it was just a matter of time until you got back together anyways," I aggressively spout, trying to get the words out before he can cut me off again.

"Listen, I was being stupid. She wanted to keep dating, so I tried but I couldn't do it anymore. There's a bond I can't explain with her. I kept holding on to it not because I wanted to but because it felt like my only choice." He sighs deeply. "I know I feel connected to her like this because I lost my virginity to her, but it sucks. I don't want anything to do with her anymore, but that feeling, that bond is what keeps bringing me back to her."

Hearing him voice those words directly to me makes it more real, more vivid than anything has so far. The image of them tangled up in the sheets has my stomach twisting in knots. They have a closeness I'll never be able to have with him, and that realization sucks. It really freakin' sucks.

I can't help the bite in my next words.

"Well, how would I know any of that? You cut me off and left me like I wasn't important to you. Once you had a gorgeous girl on your arm, you forgot all about me. You never even asked how I felt about you two dating or how I was doing once you blocked me. I was left to wonder if you even cared about me at all anymore."

I was standing now, death gripping the phone from the anger surging through me. How dare he make me feel bad, like he's the one who was hurt. He didn't care about our friendship or else he wouldn't have just cut me off and tossed me aside for sex with a pretty girl.

What a hypocrite.

"Did you even think of how I would feel when I heard that you two had sex? I didn't even get to hear it from you! I had to hear it in the locker room from girls who don't know you half as well as I do."

"I didn't—"

"No, you didn't," I sharply cut in. "What about the first time you cut me off and blocked me? You never even gave me a warning or asked me how I felt about never talking to you. I had no idea if I was your friend anymore or if we'd ever talk again. Was it even hard for you to cut me out just so you could get some? Like, was her vagina magical or something? Was it worth the possibility of losing me forever?" I finish my rant, my quick heartbeat pulsing in the fingertips death gripping the phone. If he was here, I swear I'd smack him across the face.

Tense silence rings over the phone. Guilt for berating him creeps in as my eyes moisten. The long silence breaks with a sigh on his end.

"Char," he squeaks softly, voice breaking.

I can almost hear his brain churning to find the right words, but I don't care. I want to hang up on him to make him feel a shred of what I feel right now. What I've been feeling this last year each time he's discarded me like some piece of trash only to be pulled out as a second option. I rarely explode or feel my emotions like this, leaving me inappropriately armed for how to handle the violent thrash of them inside me.

Who knows what's gotten into me lately, but even if it's a bad thing, I don't care. It feels good to allow myself to fully feel for once. These emotions surfacing as of late are making me feel like a new person, and I'm going to embrace it. I'm not going to shy away from my feelings anymore. I'm not going to let him walk all over me and use me when he wants for his own emotional comfort.

Thoughts I've always pushed to the side keep popping up the longer he stays silent, driving the anger to embed itself deeper. Steady tears drip down my cheeks from anger and hurt, and I don't care if he can hear it. I hope it makes him feel worse.

"Let me come over. I'll explain it all to you better. Please don't cry."

"I-I-I'm n-n-not crying," I stutter, unconvincingly.

"Char," his voice quietly breaks again.

"Stop calling me that! I'm not your Char right now."

Ben calling me his special nickname for me is the last straw. I don't want him to be able to feel close to me right now by using my name his favorite way. That was a sweet name he's always called me, but he's *not* allowed to use it right now. He does *not* get that privilege after treating me like I'm disposable.

He sighs heavily again over the phone. Not an angry or irritated sigh, but one more out of empathy. In the rare times I've cried from anger, usually from when I accidentally hurt myself as a kid, he would sigh like that and then give me a big hug. When I was younger it helped me get over the emotion quicker and made me feel better, but now the thought of him hugging me just ticks me off more.

"Charlotte, I want to explain this all to you in person... if you'll let me."

"Explain what, exactly? What is there to explain, Ben?" The anger's edge softens at his pleading tone, a small shred of guilt surfacing again for still being so short with him, but I hold onto it, nonetheless. This whirlwind of emotions is exhausting.

"A lot of things. I just... I've been wanting to talk to you for a while now. But I don't want to do it over the phone."

"What, did you get Tree pregnant or something?"

A ball rises in my throat, an overwhelming wave of nausea hitting me and dread that my accusation might be true.

"Jesus Christ, Charlotte, no. If you'd listen to me, and let me explain, then you'd understand."

He's treating me like a child being scolded. The nerve of this guy.

"Do *not* talk down to me like a child."

"Then don't act like one! Be an adult and let's have a fucking conversation!"

"Don't you swear at me Benjamin Beltre!"

"We're eighteen, Char. Damnit, we can swear. You don't have to be a goody-goody forever. You'll run into plenty of adults at college who swear, and you're going to have to listen to it."

I pause, taken aback by how he's talking to me. He's never sworn directly at me, and he knows how much I hate swearing.

"I'm going to let you cool off, and we'll talk tomorrow, okay?"

"No."

"Really, Char?"

"No. I don't want to talk to you tomorrow. I don't even know who you are anymore."

To be fair, I don't know who I am anymore either, I want to say.

"Whatever. Fuck it. I'll talk to you when you cool off."

The tone beeps three times, signaling he hung up.

I lower my phone, staring at it— more offended than I expected. I can't believe he actually hung up on me. Drops of my tears smear and bubble on the surface of my screen. Wiping my tears on my skin first, then wiping off the moisture on the screen, I put my phone on my computer desk to charge.

Ben and I have never fought like this. He's never treated me this way. This is the *worst* feeling.

I hate this.

Tears fall harder down my face, soaking the skin down my neck onto my collarbone.

Clarity begins to settle in as the tears release the tension and anger held in my chest. Yes, he "disposed" of me because of a girl, but he *did* find subtle ways to make sure I knew I wasn't forgotten at times. When I was cut off, he'd leave a note in my locker with an inside joke from our childhood, or one that just had my name on it and nothing else. No one else called me Char so he knew I'd know it was from him. Then there were times in class where he'd give me a soft smile or stick his tongue out at me even though he would sit all the way across the room.

In the heat of the moment, I forgot about those small hints he left showing he was still thinking of me. Granted, he didn't do those hints often, but just enough to let me know that he still cared about me.

Mentally and physically exhausted from the night, I crawl into bed.

As I bring the sheet up over my shoulder and nuzzle my head into the pillow, I ponder if I overreacted. Even if I did overreact though, I didn't deserve to be yelled at. I mean, what I said *is* true. He used to be so open with his emotions with me but the last couple of years, that's dwindled. Maybe this is just what happens as we grow into adults; we share less of ourselves with other people, even our best friends.

I turn over, unable to shut my mind off enough to drift off to sleep.

Is he right? Do I need to grow up? Am I really acting like a little child because I won't swear or get into what everyone else gets into in high school? I've always felt like a loner—never left fully out but never let fully into social groups. Maybe this is the reason I was never included... They could see I wasn't on their level—see I hadn't grown up yet.

"Ugghh," I expel with a huff, turning on my back and covering my head fully with my sheets. I hope this fight doesn't affect our friendship again. We were just getting *us* back. I don't want to lose that again so soon. I'll wait and see how he reacts tomorrow or try and talk to him later in the week before school ends.

Yeah, I'm sure we'll be fine, I reassure myself. *We'll be fine.*

I roll over one more time, finally drifting to sleep thinking of Ben and his sweet smile, and all the good times we had growing up when things were easier.

Chapter Six.

My nerves get the best of me. My first class with Ben arrives, and I have no idea how we're going to interact.

I made sure to wear something I considered cute to give myself a better shot at drawing his attention. He once whispered to me that I looked cute when I wore sundresses so I figured a long yellow sundress with brown sandals might help ease the tension. I've never dressed up intentionally for him, let alone anyone before.

God, this is probably a terrible idea.

A few people turn their heads to stare at me as I walk down the hallway. Is it the dress or because I actually straightened my hair today and wore some eyeliner? Ugh, now I'm even more self-conscious. What was I thinking? I wish I'd brought extra clothes to change into.

Ben's sitting at the back, far away from the usual spot he grabs us. He must still be mad then. I move toward him but stop when I hear my name being called from the hallway.

"Hey Charlotte!" Jared says grinning widely from the doorway. Upon hearing my name, I catch Ben, in my periphery, turning around and perking up to stare directly at us. I ignore him, turning my full attention to Jared.

"Hey, Jared. What's going on?" I casually hug my books closer to my chest.

"You're for sure coming to my party on Saturday, right? It starts at five." He leans on the doorway, folding his arms together nonchalantly, his red T-shirt tight enough I can see every muscle outlined underneath.

It's common to see him shirtless at practice but for some reason it's just now hitting me how buff he actually is. I glance quickly to the perfectly outlined six-pack under his shirt.

A familiar, wet tingling sensation revisits the spot between my legs. My lips curl in under my teeth in frustration at my body's unbelievable gull to act like this in public.

What the heck is wrong with me? Calm down or else he'll notice and then what would I say? Sorry, your abs are turning me on? I need to go take care of myself real quick, BRB?

I sneak a peek behind me and catch Ben staring intently at us. For sass, I flip my hair over my shoulder and turn back to Jared.

"For sure! I promise I'll be there at five, right when it starts. How long does it last? It didn't say on the invite." The heat of Ben's stare on my back radiates through me. Talking to Jared while Ben watches like this feels good. It makes me feel in control of the situation, of his emotions toward me. Who knew all I had to do to elicit an emotion out of him was talk to another guy?

Jared lets out a low chuckle and winks. "It ends when it ends. You can stay however long ya like."

I blush. It was pretty cute how he said that. I brush my hair behind my ear, still holding my books in my other arm lightly to me. "Alright, I'll see you Saturday then."

He nods and walks off with a noticeable bounce in his step. We don't have any classes together, but sometimes I'll see him in the halls or at practice. The last two days are the most we've interacted in a long time though. Is he trying to make friends with everyone before we all go our own separate ways?

When I turn back around, Ben's resting his chin on the back of his chair, staring at the ground, brows furrowed and lips pursed in contemplation. He only wears that expression when he's had to make big decisions.

I rack my brain, trying to remember if there's something big happening in his life but nothing comes to mind, which couldn't mean anything since we haven't been as close lately. My heart dips into sadness. I miss us.

Bucking up some courage, I step to walk over to him to make up, but as soon as I move, he lifts his chin off the chair and makes eye contact with me, his face going blank before his full lips straighten as if still mad then turns around to face his computer away from me.

I jerk my neck back in surprise and annoyance. Fine. If he's going to act like that then forget it. I'll go sit in our usual spot and treat him how he's treating me.

Setting my books down beside my keyboard, I steal one more glance at Ben and stifle a laugh as Greta sits down next to him, scooting her chair as close as possible until they're almost touching leg to leg. He cringes, withdrawing an inch before planting an awkward smile on.

Serves him right. I stick my nose up, turning back to my computer with a satisfied smirk.

The rest of the day's interactions with Ben go the same way. He perks up when he sees me, eyes slightly wide, then quickly looks away. I decide to ignore it. I don't care. He's the one acting like a child after telling me to grow up so, whatever. I'll let him sort that out on his own.

As the day goes on, I receive increased attention from a lot of my classmates which is an unexpected confidence booster and helps me feel more comfortable in my dress. Being invisible isn't bad, but this new attention elicits an ego boost I could get used to. I should have started wearing dresses to school much sooner. I could've had a totally different experience here.

The last bell of the day rings, so I make my way to my locker to grab my keys and backpack after my oddly thrilling day. I walk down the hallway, a small bounce to my own step when a heavy arm hangs over my shoulder.

Smirking, I tilt my head up expecting Ben but instead see Jared, smiling down at me. His blonde hair's still in the bun from earlier, but a few wisps are left untamed near his face. He smiles at me differently, softer, and studies me more deeply, intimately.

My cheeks give away my reaction to his intimate attention, but I act unfazed, smiling softly back and letting him keep his arm over me.

"I'm glad you're coming. We're gonna have a blast. Everyone from the cross country and track team's coming. We're gonna order pizza, play games, and maybe even *swim*."

The idea of everyone seeing me in my bikini makes me want to crawl back into my turtle shell.

"Well, I probably won't swim, but it all sounds like a great time. I'm looking forward to it." This feels nice. Having someone excited to include me in this way is something I could get used to. I just needed a little push. I'm grateful to Jared for that.

He side hugs me harder, pushing my cheek against the right side of his chest. Sandalwood with a hint of citrus fills my senses. It's very different than Ben's scent—leather and mint.

My body rebels against me and throws me a reel of the mysterious biker riding shirtless on his motorcycle. A shot of adrenaline rings through me with the pleasure sensation following down below.

Okay, now I feel uncomfortable being under Jared's arm given my current...situation. Shoving the image out of my mind, I instead focus on the fact that I'll be home soon and can log onto Xypher to take care of the problem. I quicken my steps, in turn quickening Jared's since he's insisting on keeping his arm around me.

"Are you okay? We're basically jogging to your car. Am I making you uncomfortable?"

His question slows my pace. How sweet of him to care if he's making me uncomfortable or not.

"Sorry. Yeah, I'm okay. You're not making me uncomfortable," I reassure him with a subtle grin.

His eyes soften as they search mine. He gives me another squeeze on my shoulder, pulling me into him again. Butterflies flutter in my stomach at the acceptance of his touch and the reciprocated smile.

He finally removes his arm, only to open my car door for me. I widen my eyes at the gesture and go to thank him, but my voice is drowned out by the roar of a motorcycle speeding out of the parking lot.

We both turn to see Ben pop a wheelie before speeding away onto the road. I roll my eyes. What's gotten into him? I hate this obnoxious side of him. Nine times out of ten he'll keep his cool, but when he doesn't, he's the one who acts like a child. I exhale forcefully at his obvious childish actions. And he had the gall to tell *me* to grow up.

Jared gently shuts my car door and waves to me as he walks off to his truck. Once I'm sure he's gone, I scan my surroundings to make sure no one else is looking and slide my hand up my thigh to find how drenched I am. I shiver at my own gentle touch, a quick shoot of anticipation rushing through my body, urging me to speed home to explore myself again with the biker boy.

Disappointment creeps in when I notice Dad's home.

Crap.

Whatever, I'll just have to be quiet.

I drop my bag by the stairs roughly to signal I'm home, shout hi into the living room and rush up the stairs, skipping every other step.

My lips curl ever so subtly, excitement building quickly inside me. I keep my bedroom lights off so it's only the light from the laptop once more and whip my dress off, throwing it on the floor, prepped and ready for my alone time. Xypher's website greets me automatically with BikerBB64's profile showing five new videos posted since yesterday. Upon initial investigation, he usually only posts one video a week, but to do five in one day just as I discover his profile?

Thank you, universe.

The new videos are ten times more seductive, heightening my current situation to new levels. The first video reveals him sitting on his bike with his shirt off in tight leather pants, breathing heavily and flexing his abs, staring at the camera with his head cocked, giving attitude like I disobeyed him to sultry music.

The next one shows him flexing his hand, highlighting his veins and tan skin. In the last three, he dances to various sounds, seductively of course, moving his hips in circular motions, pulling his shirt up, flexing… All the good things.

The flexed arm video draws my attention the most. I don't know why it's *so* attractive to me, but it's getting me going so bad I can't stand it. An intriguing idea occurs to me.

What if I picture his hand instead of mine touching me?

I intently memorize every detail about the hand; the shape, the texture, what it'd feel like on my skin…Inside of me.

"Knock, knock," Dad says knocking on the door, opening it without waiting for me to answer.

A thud shakes the entire upstairs as I fall off the chair in a panic. I rollie pollie on the floor to my bed and rip my comforter off it, throwing everything off my bed to cover myself as much as possible. My teeth grit together from the intense stinging in my tailbone from the fall as my dad fully opens the door. In horror, I stare at my computer that's still open to the viral biker's hand, the seductive music playing quietly.

"Woah! You okay, champ? Did I scare you?" He studies me questioningly, brows furrowing at my odd behavior.

"Oh yeah, no worries. I was just in the middle of stretching and I hadn't fully changed my clothes yet because I was hot," I say with clenched teeth.

As much as I try to sound normal, the words spill from my mouth in a rush. With bated breath, I wait for his response and some sort of confirmation that he doesn't suspect anything.

Relief washes over him. Looks like he bought it.

"Why are the lights off? Will you melt if I turn them on?" he chuckles, flicking the light switch.

Good, he's joking.

I joke back, hissing when the light comes on acting like I'm a vampire shielding myself from the brightness. He laughs. I smile back, relaxing my shoulders while ensuring the covers tight on me.

Oh, right. I'm on the floor.

I gather the comforter wrapped around me and am about to stand up to sit on the bed when I catch him turning to my computer. As if in slow motion his head turns toward the screen.

In a panic, I leap forward to shut the laptop, but trip, my feet catching under the loosened covers pulling my feet out from under me. I land hard on the floor, catching the brunt of the fall on my elbows.

"Charlotte! Are you okay? *What* has gotten into you?" He reaches to help me up, concern brimming his face.

"Sorry, I'm okay," I chuckle trying my best to play it off. "I was trying to stand up and got up *way* too fast."

My mind races for a way to get him out of my room to end this brutally awkward encounter.

Lightbulb! That's it!

"Are you hungry? I'm *starving*. Do you want to pick up some Chinese food and bring it home? We haven't had that for a while, and it sounds *so* good. I could use some sweet and sour chicken."

He pulls away, studying me curiously. I can tell he caught on to my change in topic as a distraction but is fighting the urge to ask more questions. He puts on a smile that doesn't meet the eyes.

"Sure, hun. Why don't you get dressed and I'll meet you downstairs, alright? We'll surprise Mom."

I nod, releasing a sigh of relief. The door closes with a quiet *click*. I stay still, listening to his footsteps retreating down the hallway before moving an inch. Once deemed safe, I uncurl from the blanket and shut the laptop before laying down on the floor. I close my eyes and try my best not to relive what just happened. My heart pounds in my ears so hard it makes my eyes bounce with the beat beneath my eyelids.

This absolutely *cannot* happen again. I was being reckless and didn't think about the consequences. My parents *cannot* know I do this.

If I ever feel like doing this again anyways... That was traumatizing as hell. Who knows if I'll get the urge again. Maybe this was the wake-up call I needed to stop.

I get dressed in a daze and make my bed, avoiding my now closed computer screen.

I'll deal with it later. I don't need to sort all this out now.

The drive to pick up Chinese food is uncomfortable at first, to say the least. Dad doesn't say much, and neither do I. Shifting in my seat, I search for a conversation topic to break the silence, but I'm coming up completely blank. I only pray he won't bring up what happened in my bedroom. Luckily, a break in the tension occurs at the gas station when we run into my fourth-grade teacher, Ms. Roche.

She remembers me right off the bat. It's heartwarming to reminisce over how I was the best reader in the class, although I could have done without her telling my dad about the one time I got caught cutting the girl's hair in front of me with scissors, and admitting to her when I got caught that I didn't know if regular scissors could cut hair or not. He shoots me a jokingly stern frown and eyebrow raise, making us laugh.

I'm grateful for her presence, giving us a reprieve from the tension, especially because the rest of the drive is completely normal. All the awkward moments from before vanish.

Our timing is perfect. By the time we pull into the driveway, Mom is just pulling in and by the dancing in her car, she's definitely excited to have her favorite Chinese dish of pork soup dumplings and egg rolls waiting for her.

The rest of the night goes as usual—joking around about their books, poking fun at each other and watching Tidal Wave, our favorite natural disaster movie.

My emotional cup is full by the time I walk upstairs to go to bed. Everything's going to be just fine between me and my father, thank God. Here's hoping he doesn't tell Mom about it either so we can forget the entire encounter ever happened.

I check my phone, which surprisingly has no messages on it and curl up in my bed, comfort finding me immediately.

My thoughts drift aimlessly, the interactions with Ben filling my brain, preventing me from relaxing all the way. As my mom taught me, I acknowledge the thoughts and then do my best to let them go, attaching no emotion to them.

His eyes widening each time he saw me in my dress...

The subtle movements of his lips indicating some sort of emotion hidden behind his solemn face...

We're in such a weird place right now. I don't know how we move forward from here. Especially with the fact that he hasn't texted me or made any moves to reconcile. Of course, I guess it has only been like a day. Maybe we'll sort this out tomorrow or by the end of the week.

Yeah, we'll be okay...We have to be.

Chapter Seven.

The next day at school is rough. A stark horniness sets me on edge, distracting me all day. All of this is so new to me. Am I really going to have to start masturbating every day to feel normal? That would definitely hurt my ability to be a socially acceptable, functioning human being.

Each time I get called on ends with a frustrated glance from the teachers. I'm completely checked out, the only focus possible being on those videos of the biker boy waiting for me at home.

Today's outfit choice is a blue and white spotted dress to see if I can get another reaction from Ben. Unintentionally, it brings the attention of Jared once more, causing us to replay our walk down the hallway and him putting his arm over me every chance he gets.

Ben's facial reactions upon seeing Jared and I together, or when just seeing me in general, get more obvious.

Anger. Jealousy. Hurt.

They all flash on his face in that order. By the end of the day, he looks like he's going to punch something or someone.

I don't know why he's getting so worked up. I've seen him and Tree together like this tons of times and *I* didn't freak out...well not outwardly. I keep myself in check even if it hurts or angers me at times. He's acting like I'm committing the biggest act of betrayal by hanging around Jared. We're all just friends so I don't see the big deal or why anyone has to make drama out of this.

Hopefully we can sort this out before Ben's graduation party. If not, maybe I'll pull him aside and talk to him at his party either before or after everyone leaves. I don't want our friendship to end over a stupid argument over nothing.

Jared walks me out to my car again at the end of the day. I scan the parking lot for Ben, but he's nowhere to be seen. Jared gives me a big hug with a tight squeeze around my mid-section, pulling me fully into his chest and letting his cologne wrap around me.

Maybe I should explore this with Jared. He's putting in the effort lately, and I'll admit, I like it. Plus, he's not bad to look at either. I've always noticed how in shape he was but never thought anything of it. He's not a thicker, muscular build like Ben, but a lean cut, built for running with legs clearly displaying the power contained within them. I mean, the guy's calf muscles pop out with every step he takes.

He holds me for a second longer than he needs to, continuing to smile down at me. I return one back, getting in my car and he shuts the door for me like a gentleman.

"See you tomorrow, Charlotte."

Rolling down my window, I reply, "Yeah, for sure. Isn't it nuts? That this is all over? That we'll officially be done with high school?"

He leans over the open window, folding his arms and resting his chin on them in a relaxed manner.

"It really is. This last year was way more stressful compared to the previous three. Too bad everything is ending right when it was getting good."

"What do you mean? You've got this amazing scholarship for track and will be venturing out into the real world. You're nothing like me. I barely scraped into college, and I've never done anything special to be remembered for. I have a feeling my adulthood is going to be just as average as my adolescence."

I end the statement discouraged, looking down into my hands lying in my lap, twiddling with the folds of my dress. These thoughts have lingered in me for a while, but I haven't yet had the courage to have this conversation with Ben or my parents. I'm surprised I was able to be this vulnerable with Jared.

His knuckle grazes my chin as he tilts my head up. He lifts his head off his arms, eyes boring deep into mine. Wow, I never noticed the multitude of gold specks in between the bright green of his irises. The colors blend to create a beautiful combination.

"You are anything but average, Charlotte. You can achieve anything you put your mind to. All it takes is setting a goal and being resilient enough to discipline yourself into doing all that it takes to reach that goal."

I smile gratefully. He smirks back, his eyes slowly drifting down from my own to somewhere different. My mouth. I bite the inside of my lip, trying to contain the urge to turtle up.

The pulse between my thighs beckons to me, calling me to touch it, feel it, delve into the wetness of it. Heat sears my cheeks, forcing me to look away in case he can tell what's happening.

He chuckles, releasing his knuckle from my chin and pushes off the car, standing up while keeping his hands on the car door through the open window.

"My parents always preached that anecdote to me, and I believe that's one of the reasons I've been so successful here. Even though they were a little harsher than most, it taught me that if I want something, I can get it if I work hard enough. It's all about mastering your mind and body."

He pauses and peers up at the sky. "Sorry to get all life coachy," he says, looking back at me as he rubs the back of his neck. "If you ever want any tips on motivation or finding what you want to do, let me know. I'd be more than happy to help you."

Why's he so eager to help me? Does he really mean it?

"Thanks for the coaching moment and offer, Jared. I may just take you up on that sometime, but I gotta get home. I'll catch ya tomorrow."

A deep rumble drowns out the last of my sentence, pulling my attention to the road.

NO FREAKING WAY.

Ecstasy is tied to that man and his bike. I could spot him anywhere. It's the biker boy! *Holy shit*! Does he live around here then?

Everything else in the world turns black as my sights pull him in. He slows down as he nears the school parking lot and in slow motion glances my way. My breathing grows faster, and I squeeze my thighs together, my body now trained to expect pleasure when he's around. If only that dark visor lifted up for a moment, giving me something to confirm he's real and I'm not hallucinating right now. But just like that, the motorcycle growls as he speeds off past the entrance and doesn't look back.

"Charlotte? Charlotte..."

"Huh?" The rest of the world's sounds return.

"You alright? You looked like you saw a celebrity or something. Did you know that guy?" He hooks his thumb over his shoulder where my fantasy just vanished from.

"Uh, no. Sorry. Just zoned out for a sec. Sorry," I chuckle awkwardly as I grapple with my reality.

No way did I just see my secret obsession in real life. No freaking way.

"No worries. I'll see you tomorrow, okay? Drive safe."

And with that he turns and runs toward the track, ripping his shirt off in the process. I stare at him through my rear-view mirror, mesmerized by the muscles in his back moving in tune with those powerful legs of his. He's not even in track shorts yet, why'd he take his shirt off? Did he remove his shirt for me?

I need to get out of here...

My parents are home, but I want it so badly, I'm willing to chance getting caught again. To make sure they can't notice anything, I check the back of my dress in the side-view mirror of my car to make sure I haven't soaked through it from how wet I am. The cloth looks dry, thank goodness. I chose not to wear underwear today for easy access in case I found time and felt up to pleasuring myself. Turns out, not wearing underwear is comfortable. Sounds like the commando way might be the way to go moving forward.

Their keyboard clacks echo from the dining room as they both furiously type away on their laptops. They must have a tight deadline to hit. Typically, when I find them in this condition it's a bad idea to disturb them. So instead of saying hi, I give each of them a small side hug with a squeeze that's returned with a small pat on my arm as acknowledgment.

Excitement builds as I dart up the stairs. This is perfect. There's no way they'll walk in on me with how engrossed they are in work right now.

Discarding my phone on the bed, I sit in my chair, excitedly opening my laptop at last. The biker boy's page on Xypher is still pulled up from last time. Oops. I completely forgot to close it out. I hope dad never came up here to snoop.

That thought almost sways me to not do what I'm about to do, but then I glance at all the videos again and decide, screw it. I quickly lock the door, making sure to keep the lights on this time so it doesn't seem suspicious.

Satisfied I'm safe, I gravitate toward the video of his arm and hand again. Veins clearly bulge out on his forearm and the back of his hand when he flexes. As he keeps his fist in a ball to show his strength, it makes me wonder how all that strength would feel inside me.

My fingers slide under my dress, ruffling up the lower half and letting it rest on my upper thighs. Two fingers trace along the inside of my thigh as I imagine they're his teasing me and grazing against my skin but not entering right away.

My chest rises and falls faster with each touch. I rest my head along the back of the chair and close my eyes, fully allowing myself to dive into the fantasy. He heavily pants underneath his helmet beside me, eager for his turn to touch me.

I'm dripping onto the chair under me in unbearable anticipation, aching and breathless from the wait. Unable to take it anymore, I thrust two fingers deep inside myself in one quick motion, cupping my hand to my mouth to prevent the loud sound that escapes from giving me away. My back arches and my neck strains against the back of the chair from pleasurable tension.

It feels so good. So *fucking* good. I rarely swear, but it feels *so* right to say in this situation. I can't believe how naturally swearing comes under these conditions, but *fuck*. There are no other words capable of matching the pleasure filling my body at my touch.

My nails almost tear into the skin on my face, my palm clasping over my mouth so hard, I'm almost suffocating myself to keep silent. My other palm glues down flat to get a harder grip into myself. Two fingers don't feel enough anymore so I move a third finger in, squeezing tightly beside the other two. I release my other hand from my mouth, lurching forward to get deeper, biting my lip hard to keep from crying out, barely feeling the pain amidst the pleasure.

My dress straps fall down my shoulders, exposing my breast that's now being coddled by my hand. I grind in rough circular motions to explore every part I can, panting and gripping my left breast hard, tensing more and more with each movement. Pressure builds in my core and my muscles tense. I'm getting close.

How? How does this feel even better than the other night? My heavy eyelids lull open, my eyes rolling back from pleasure as my toes grip the carpet. My body tenses up, harder and harder until I can barely get a breath in. Stars fill my vision as euphoric release hits me, and its pulsing grip sucks on my fingers. Whispered moans escape as I writhe against myself through blissful completion.

That felt so fucking good. My God.

I sit forward and wipe my fingers on my dress, disheveled and breathing heavy, trying to get my bearings back.

A small amount of shame resurfaces but I shove it down hard, instead letting myself revel in the ecstasy I brought myself. Ben's right. I'm an adult. I'm allowed to make my own choices and keep secrets about myself. It's harmless pleasure. I'm not doing anything wrong at all.

After exiting Xypher and erasing my browser history for good measure, I go to stand up but freeze at the rev of an engine.

Is that Ben? Is our fight finally over?

Rushing to the window, I fumble with my dress strings, pulling them back onto my shoulders to make sure I'm covered. But it's not Ben. It's *him.*

My heart races, a sudden coldness hitting my core, replacing the previous warmth that was just there. He's staring down at his phone. Mouth parted, I watch in shock as he sits on his bike in idle like he belongs here.

Like he's just pulled up to home and hasn't a care in the world. What's he doing? Does he know I live here?

His gloved thumb taps the screen at the same time my phone dings.

What the...

His helmet snaps toward my window.

Oh shit!

Like a heavy sandbag, my body drops to the floor, taking the breath out of me from the impact. *Ouch.* My chest and knees took the full brunt of the hit on the hardwood, leaving a residual sting in my nipples and bones.

R.I.P, my boobs.

Why did my phone go off at the same time he tapped his? There's no way...

Staying on the ground, my elbows scrape against my floor as I army crawl to my bed and pat around for my phone.

Gotcha!

The bright screen makes me squint, but the thudding in my chest only increases at what I see.

UNKNOWN

You're so beautiful when you touch yourself to me, Charlotte.

The unknown text has no number attached to it no matter how many times I click the name. No freakin' way is the man I just masturbated to texting me that. Are you kidding me? Panic ensues with racing questions as his motorcycle still idles outside my house like it's waiting for my next move.

He saw me? How the hell could he watch me masturbate to him? How many times has he watched before... And why is it so hot to imagine him secretly watching me get off?

A dull warm throb returns as my breathing increases. Would he come upstairs if I invited him in right now? My arms twitch from the power of my pounding heart as I text him:

ME

I don't know how you got my number... but are you BikerBB64? And if you are him and sitting outside my house right now... did you want to come in?

I can't believe I just sent that! Who am I?

Probably not a smart thing to do in case this dude is a serial killer, but my curiosity is getting the better of me. Plus, I don't care if he reveals himself to me or not. He can keep his anonymity. It's not like he needs to take the helmet off to play with me...

My toes curl, and I bite down on a mischievous grin.

A minute passes and I have no idea if he's reading it or what's going on. So, daring a peek, I get on my knees and look over the windowsill. The bright light of his phone shines in the reflection off his visor. Both of my lips curl under my teeth and my fingertips drum on the wooden windowsill as I anxiously await his next move.

But instead of getting to live out my fantasy, he shoves his phone in his side pouch after obviously reading my message and speeds off, leaving me empty, wet and alone.

Did I do something wrong?

The rejection stings, setting my ribs tight and bringing about that familiar dull ache in my chest. With now two boys under my belt ignoring me, one who apparently has decided to stalk me, I swallow the lob in my throat and sulk into the bathroom to shower off the leftover pleasure coating my leg along with the cold emptiness settling into my soul.

Getting ready for school the next day is bittersweet. Fighting the self-consciousness from being rejected by my latest obsession, I wear the next dress in my closet, a long pale blue sundress flowing down to my mid-calf and bunched up in the middle, pushing up and accentuating my breasts. I pull the middle strings tight, tying them to allow the tops of my breasts to pop up more. My eyes linger on them in the mirror. They seem bigger. Is it from my newfound explorations?

I bought this dress years ago for a Renaissance fair but never had the courage to wear it. Instead, I wore leather pants and a long white shirt. Safe, unnoticeable and comfortable just like me most of my life.

But this last week has been different...I've felt empowered for the first time ever and not just from the attention I've gotten from Jared but from the extra attention I've given myself. The ghost of a smile paints my lips. Yeah, who cares if Ben nor the biker boy want me.

My breasts bounce when I fling my backpack on, filling me with an overflowing lightness. Yeah, I'm freakin' hot. I don't need them. Like a string pulls my shoulders back and chest out, self-confidence returns with a vengeance.

I wish I'd found this confidence in myself sooner. My high school experience might've been much different than the low-key, isolated one I chose. I'll just have to make college a different experience. One full of fun memories, life lived and new experiences.

I smile at the prospect as I park in the school parking lot. I have a feeling my life is about to get vastly better, and I'm excited for it.

When walking through the school hallway, more than a few heads turn my way, making me blush and causing me to return the attention with a painful smile.

When I got dressed this morning, I noticed my lower lip had slight bruising and swelling on it from how strong I had bitten it to keep quiet last night. I hope that isn't the reason heads are turning to stare at me and it's just the fact I look good in the dress. I tried to dig up whatever old makeup I had laying around to cover it so they shouldn't be able to tell, but I'm still paranoid. If anyone asks what happened, I'll probably freeze and stumble over my words.

What would I tell them? Oh yeah, my lip's bruised because I masturbated so hard last night, I couldn't keep my mouth shut and almost screamed out into the house alerting my parents to my sexual activities. That'd go over well.

I'm adjusting my backpack in my usual seat in first period when Ben walks in. He takes one look at me and blushes a deep shade of red.

Ben actually blushed?

My cheeks burn to match his. His eyes lower and widen for a split second, a second that wouldn't have been noticeable if I didn't know him so well, before he meets my gaze and quickly looks away. An ever so subtle lip curl twitches at the edge of his mouth as if he's trying to hide a smile. I mirror him with a smirk of my own, hoping to break the ice, but unfortunately, he still moves to the other side of the classroom away from me.

I slouch, deflated from the small hope I held for a second and rotate back to my computer. Why's he not sitting next to me? I thought his initial flicker of a smile meant he wasn't mad at me anymore, so why the distance? Does he hate me now? Maybe he's back with Tree, I think sadly, leaning my cheek on my left hand that's propped up by my elbow off the wooden desk by the keyboard.

"Alright class, I know it's the last day, but I still want to see the resumes I've asked you to type up. Go ahead and open them on your computers. I'll go around in alphabetical order and review. If you have any questions, feel free to write them down so we can discuss them when I get to you. Otherwise, you may talk, quietly."

Mrs. Coxe is the best. I'm going to miss her. She always makes sure we keep to our rules but with some amount of freedom. I can only hope I find some professors at college that make me feel as comfortable as she does.

I lazily click open my resume and leave it on the screen to wait my turn. This is so pointless to do without any work experience. It's like, *here you go. I went to school and now I'm totally unprepared to do the job I'm interviewing for…hire me.* But maybe that's just the cynic in me.

I peer at Ben discreetly to see if he's looking at me too.

Sigh.

He's not. He's caught up in a conversation with Greta who once again sits right next to him.

What a good guy. As much as she annoys him and as much as he teases about running away from her, he always entertains her with kind conversation. I've always loved that about him.

Oops, I stared too long. Ben locks eyes with me, his lips curving into a mischievous smile before turning away again.

Embarrassed, I turn back to my computer, placing my cool palms on my cheeks to calm down.

I wonder where we'll both end up in life. Will this be the end of our close friendship? I can't imagine we'll stop being friends altogether, but maybe our best friend phase has run its course. A twisted tug of sadness hits me in my core from that reality along with nostalgia for the times we may not get again.

His family's farm has always been one of my favorite places to escape to when I've felt overwhelmed with life. If I could describe heaven, it would be there, helping in the field or with the livestock. Sometimes when Ben isn't around, I'll hang out with his father in the shop while he fixes machinery. Even just sitting here now, I can smell the exhaust from the tractors or the fresh cut hay in the field after him and his father have mowed it down and raked it. Mmm...my own personal euphoria.

I used to run over to his house on the weekends before Tree existed. When he'd come meet me straight out of the field, *God*, he'd smell so good, like fresh dirt and sweat. Whenever I hugged him, especially on those days, it was hard to let go. My body would completely relax like he was my own personal therapy human.

Not to mention, his parents are practically my second family. I've been to plenty of family dinners, holidays, family game nights and even a few vacations with them.

Although now that I think about it, my parents never returned the favor. Ben's rarely been invited over to my house as part of the family or treated as such. I never realized that before. I wonder why that is.

My parents on the surface seem to like Ben a lot. Maybe before the summer is over, I'll ask if my parents are okay with inviting him over a few times for game nights and including him as part of the family so we can have those last memories to share together before the good times inevitably end.

"Okay, Charlotte, let's see what you got," Mrs. Coxe says from behind me.

"Huh? Oh, sure."

I scoot my chair back and give her a full view of the screen before fading back into my daydreams.

Jared leans on the classroom door, hands fully in his pockets as he waits for me after class.

"Beautiful dress today, Charlotte," he says putting his arm around me per our new routine. "I'm sad that after today I won't get my daily dose of you in your dresses. We'll have to make sure we meet up over the summer, so I can get my fix," he jokingly says with a wink.

At least, I *think* he's joking. He needs a daily dose of me in dresses? He wants to hang out during the summer? A hot burn tingles my face at the implication.

I walk with him to my next class, not bothering to check for Ben. I'll let things flow and fix themselves naturally between us. Plus, I'm sure approaching him while Jared has his arm around me won't improve the situation. I make a mental note to ask him why he hates Jared so much one of these days. He's a nice guy. Plus, all the other girls are friends with him. If he was a bad guy, he wouldn't be so well liked, right?

Jared leaves me at my next class with a tight side hug which I reciprocate with a head on his shoulder and a wave goodbye. No other teachers bother to teach anything of substance to us seniors, so I'm able to spend the rest of my day zoning out about Ben, Jared and my new anonymous stalker.

Does he go to my school? Is he even in school? I can't tell his age at all by his posts, but regardless of his age he seems...experienced. Is his face as hot as his body? If I text him again, will he respond? I shake my head at the ridiculousness of the idea. No. I invited him in and he stiffed me. He doesn't deserve my attention right now.

Everyone else in class bonds over their excitement for all the graduation parties this weekend and what events are being held at each one. I don't have any others to attend besides Jared's and Ben's this weekend. I'm surprisingly excited about going to both.

Look at me being a social butterfly.

I'm determined to be more outgoing at both parties and have a social summer. Currently, I'm more excited for Jared's party at this point because it doesn't involve worrying about how Ben will react or might be feeling since he won't be there. I'll be totally free to enjoy myself for once. And if the biker boy wants to see me, he apparently knows where I live so he can come get me if he wants to that badly.

Hmph.

Someone grabs me from behind and pulls me into a hug.

"Hey girl! I cannot believe it's our last day. We're like officially adults now!" Shirley walks around in front of me with a sidelong smirk. "Also, I have a few questions for you."

My stomach jumps in anxious anticipation of what questions she could possibly have. She practically falls into the chair next to me.

"Okay, so first off have you seen the biker boy's post I sent you yet? His videos are sooo *fuckin'* hot. If you don't check them out, you *will* regret it. And look, I know you don't want to create a Xypher account, but it doesn't cause any harm to do it. Plus, if you create one, then you can follow me, and I can send you all the hot guys I follow. It'll be how we bond over the summer and keep in touch," she exclaims with a giggle.

If there was such a thing as being a lush for men, she was it. I curl my lips in at the comment to fight a grin, knowing I have to lie. If I'm honest about creating an account and stalking his profile, then for some reason I feel like she'll know what I did…know that I pleasured myself to that profile multiple times, am starting to have an unhealthy obsession with him and that he's reached out to me. I don't want to share that part of me with her, nor anyone.

"How about this. How about you help me create an account sometime this summer so we can be connected through Xypher once we both go off to college?"

She lights up at the idea. Good, she bought it.

"Perfect! Text me, and we'll get together and create one and explore *all* my favorite profiles. Who knows, maybe we'll find the perfect guy for us on there." She stares up at the ceiling dreamily.

I smile at the dopey expression. Yup. Such a lush.

"Great," I chuckle.

"So... are you dating Jared?" she asks in a hushed tone, leaning towards me.

In the middle of bending down to grab my notebook, I almost lurch out of my seat in shock. Dating? Me? Jared?

"What makes you say that?" I say cooly, hoping she didn't notice my actual hidden reaction.

"Oh, you can't hide it from me, Charlie. I know the only reason you've been wearing dresses all week is to catch his attention. Plus, his arm's always around you in the hallway and to be honest, it looks like you enjoy it."

Oh...I didn't think about everyone being able to see how Jared and I were acting. I've been in my own world, oblivious to the people around us. The only person's reaction I ever thought about was Ben's. Self-consciousness creeps back into my gut. What have people been saying about me behind my back?

"Well first off, I didn't start wearing dresses for him nor anybody for that matter."

Lies.

"And Jared sorta just started waiting for me after my classes and acting like that on his own. I mean, he's cool and all, but I'm pretty sure we're just friends."

"Mmm. I see," she says like she doesn't believe me in the slightest. I hadn't bothered to put the time in to delve into what's happening between Jared and me. Maybe it's worth investigating... I am single after all, and he does seem interested.

"Well, regardless of what's actually happening, it's pretty obvious he likes you. Do you like him back?"

"What's with the third degree, Shirl?" I snap with a bite in my tone. Being interrogated about my personal life is not something I'm up for with her nor anyone else right now.

"Sorry, I didn't mean to hit a trigger. I was only curious. Jared's never dated any girls at our school, so I find it interesting is all."

I nervously play with the drawstrings on the bosom of my dress, contemplating what to say.

"No," I pause. "We're not dating. Honestly, I have no idea what's going on. As far as I'm aware, we're just friends, even though we *have* gotten closer this week..."

"*Girrrrl.* No one is interested in being *just* friends when they act like that. Especially when they walk you to your car every day and are all over you all the time. I mean, you *have* noticed how he looks at you, haven't you?"

Yes, but not really? There's a small bit of intensity to it, but it's not like it's all the time.

Sigh.

Being out of touch with my emotions is getting really inconvenient. I shouldn't be this oblivious to everything everyone else can see, especially when it makes me sit here clueless.

"I mean, I have noticed he's looked at me... differently, but I don't know. Nothing's happened."

"All I know is that if Jared was looking at *me* like that, I'd be all over him. You should be flattered. Like I said, he's never chosen any girls here to go out with. You're the first."

"Chosen? Are there literally girls lining up to date him or something?"

"Yes! How've you never noticed?"

Well, because I only paid attention to the girls who always went after Ben, which always seemed to be a lot.

I forgot about other guys who might be tagged as desirable, yet unreachable.

"I don't know. I've uh, never been in this situation before, I guess."

Shirley rolls her eyes.

"Always so innocent, Charlotte." She chuckles trying to play it off, but I swear it sounded snarky like she was annoyed.

"Was that supposed to be a dig at me?" I retort, not caring if she registers my snark back. The comment she made is rude and meant to hurt me on purpose.

Her eyes narrow for a second, flashing her true feelings. Then it hits me.

"Do you like Jared? Is that what this is about? Are you jealous?"

She scoffs, defensively crossing her arms and stands. "No. I was just curious to find out if the rumors of you two dating were true, but I didn't expect you to be so oblivious about it."

"Listen Shirl, I don't care if I date him or not. I can put in a good word for you if you want? I don't want any drama or to have you be mad at me for no good reason. Like I said, I didn't even think much about dating him. If he likes me as you say, then I'm sure he'd hear me out if I said I wasn't interested and hyped you up instead."

A small twitch of emotion flickers under the surface, her eyes darting to the side slowly as she contemplates my offer. She finally meets my gaze with a smile.

"Really?" she mutters quietly, relaxing her body and sitting back down.

"Absolutely, Shirl." I mean it too.

I place a comforting hand on her shoulder to prove I'm not a threat. Jared's affections don't mean that much. Sure, it's been fun the last week, but since Shirley's always liked him a lot, then I don't care to step aside. If I never talk to Jared after his graduation party, that'd be fine with me.

"Why didn't you tell me this before? I could've put in a word for you sooner or at least stopped the behavior if it was making you uncomfortable."

I know I don't owe her anything, but I hate needless drama. Especially over stupid things like boys.

Especially boys who act weird, never say what they mean or throw fits. Or boys who secretly send you a flirty message and then drive off, never to be heard from again.

Tsk. Freakin' babies. All these boys are babies.

Her eyes soften. "Thanks, Charlotte. I know we haven't been the closest of friends, but to know you care about my feelings means a lot."

"So, what do you want me to say to him? Have you guys ever really talked before or flirted you think? You're going to have to tell me exactly what you want me to say because I'm new to all this stuff."

She brightens with excitement at the prospect. "You're the best! I really did *not* expect you to be this cool about it."

I nod in appreciation, sitting back and waiting for her to tell me what she wants me to say.

"Okay, first ask him if he likes anyone on the track team. Then when he starts talking, say you have a good friend who would be perfect for him and talk me up. Like tell him that I love running, obviously, that I plan to run in college, and that you think I'm hilarious and cool to hang out with."

Her plan doesn't sound very convincing. I'll have to come up with something before I talk to him. She's cool and all, but I don't know much about her that qualifies as a *wow* factor. I'm sure I can sway it to make it sound like he has to check her out if she's right about how he feels about me. If anything, the effort's worth it.

Maybe this will bring Shirley and I closer, dare I even say something resembling best friends? It'd be nice to have a girlfriend around, especially if things don't resolve between Ben and me. A painful twang punches my stomach at the idea of Ben leaving my life.

The low-pitched bell rings, indicating the end of the day is here and high school's officially over.

Shirley gives me a big hug and leaves the classroom. She bashfully smiles at Jared who barely glances at her before motioning to me to get under his arm like I was wrong for not being there already. Another twang stirs in my stomach; except this time, I'm not sure what causes it. I smirk, ignoring the sensation and snuggle in under him.

He smells even better than this morning. Did he put more cologne on before coming to get me? Is that normal for friends?

I shake the notion off, instead focusing on how to bring up the conversation about Shirley to him. Too in my head, I don't realize we aren't speaking until we get to my car, and he asks what's wrong.

"Huh?" I say, pulling out of my concentration. This would be a good time to bring up Shirley, but I haven't thought of exactly what to say yet. Guess I'll just wing it.

"I said are you okay?" he says with an amused chuckle, removing his arm around me and standing in front of me as I lean against my car door.

"Oh yeah. I was just thinking—"

"Thinking about what?" he asks curiously, leaning closer to me, cutting me off mid-sentence.

“Well, I’d tell you if you let me finish,” I sass back with a smirk.

He rests his palm on the car door next to my left shoulder, half sealing me to my spot. My stomach flips from being this close, the suggested intimacy way more than what we’ve been doing thus far.

I clear my throat, trying to get rid of any noticeable anxiousness in my voice and redirect the vibes coming off him.

“I was thinking of something I wanted to ask you.”

His face lights up. “I love questions. Give it to me.”

“I was wondering if you liked any of the girls on the track team because I know of a great girl for you.” Shoot, that was rushed.

He pulls his arm away from me, studying me like he’s unsure about my question. Why’s he taking so long to answer a simple question? The awkward silence is killing me.

“Because Shirley is great for you, you know,” I blurt out, unable to stand the silence or his intense analytical stare any longer.

Crap. I blew it.

That wasn’t convincing in any way. I didn’t give him any of her strengths or make her sound unique at all.

“Is that so?” he asks, putting his hands in his back jean pockets, watching me intently like I'm an equation he can't figure out.

“Mhmm. She loves video games and running, obviously…” She's going to hate me. I am blowing this so hard.

“She's cute, yeah. I've noticed her before. I haven't thought of her that way though, if I'm being honest.”

“Well, you should check that out.” *Kill me. Just kill me. I am so awkward.*

He smirks slyly at my obvious awkwardness.

“Don't laugh at me,” I giggle, pushing him playfully in the chest.

“I can laugh at you if I want, Charlie,” he says, teetering back and forth on his toes. He moves next to me again and leans on the car door. Ben walks right in front of us, distracting me from the conversation Jared tries to continue.

He doesn't bother glancing in my direction. I barely catch sight of his eyes before he's fitting his motorcycle helmet over his head and hopping on his bike. My chest tightens. I miss him so much.

“Why are you always staring at Ben?”

“Huh?” I say, caught off guard from the question.

"Why are you always staring at Ben?" he asks again rather sternly, bouncing a deep stare back and forth into each one of my eyes.

"I am not *always* staring at him. I may have been *glancing* at him more recently but only because we haven't been as close lately. We fought over something stupid and have barely talked since. I'm just trying to figure out what's going on. Fights like that aren't worth losing friends over, in my opinion, so I'm trying to figure out how to navigate it is all." I look down at my feet, now feeling uncomfortable with the conversation.

"Ah. I see."

Studying him, I notice his gaze lingers anywhere but me, and his pained expression of tight lips and furrowed brows worries me.

"Are you okay?" I touch his arm to comfort him.

His shoulders loosen at my touch, and his face softens. He puts his arm around me again, allowing me to lean into him where I wrap myself up in his fresh woody and citrus scent. His cologne makes me want to lay on the beach by a campfire at night. It's relaxing but also makes me want to be adventurous, to try new things and hang with friends around a fire on a cool summer evening.

"You're a hard one to figure out, you know."

I tilt my head up at him, furrowing my brow at the accusation. "What do you mean?"

I pull out of his embrace and put my bookbag in the backseat. When I turn around, I notice the parking lot's almost empty. Everyone must've booked it out of here now that school's officially over. "Wow, everyone's gone already."

"I didn't notice."

Now I'd almost rather him look away. His intense stare into my soul is staggering. I turn away, unable to bear it and shift on my feet, trying to think of how to escape his gaze.

"Well, hey. I'm gonna get going. You should definitely talk to Shirley though. If you want, I can write down her number for you?"

"That's okay," he says shortly. His face softens quickly at his next words. "My graduation party starts at five tomorrow. You're coming for sure, right?"

"Yes. I wouldn't be telling you I was coming all week and then not show up. Geez, I'm not that bad of a flake."

He brightens from satisfaction at my answer. "Good."

He opens my car door as I tuck my dress underneath me and slide into the driver's seat. He folds his arms on the open window of my car door, resting his chin on them with a soft smile.

each move of his leg brings out another curve in his skin and how sometimes, just sometimes, I'd catch him watching me and I'd wonder if I'd imagined it. I never wanted to believe any guy noticed me because he thought I was attractive, I always just assumed they were looking past me to someone else.

He's been there all along. I've just been too oblivious to consider the possibilities

I unpack my school things for the last time and sit on the couch in the living room, reflecting on my promise to Shirley and how she'll think I'm a backstabber if I end up pursuing Jared after all. She's the one who told me he liked me in the first place, and I assured her I wasn't interested even after hearing the possible truth.

But is that enough of a reason not to date a guy? I'm allowed to change my mind, right? I exhale forcefully, leaning my head back against the vanilla padded plush backing of the couch and stare at the ceiling, turning over more scenarios in my brain.

His graduation party's tomorrow so I have enough time to figure this out, right?

Ugh, this makes my brain hurt. I don't want to be a crappy person, but Shirley and I aren't *that* close of friends...but is that enough of an excuse to be a bad person? Is a guy worth all this possible drama?

I lose track of the conversation in my mind when images of Jared invade again. His abs, his toned legs, his full lips that are always moistened, the slow flick of his tongue when he'd lick his lips right before speaking to me. Heat sears between my legs, the wetness already accumulating.

My palm loudly smacks my forehead in exasperation. Am I now completely controlled by my inner urges? *So frustrating.*

Yet, before I know it, I'm back in my room, turning off the lights and touching myself to the biker boy once again. This time though, I'm aware I may have an audience. Knowing he could be watching me, spurred me on, swiftly bringing me to orgasm. Except afterwards, instead of feeling guilty, I was disappointed. My biker didn't reach out or drive by or anything. What the hell was the other night about then?

Ugh.

Whatever. I shouldn't be worried about him anyways, I have someone who doesn't hide behind a helmet who actually shows me he likes me. Screw the biker.

Ugh, these mood swings are going to be the death of me.

Downstairs, I find Mom and Dad sitting on the back patio with their laptops open, conversing quietly. I slide open the double-sided glass doors and greet them.

"Hey! When did you guys get home?"

They're both beaming.

"Oh, about twenty minutes ago," Mom says brightly.

Wow, I didn't even hear them. I hope I was quiet enough in my bedroom.

Panic shoots through me at the possibility they overheard me or the music coming from the video when my biker boy lifted up his shirt and spanked the back of the bike sexually one quick time before the video would replay.

"What's that face for? I've only seen that look when you were doing something you shouldn't be." Dad's laugh sounds strained, his smile once again not meeting his eyes as his brows crease.

Oh, God. Is he thinking about the other night? Did he catch on to what I was doing? My pulse quickens as I race to come up with an excuse for what I was doing upstairs.

"Oh honey, stop pestering her. It's her last day of school after all. We officially have a college girl in the house!" She winks at Dad and gives me a big hug. God bless her. "How do you want to celebrate tonight?"

Hiding my sigh of relief, I say, "Let's just stay in and play games tonight. I'm going to be at graduation parties all weekend so I'm going to need to save up my social energy for those."

"Sounds good. I'll order the pizza."

She walks inside to call the pizza shop, leaving me with my father, the man who I've never had an awkward moment with in my life until recently, and who suddenly seems harder to be around because I don't know how to act in front of him. He smiles uncomfortably at me, as if he feels the same way before returning to his laptop and begins typing, presumably to work on his current book.

Taking my chance to escape further awkwardness, I go inside to pick out what games we're going to play tonight. I know we'll have all summer to hang out, but I don't want these moments to pass me by. My parents are everything to me, and I can't imagine not being close to either one of them. I have to fix Dad and I's relationship before I leave for college. There's no other option.

Dad and I get into our competitive spirits quickly once the games begin, absorbing all the previous tension. I'm happy to be back to goofing off with him and feeling like the little girl he's always been so proud of.

We finally call it quits around one in the morning after a great night, making me forget all the drama between Jared and Shirley.

Crap. Until now.

Doing what I can to stop my mind before it can jump over a ledge into a pool of overthinking, I snuggle in nude under my covers, enjoying the coolness of the silk on my skin. Clothes feel too constricting tonight, as if my mental state's suffocating me physically as well. I'll have plenty of time to deal with the Shirley debacle before Jared's graduation party tomorrow. Future Charlotte can handle it. I hope.

I lay my phone on the other side of the bed next to me and bury my face in the pillow.

It hadn't even been five minutes when a low light and vibration from my phone wakes me up.

BENNY BOY

Hey

Adrenaline energizes me, shooting me up as I stare at the screen, excitement rolling through me. It's Ben. My breath uneven, I type back hesitantly.

ME

Hey.

BENNY BOY

Let me in.

I look around in confusion.

ME
What? Where are you?

In disbelief, my mouth drops as a soft knocking sounds on my bedroom door. No way is he here. My parents are lax with the rules here but not *that* relaxed. If they find him here this late, we'll both be screwed.

I bundle up my comforter, quickly wrapping it around my naked body and open the door to see Ben standing in his full motorcycle gear right in front of me. I can't believe it. He's never done anything like this before. How'd he get in? I panic, worried that something terrible happened. Why else would he risk getting in trouble?

His honey brown eyes widen at the sight of me, his full lips parting and tongue flicking the roof of his mouth just long enough for me to notice it before his face goes blank. The soles of his motorcycle boots quietly thud on my bedroom floor as he sits his motorcycle helmet on my desk.

Grasping the door handle with one hand and pressing my palm flat on the door with the other, I press the door shut behind him quietly, making sure to not release the tension of the knob until it's fully settled into the doorjamb to avoid even the sound of a click. My shoulders wiggle the comforter up a little more to make sure I'm still fully covered before turning around. When I do, I find him sitting on the bed looking down, slowly rubbing his thumbs together with his elbows resting on his knees.

I haven't seen him look this solemn…ever. My heart races as I shuffle over to the desk chair, being careful not to trip over my comforter and almost flash him like what happened with my father.

He takes a deep breath, then with a noticeable effort, raises his head. Pieces of his un-gelled hair fall over, staying just out of his eyes. I want to comfort him and sit next to him, but I don't feel comfortable being naked and all underneath my blanket, so I stay where I am.

"What's going on? Are you okay? Did something happen?"

We lock eyes as I search his for an answer…any answer to tell me the cause for this late-night surprise visit. He silently studies me, slowly moving his gaze down to my bare collarbone and then at my hand grasping the comforter to my chest.

"Why aren't you sitting next to me?"

"Oh, I uh, want to, *but* I currently don't have any clothes on under my blanket, sooo…," I reply slowly, carefully.

His eyes perk up. "I can step out of the room if you want so you can get dressed. I want you sitting here on the bed with me."

That wouldn't work. If my parents come out of their bedroom and see him standing in the hallway outside of my door, that could be *very* bad. Let alone make the situation even more awkward with my father and possibly cause an irreparable rift. I can't imagine what my mother's reaction would be, but I don't think she'd care, honestly. She trusts me wholeheartedly. Dad though, he's very protective of my innocence as he's proven constantly lately.

"No, that won't work. I don't want you to get caught and you absolutely will be if you're standing outside my bedroom door. Just go to my closet and face the clothes. I'll grab something from my dresser."

He nods, the corner of his lip twitching up, and walks to the closet, facing the other way.

"If you peek, I'll slap you so hard it'll make you scream and then I won't care if you get in trouble."

He whispers out a chuckle, "Got it, boss."

I clutch my comforter tightly and waddle to the dresser, dropping it only inches to fit my shirt on and a pair of shorts. Not wanting to mess with the bra, I re-cover myself with the comforter to hide the fact that I wasn't wearing one and sit on the bed.

"Done. You can turn around now."

He obeys, his black T-shirt catching right above his pant line from the movement, showing the tiniest amount of olive skin. That inch betrays him, revealing the dip in his V-cut diving into his midriff. He chuckles at me again and knowing that he caught me staring, I blush sheepishly. There's something electric between us, something newly born making me avert my gaze as I feel the bed sag where he sits next to me.

"I've missed you a lot this week, Char. I'm sorry we fought on the phone the other night. I was having a bad day, and I took it out on you. I wanted to approach you all week, but you seemed like you had other things going on..." he trails off slowly, carefully laying out his implication.

"No? I was waiting for you to apologize for swearing at me and treating me like a disobedient child."

Facing me, he throws one bent leg on the bed while the other stays on the floor, a position signaling he's willing to be vulnerable with me. He's apologizing and he's here now. I shouldn't be so mean.

"I'm sorry, Ben. I just..." I try to find the right words to say, but he beats me to it.

"Dating Tree wasn't something that was supposed to last. It was all infatuation because she gave me what my body wanted, and I risked losing you for it. I'm so, so sorry, Char. I was stupid and immature, and I should have never let it get that far," he blurts out, brows cleaving together.

I cock my head back in shock at his admittance but stay silent as I wait for him to continue.

"I didn't like her at first, but then she kissed me, and it felt good to feel wanted that way. I'd never let myself feel that way with any other girls so when she broke that barrier, it unleashed something in me. I was controlled by lust. It was dumb to let lust almost ruin our friendship, and I'm sorry it took me so long to realize it. Please forgive me, Char."

Hearing him admit those words, how he wanted her so bad physically, how he couldn't help himself and knew he was risking our friendship made me want to hurl. I can barely stand the disgust at the truth of it, but since he's being honest, I should be too. It's time for us to have this conversation and move past this. I *want* to move past this once and for all and move forward back to normalcy.

"I never thought you'd be that kind of guy." I want to say more, but the right words elude me.

He stays quiet, brows furrowed and searches my eyes, begging for forgiveness. My heart wrenches as his silent pleading reaches my soul at how sorry he is.

"I'm sorry, Char. Really." He grabs my hand and wraps it in both of his, setting them on the comforter in my lap. His gentle touch triggers a lightning bolt that slams through me all the way down to my fingertips, causing a quick twitch. I bite the inside of my cheek and try to collect my thoughts, which feels impossible to do when my mind's blank. I remove my hand and sit up straight.

"Thanks, Ben. That honestly means a lot. I was hurt you didn't tell me why I was unable to talk to you or that you'd even let it get that far. It felt like you cared more about her than me." I take a deep breath and let everything I've been holding in for far too long spill. "And what's even worse was I had to find out you had sex from someone random in the locker room. The fact that you wouldn't even tell me about it or talk to me killed me. It was such a stab to the chest. It felt like you died, and every time I had to see you after that, it was a wound that continued to get reopened for months until it numbed over."

"I know, I know. I was stupid. I wasn't controlled by my brain at the timc."

"Why wouldn't she let you talk to me anyways? It's not like I was a threat."

Now it's him who's avoiding eye contact, finding something far more interesting on his hands.

"She thought you were. She said we shouldn't have best friends of the opposite sex and that if I wanted to keep getting satisfied, I had to stop talking to you altogether. She hated you."

My neck flinches back. "She hated me? She doesn't even know me," I scoff.

He continues looking down as his true admittance fully sinks in.

"Wait, you stopped talking to me because she threatened to withhold sex from you, and you obeyed? You put sex before me? Am I that low on the chain that it was easy for you to make that decision?" I blurt angrily, the previous jagged wound cracking open inside of me.

"I know, Char. I'm really, really sorry," he says, finally meeting my gaze again.

"Is sex really *that* good that you were willing to throw our friendship away? I mean I know it feels good to get off, but like—" I stop speaking, horrified I may have revealed too much.

A spark of excitement surfaces in his beautiful brown eyes, a grin cracking wide on his face.

"Oh, yeah?" he asks with a ferocious smile that lights my blood on fire. It's a dominant, interested look that brags that it enjoys the thought of me in that state of pleasure.

"No, I mean..." Words elude me, tightening that tight rope of tension rebuilding between us. Standing to get away from the uncomfortable situation I've created, I lean on my door, settling my hands behind me as a cushion. Then I notice the comforter still on the bed next to him.

Crap.

My cheeks heat, knowing I'm completely exposed underneath my shirt.

This type of vulnerability is new territory with him. I mean, sure I've been vulnerable with him in other ways, like when I'd cry or when I'd get hurt and he'd come help me feel better by giving me a hug or coming to my rescue, but nothing ever resembling a sexual vulnerability.

Ben slowly stands up, the corners of his mouth turned upwards just enough to show amusement. My heart instantly beats faster with each step toward me, his motorcycle boots echoing quietly on the hardwood of my bedroom floor.

His eyes flash in a way that makes my knees weak. I flatten against the door, attempting to melt into it. My nerves go wild at the intimidating way he approaches me—in that calm stalking manner.

What's he planning to do? Why's he coming near me in an almost predatory way?

I look away, unable to maintain eye contact for fear my heart will beat out of my chest if I hold his stare any longer. His hand meets the door and glides down the wood to land right beside my ear. He shoves his other hand in his motorcycle pants pocket, taking a firm but relaxed stance, pinning me to the door but with room to move if I want to escape.

"You sound breathless," he whispers, his hot breath tickling my face.

The tension suffocates me, taking away my ability to speak. The way he's watching me, with his smoldering intensity, makes my thighs clench together. We're an inch from being chest to chest. I study him deeply, trying to read what's happening between us as I bounce from his left eye to his right. His lips draw my attention next, parting slightly. He catches his breath, and I notice him focusing on my mouth. A slow drag of his tongue wets his bottom lip and lingers there for a split second before going back in his mouth.

I'm drenched between my thighs, the unbearable urge screams through my body, daring me to taste him, to pull him into me and press my lips on his. I push my backside into the door harder, holding myself back.

He smirks like he knows why I moved. I swear he can read my mind.

"*So*...you've gotten off before?"

"Mhmm."

"By who?"

"What?" I say, thrown off by the question, my cloudy judgement preventing me from thinking straight.

"Who. Got. You. Off?" He says pointedly, accentuating every word.

My gaze drops to his chest. I didn't want to admit it out loud, especially to him. I didn't want to embarrass myself. Plus, what if it makes him think less of me?

Thankfully, he doesn't press me harder for an answer. He pushes off the door and sits back on the bed, leaning forward on both of his elbows, looking down at his hands clasped together.

My body feels weak against the door, like all my strength was being used to hold myself back and when he withdrew, he took all my energy with him. I want him to push further. I want him to want me, but I'm not going to be the one to initiate. I'm not going to be the one to cross that line without knowing he wants me too.

This. *This* is exactly what I've been feeling toward him. I've been hiding, lying to myself about what I've wanted. All those glances at him, the temperature rising when I look at him, the enjoyment of the flirting, the hurt of what he's done with Tree...

"What are you doing tomorrow night?" he asks casually, still avoiding my gaze.

"Going to Jared's graduation party. Why?"

His head shoots up, a flash of anger showing before turning more serious. "Why do you hang out with that guy?"

"We don't hang out. We just interact at school," I retort with attitude to match the one he's giving me.

He snorts sarcastically. "That's what you call friendship? His arm hanging over you constantly, you dressing up for him, then you two strolling around like lovebirds...If I didn't know you so well, I'd think you were dating. Matter of fact, the whole school thinks you guys are dating."

So, we're doing this again. I'm not going to give him easy answers if he's going to be like this. Why can't he talk to me about other guys like a normal human?

"Well, we're not dating—"

"But he wants to," he interjects.

Well, I can't deny that, especially after what Jared said to me when he left me at my car this afternoon. Okay, what now? I'm not going to lie to him about it. Looks like sassy admittance is my only option.

"Yeah, and?"

"Oh, so you know. So, what then, are you wanting to date him? Is tomorrow going to be your coming out party?" he spits viciously, his hands curled in fists, veins popping out on his hands and forearms from clenching them so tightly.

"What the hell is your problem?" I spit back.

"Wow, using swear words. I must have really hit a nerve. Guess I was right. I hope you two have fun tomorrow. If you two do start dating, do *not* bring him to my party." He pauses, knuckles relaxing and opening his fist in surrender. "You're still coming right?" he asks, softly.

"Well yes, I plan to, but do you even want me to come? And of course, I won't bring Jared. I know how you feel about him." I gather my courage and walk toward him, leaving the safety of the door. "Ben, I have no idea what's going on with you anymore. One minute you seem to be flirting with me, the next you're berating me over Jared and making me feel shameful for getting the attention of other guys. What *is* this? What exactly is going on in that head of yours?" I demand, throwing my hands up, not caring what's being exposed.

Our voices are getting louder, but I don't care. I'm not going to let him bully me.

His eyes focus on his hands again. "Answer me this," he finally says. "Do you want to date Jared?"

The question churns in my mind as I decide how much to tell him. "I don't think so. Shirley likes him and wants me to set them up, but if he doesn't want her then maybe? I don't really know. It's all so new. You know I've never dated anyone before. I don't know how to do any of this."

"So you're okay with being someone's second choice?" he sneers.

Rage flares at the flagrant insult. With arms straight at my sides, knuckles white, I'm now fighting a different urge…the urge to punch him in his smug fucking face. "You're *such* an asshole."

"Well, that's a sad answer. And for someone who cares about you to be called the asshole when he's always been there for you and wants you to have standards."

He aggressively gets up and grabs his helmet, but when he opens my bedroom door to leave, he stops dead in his tracks.

My father stares at him on the other side of the door, his eyes brimming with rage. My heart drops. Oh, God. I hope he doesn't think the worst, especially after the other night.

"Ben, what the hell are you doing here this time of night? We gave you a key in case of emergencies, not to do late night visits. I expected more out of you," my dad fumes, standing with his hands on his hips, his nostrils flaring.

Ben's knuckles tighten on his helmet. I didn't know they gave him a key. When did they do that? Are my parents close to Ben behind my back?

"I'm sorry, sir. I wanted to talk to Char about something, but I didn't want to do it over the phone. I promise nothing disrespectful happened under your roof. I came with good intentions."

My dad's hardened expression softens minutely because he knows Ben's a good guy and is good on his word.

I, on the other hand, am still fuming. Nothing disrespectful, my ass. He was being a dick.

"Next time call instead or come over at a decent hour. Okay? I do not want to have this conversation with you a second time."

That's his dismissal, and we both know it.

Without looking back, Ben walks out of the room, leaving me cold, alone and hurt from the whiplash of emotions during that entire encounter. The sound of his motorcycle starting up outside cuts me like a knife as my dad surveys me and the room.

"Sorry, Dad. He showed up and wanted to talk. I should've let you know he was here."

But inside, I don't care that I didn't let my father know. I only apologize because I know he expects one. I liked the secret encounter at first. If things had gone differently and Ben pursued me, I would've never let my dad know he'd been here. I'm eighteen and it's my life. I'm allowed to keep my own secrets and lose some of my innocence...right? Ugh. One of these days I'll fully convince myself I'm allowed to be independent.

He puts on a forced smile and nods. "Make sure that you do."

And with that last word, he walks off.

My jaw clenches. That was rude. I'm getting sick of everyone treating me like a disobedient child. I shut the door, harder than I need to, and climb into bed, my head spinning from the entire day's events.

Chapter Nine.

I toss and turn all night, moving in between sleeping and waking from either being turned on at the thought of Ben, making me want to spend some quality time with the biker boy to satisfy that desire or angry at him and my father. At least I have no plans for the day until Jared's party so I can rot in bed if I want to.

Ugh, Jared's party. I was looking forward to it yesterday until Ben's comment. Now the thought of going makes me feel guilty, which is absurd because it's not wrong to go. Jared's my friend and even if he does like me or if I end up liking him, it doesn't matter.

It's none of anyone's damn business, I stubbornly declare.

The dread of facing reality keeps me in bed until eleven, sulking and irritable. I hate that Ben holds the power to make me feel this way, completely ruining my mood and motivation.

"Ughhh..."

Uttering a groan, I sit up in bed and plant my feet on the hardwood, letting the coolness sink into my skin.

That's it. Enough. I'm giving myself one more hour to sulk and then I'm going to buck up and get excited for the graduation party.

The rest of the day drags by, the excitement never coming like I hoped. Sick of the stuck mood, I go on a run to clear my head and then join Mom for lunch while Dad works at some writer's conference. Apparently, he talked to Mom last night about Ben being over, and he was *not* happy.

Apparently it took her hours to calm him down and convince him not to ground me this entire weekend nor ban Ben from the house.

"Ban him from the house? Isn't that a bit excessive?" I scoff, raising my eyebrow.

"Honey, it was one in the morning, and he snuck into your room. Can you blame him? Ben should've known better."

"It's not like we were doing anything. He wanted to talk to me about something, but he wanted to do it in person. I don't see the big deal."

"And why couldn't he have come over during normal hours to have that conversation? Don't be so naive, honey."

Anger bubbles in the pit of my stomach, fit to burst. If one more person speaks to me in this condescending tone, I swear I'm going to lose it.

"When will everyone stop talking to me like I'm a child," I yell at her. "Ben's been my best friend since we were kids. You *know* him. Plus, I'm old enough to have boys in my room if I want."

She turns the car off in the driveway but makes no move to get out. She releases a deep sigh, running her fingers through her hair and frowns at me in disappointment, stirring my anger further.

"What's with that look?" I snap.

I've never talked to her like this before in my life, but I can't help it. People need to let me grow up. I can't always be who they want me to be. That innocent girl who always does what she's told and keeps to herself... I'm not her anymore. I don't know what happened to her, but she's gone, and I'm glad for it.

"Charlotte, stop it," she snaps back.

I sit back and cross my arms across my chest defiantly, looking forward to avoid her heated stare.

"Yes, you are eighteen, but that does *not* give you the right to disrespect your father and I in *our* house. Yes, you are an adult by societal standards, but you still need to respect the fact that we pay for the clothes on your back, feed you and provide a roof over your head. We are not to adhere to your rules, but you to ours. I've stood up for you to your father lately, but don't push me away. Don't force me to set stricter boundaries in place because you feel entitled. I don't know what has gotten into you lately, and I don't care. No boys are allowed in your room at any point. You will not talk to either I or your father like this anymore. Once you are away at college, you can do as you like. Do you understand?"

Sadness rings in her voice behind the strict tone, like quiet choked sobs are being held back. She always hates it when we fight, and this is definitely the worst fight we've had. Great, I've made my mother cry. Am I turning into a bad daughter? A bad friend? A bad person?

I nod, silently agreeing to her conditions without looking at her and get out of the car to go up to my room. This crushing weight on my chest and knot in my throat is unbearable. I need to talk to someone other than my parents right now or I'm going to die inside.

There's only one person who can make me feel better in this moment. I don't care what's happening between us, I need him right now. I need *us* right now.

The first ring barely finishes before he answers.

"Hey."

That's all it takes. Tears fall down my cheeks as labored breaths break through between sobs.

"Char, what's wrong? What happened?" His voice laces with concern.

In between hitched breaths, I tell him everything. He stays quiet until I'm completely done and all that can be heard over the phone is my soft sobs.

"You are *not* a horrible person, Char. You and your family are just going through growing pains. I'm dealing with similar stuff on my end with my parents. It's not easy shedding your old life for a new one, but it'll be worth it. I guarantee when you fully grow into your new self that you'll still be the great person you are, and you and your parents will be back to being your regular old selves. You just have to understand that growth and change can't occur without pain. It sucks but it's reality. You just have to stick it out and push through the good and the bad. Don't set too many expectations and ride the waves. You'll be okay, I promise."

A slight whimper slips out as the cries lesson, relief washing over me. He's right. I'm going to be okay. My parents and I are going to be okay. I'm going to change and grow as I get older; it's just going to be way more painful than I want it to be.

"Thanks, Ben. You always know what to say. And thank you for picking up the phone even though we've fought a lot lately..." I pause. "We're going to be okay too, right?"

A motorcycle revs outside the house, drowning out the rest of my sentence. No way he rode over here while we were on the phone. I race downstairs, still clutching the phone in my hand with him on the call and fling open the door.

There he is in his black leather bike pants and red bike jacket, kicking down the kickstand on his red and black Ducati. He lifts his leg over the seat and gives me a simple wave as he leans on his bike. Before he gets the chance to unhook his helmet, I'm already wrapped around his torso, giving him the biggest hug and melting into him for comfort.

His muffled chuckle vibrates my chest as he hugs me back, setting his head, still in the bike helmet, on top of mine and squeezing me back just as tightly. I bury my face in his jacket, his scent of mint and leather calming me, relaxing my body bit by bit.

"It's okay," he says, stroking my back softly. "It's going to be okay."

I squeeze him harder, afraid that if I let go, he'll disappear.

Time stops as we hold each other. His easy breaths keep the rhythm steady to calm my own. I don't keep track of how long we embrace, and he's kind enough to keep holding me until I loosen my grip.

Moving out from under his helmet, I flip his vizor up to see his eyes, my left hand still on his waist and his on mine. His eyes crease, twinkling before softening as he raises his hand up and grazes the tears left running down my cheeks. The grip patches on his motorcycle gloves are like sandpaper, making small claims into my skin with each caring stroke of his thumb.

I grab his gloved hand and smush it against my cheek, closing my eyes, thanking him silently for being exactly what I need right now. He pulls his hand away, tilting my chin up to look into his eyes. They're back to being playful as he slowly moves his hand toward my nose and gives it a quick flick. I retaliate by slapping his vizor down and letting out a giggle.

"I'm glad I got you to smile," he chortles. Suddenly, his demeanor changes and even with his face hidden beneath the helmet, my body can sense it.

My cheeks blush heat as a bolt of adrenaline rushes through my body at the lower tone in his voice. I reach to pull his vizor up again, but my phone vibrates in my pocket, distracting me. It's Shirley.

"Girllll, when are you heading over to Jared's? Wanna ride together?"

Shit.

I completely forgot about the party after the fight with my mom. I pull my phone back from my ear and check the time. It's already four-thirty and it takes me at least twenty minutes to get there.

"Hey Shirl! No, I'm gonna drive separately. I'm running a little late. I'll text you when I leave, okay?"

"Ok, but don't be *too* late, because I need you to be my wing woman! That way Jared and I have the rest of his party to hopefully hook up."

"Sounds good," I chuckle awkwardly and end the call.

"You're still going to Jared's?" he questions, disappointment painting his tone.

"I have to. I already promised him and Shirley I would go." I wish I didn't have to lingers on the tip of my tongue but remains unspoken.

Any meek feelings that existed under the surface for Jared are gone. Even the biker boy seems like a distant memory of obsession right now.

"Stay with me," he pleads softly, grabbing my waist a little more firmly.

"I can't," I whimper, swallowing the lump in my throat. But God, do I wish I could stay with him. Every fiber of my being is telling me to stay and say the hell with

Jared's party, but I promised myself I'd make friends and if I just slip back into my old habits I'll be screwed once Ben leaves for college.

"If I didn't promise them I'd go, I'd stay with you, I swear. But I can't ditch Shirley. She's counting on me tonight." Anxiety has my tongue flicking over my bottom lip and chewing on it.

"Let me give you a ride there." His hips press themselves into mine making my elbows the only thing creating any space between us.

My mouth gapes open.

"Ben, you have *never* asked me to ride your motorcycle. I've been begging you for *years* and you've never let me. Now, of all times, you're asking me to ride with you?"

I'm in complete shock. What's he trying to play at with this offer? I mean, I'm stoked, but like, what are his intentions behind this?

He doesn't respond, instead shrugging his shoulders. "Do you want to or not?"

Oh good, the bite in his tone is back. I was worried there for a second that he was being too nice.

My jaw clenches and a grimace appears in annoyance. I want to ride with him more than anything, but I also don't want to be the one who brings an unwanted guest to a party. Ben and Jared have never interacted well, and my gut's telling me if I brought Ben, it'd ruin the party or cause unneeded drama, which I *do not* need any more of in my life right now.

"I'm sorry. I promise I will next time, but I'm just gonna drive to Jared's in my car. Can we ride tomorrow instead, before or after your-?"

"Are you afraid of Jared seeing us together?" he interjects.

My stomach sinks. *Here we go.*

I can't believe he's acting this way when he knows what I've been dealing with today. Tears well up in my eyes again.

I hate this part of me. In the rare times I've cried in my life, the tears always come back super easily for the next day or so. It's like once the valve's open it takes a while for it to shut again, which makes me look like a crybaby and there's nothing I can do about it.

"Ben, please," I plead, fresh tears streaming down my face.

"I'm sorry, Char." His voice softens. "I'm not sure when we can ride together, but I'll let you know. Call me if you need me tonight though, okay? No matter how late."

I nod, giving him another tight hug. I inhale deeply and bury my face into his chest, gently scratching my cheek on his leather jacket. The roughness on the back of his jacket lumps up under my fingertips, making it hard to grab him, but I push against their resistance to keep him close.

"Oh, crap." I can't believe I forgot I was in a rush. "I gotta go!"

I let go but am held back as he hangs on, obviously letting me go begrudgingly. His grip barely loosens, his touch lingering on my arm.

Racing toward the house to get ready, an empty crack makes itself known from already missing his touch. I turn at the door to wave at him, but the motorcycle already started up, only giving me a glimpse of his back as he speeds off. Sadness and loneliness threaten to creep back in. I *do* wish he could go with me tonight.

I shut the door along with my thoughts. No. Tonight's about fun. No self-pity, no complicated thoughts. I need to enjoy tonight with my peers because this may be the last time I see any of them. I'm not going to overthink about Ben, Jared, my biker guy or anything.

Rummaging through my closet to find something to wear, I choose to forgo the dress. It feels wrong to wear a dress to his party after my intimate moment with Ben and what it might imply to Jared if I do wear one. I don't want to draw any attention from Jared *that* way anymore.

My feet bounce off the floor one by one as I dance on my faded skinny jeans with holes in the knees, slip on my flat black tennis shoes, and throw on a cute black tank top. I grab my all-black sweatshirt to take in case it drops in temperature and to cover up if I get uncomfortable. I've never been to a graduation party but I'm assuming they can go pretty late.

Sprint hopping down the stairs, I say nothing to my parents and nervously take off to my first party experience.

Chapter Ten.

His house is insane. This place is practically a mansion, with its three stories, floor to ceiling windows on each level, a huge pool already filled to the brim with people and a huge backyard surrounded by woods.

I knew Jared was well off, but I didn't know he was *this* loaded.

My God.

A valet greets me at the end of the driveway, stating they'll take my car to the lot. I'm nervous handing some rando my keys, but then again, I've never had a valet service before so I don't know the rules. He gives me a number to call when I come to pick up the car and drives off.

The doors to the mansion are wide open, adults and students filling every space. The entrance opens into a large room with a view straight to the pool through the back of the house. A large chandelier hangs in the middle of what I can only assume is the living room surrounded by a fur rug on the marble floor and white semi-circular couches on each side. A fireplace is stationed on one side and a big screen TV is drilled on top of it. I can only imagine what the rest of the house looks like.

Before I can walk to the backyard to look for Shirley, pressure appears under my chin and pushes my mouth closed.

"You are the definition of what a jaw drop looks like there, Charlie." Jared's hand pulls my face to his and he smiles down at me, his expression full of excitement. "You had me worried you weren't coming," he says, his smile softening as he meets my eyes.

My cheeks burn under the intensity of his stare, but this time a touch of nausea accompanies it. Shirley comes into view, walking toward us, an unquestionable expression of hurt on her face. I quickly remove his hand and step back.

"Hey Shirl," I exclaim as enthusiastically as I can manage.

"Hey," she says with a forced smile. Arms thrown behind my back, I turn to Jared attempting to rectify what she might have interpreted from afar. I immediately move into wing woman mode and start the conversation Shirley and I previously agreed to.

"Jared, did you know that Shirley has been in *four* beauty pageants?" Glancing at Shirley, I nod to encourage her to finish the rest of the conversation.

"Uh, no, I didn't," he replies with a confused chuckle. A brow rises as he strokes his chin.

"Yeah," she says beaming, moving in front of me to bring the focus more on her. I gladly side-step back and allow her to take charge. A promise is a promise.

Jared kindly keeps up the conversation with her even though I catch him watching me out of his peripherals every now and then.

Each time the conversation fizzles, I start up the next topic Shirley and I had agreed on to keep it going. I caress Shirley's arm and step beside her.

"Jared, did you know that Shirley is going to Jenkin's University as well?"

Both eyebrows raise in interest. *Bingo*. "Oh, really? No, I didn't know that. What are you going to major in?"

Her face lights up in excitement at the now fully drawn attention from him. I give myself a mental pat on the back. His eyes no longer veer to me in any capacity, so I assume my job is done and walk away, the ghost of his hand where it caressed my chin still lingering quietly.

Luckily, I'm quickly distracted by the magnificence of this place and I happily explore with my new freedom, wanting to see more of it. I walk to the back pool area and stare in awe at how large their pool is. It's not exaggerating to say it's the size of a small lake, shaped in an ongoing curve like fashion with beautiful clear water. A large black W for his last name, Wallace, is painted on the bottom of the it.

The pool overlooks a monstrous backyard with perfectly mowed green pathways on the sides in between two lines of trees. About a mile back, the backyard ends into a small wood where an extravagant water fountain sits, spraying water out of some type of statue in the middle. I stroll along the green pathway, taking my time and enjoying the nice weather and quiet away from the noise of the party, soaking in the beauty.

It takes me ten minutes to get to the fountain, but it's worth it as I stop right in front, admiring the beauty of it in the setting sun. The light hits the female crystal figurine in the center of it, splitting into rainbows under the mists coming out of the spouts in her hands. Two large stone dogs sit on each side of her.

"My dad had this built in honor of my mom's dog training career. She was a legend back in the day."

I whip around, my heart racing. I was so lost in thought, I forgot other people were here.

"Jared, you scared me!" I huff, gripping my hand to my chest.

His expressions apologetic. "I'm sorry, I didn't mean to scare you. I saw you admiring the fountain, so I wanted to tell you what it was about. Not many people know about my mother's professional dog training background. It's pretty cool, the work she did. She traveled all around the world, won some medals and even helped train military dogs there for a while."

I stare in awe at the crystal woman in front of me. What an amazing woman. Such power...over herself, animals and likely people.

"Why'd she stop?"

He smiles softly, albeit sadly. "She became pregnant with me." He pauses, taking a breath as if to steady himself. "Her pregnancy was rough. She was sick and bedridden almost the entire time. Then once she had me, she had post-partum depression so bad she could barely take care of herself, let alone me. My father, who is no longer in the picture, had to take ownership of me for a while. It ripped them apart. She blamed him for everything...her loss of career, her life, and for ruining her body. She wasn't a bad person; her mental health was just in a terrible place. She ended up divorcing my father and taking full custody of me in the divorce. My father, the poor bastard, was still madly in love with her. It wrecked him. He had this built right after I was born, hoping it would show her what she could still be if she wanted and how he believed in her. Unfortunately, she was too far gone. It wasn't until she met my stepdad and got into therapy that she became a good mother. I'd swear you can even say she loves me now. My father on the other hand hasn't bothered to show since divorce court. So, you could say he definitely doesn't."

A noticeable bitterness surfaces in his tone under his fake chuckle before he goes quiet, his attention on the fountain.

When I look back at the statue, she no longer seems magnificent. What kind of horrible woman would do that to the father of her child, let alone her own child. I wish she would have gotten help sooner or things would've turned out differently for Jared's sake. That's tough.

Is this why Jared pushes himself so hard and hopes to move far away from a home this beautiful? Maybe this isn't some beautiful mansion to him but a reminder of the hardships he's had to endure.

I brush his arm gently with my fingers to comfort him when I can't find the right words to say because what else is there to say to that story besides, "I'm sorry". He grabs my fingers and holds them on his arm under his hand. My cheeks burn at us practically holding hands, but again, not in a flattered way. It's uncomfortable. Wrong. Nothing like Ben's touch.

It's just friendly touching. It doesn't mean anything.

"I'm sorry, Jared. I can't imagine what that must have been like to deal with as a child. Have you lived here your entire life?"

He nods, continuing to stare at the statue, his face unreadable. "I've broken this statue three times. My stepdad always pays to fix it. He's under my mom's thumb but he seems to enjoy it. To be fair, my stepdad is a good guy, I just think he has low self-esteem. Plus, I have him to thank for my life getting better after he got my mom into therapy. But after everything, I can't find it in me to feel much love toward him. I'd rather just not have parents and do my own thing away from all the drama and baggage that comes with it."

I squeeze his arm, unable to imagine feeling that strongly about escaping your parents or the life you grew up in.

"Well at least you'll be moving out soon, so you won't have to see her anymore if you don't want to."

"Kinda. She forced a stipulation on me where she won't give me any money unless I visit home a minimum of once every three months. I won't need her money for long, but I'll need it at the start. I'll be forced to come here for the first couple of years until I've saved up enough, but after that I'm free. Fully free to escape forever."

He grips my fingers harder, almost painfully.

"Ow."

"Sorry, you okay? My anger came out in my grip there. I apologize."

He releases his grip, enabling me to shake my fingers out.

"Yeah, it's okay. I'm fine..." I say hesitantly, looking for a way to escape. "Wait. Where's Shirley?"

He rolls his eyes, minutely shaking his head and his blonde hair with it. "I left her in the kitchen talking to one of my cousins who's here from out of town."

"Oh?"

"Why were you trying to set me up with her?"

Unprepared for such a blunt question, I shift on my feet and look down, embarrassed.

"We'll talk about it later. For now, let's go back to the party, shall we?" He holds his arm out for me.

My muscles freeze in hesitation. Is it wrong to grab his arm now that I know I want to be with Ben?

"I won't bite." He winks, his mischievous smile returning.

Chuckling awkwardly, I grab his arm to appease him. I guess it won't cause any harm. Technically, friends do this, right?

The thought of Ben seeing me with Jared pops into my head, immediately making me want to pull away. My gut suddenly squirms, telling me I'm betraying Ben by doing this, but I don't know how to pull away without making it weird, so I keep my arm where it is. My phone vibrates in my pocket, so I pull it out in my free hand, hoping it's Ben. Halting in my tracks, my breath hitches.

UNKNOWN
Nobody else should be allowed to touch you.

"What's wrong?" Jared leans in to catch a glimpse of what I'm looking at.

Tilting my phone quickly away, I clear my throat. "It's nothing."

Unconvinced, he frowns, his eyebrow raising in suspicion.

"I'm good, come on. Let's go." A low hum vibrates beneath my skin as I forcefully shove my phone in my back-pocket. I can't text him back here with Jared watching. Hell, I don't know if I should text him back at all. Who is he to tell me who should and shouldn't be touching me? What game is this guy playing?

But even though I'm frustrated at his previous rejection and lack of contact, a small part of me is curious enough to consider playing the game back.

Once we get back into the crowd, everyone, especially the girls, glare at me like I'm a piece of trash who just stole their favorite toy. I immediately remove my arm from his and create distance between us.

He doesn't argue or acknowledge the action and instead goes back to the party inside, leaving me alone by the pool. Now's my chance. Being that weird person who stands alone by a bush, I snatch my phone out of my pocket and stare at the text. My fingerpads drum on the screen in debate of what to retaliate with.

ME

Who are you to say that to me? You randomly stalk me, text me once and then fall off the face of the earth. So what do you care?

To my surprise, bubbles appear showing he's texting back this time. Good. Let's see what excuse he comes up with.

UNKNOWN

I claimed you a long time ago, Charlotte. You're mine. So, I get a say in who touches you.

"Claimed me? *Claimed* me? Who the fuck does this guy think he is?" I exasperate aloud, rubbing my forehead.

ME

You've never even spoken to me and ignored me when I invited you up to my room. So you get no claim to me nor get a say in who touches me. Stop dodging my questions. Tell me who you are and why you're so interested in me.

UNKNOWN

You'll find out soon enough who I am. Now get away from him, go home and sit your ass back down at the computer. It's been far too long since I've gotten to watch you play with yourself while watching me.

I grow feverish, my eyes darting from side to side to see if he's around, but there's no sign of him. Neither sound nor visual of my suddenly talkative biker. How'd he know Jared touched me? How does he know where I am?

ME

Who's this he you are talking about?

UNKNOWN

You know who I'm talking about. You're at his house. Now, I mean it. Get away from him and get your ass home.

Oh good. Another person to treat me like a child.

Screw him. As much as I want to know how long he's been watching me, I'm not going to get scolded by some stranger who watches me masturbate.

The tightening of my thighs together begs to continue the conversation and see where it leads, but then sweet, sweet Ben comes to mind. No. I choose Ben. If biker boy wants to step up and show himself then maybe we can be friends. Maybe.

Actually, come to think of it...I'll have to block my laptop camera now...

Stealing some courage from the party, I walk around trying to get my mind off that weird text conversation and find Shirley in the kitchen talking to the guy who must be the cousin, although he looks more like a brother. His matching long blonde hair, tan skin and side profile are uncannily similar. The only difference I notice right off the bat is his height. He must be at least five inches taller. No wonder Shirley didn't mind getting distracted by him.

I tap her on the shoulder, timidly interrupting her conversation. She turns around with a big grin, grabs my hand and leads me away from him down the hall.

"I'll be right back!" she yells to the cousin.

She pulls me aside in the hallway and whispers excitedly, "Okay, you can have Jared. His cousin, Jayson is so freakin' cute and funny, *and* he actually seems interested in me."

"That's really okay. I don't want Jared. But I'm glad you've found someone you're clicking with!"

"Oh, I figured when he disappeared and left me with his cousin he went to find you."

"He did... but we just talked. He's nice and all, but I've got my eye on someone else."

A lonely ache hits my stomach, and my body warms at the memory of hugging Ben earlier, his scent fresh in my nostrils. I wish he was here. A side of guilt throws itself in the mix.

Should I tell Ben about this anonymous biker who keeps contacting me? Is it wrong if I don't tell him? Is it wrong that part of me wants to masturbate again to the biker and see if he watches? Ugh, this is all getting complicated.

"Ooooh, really? Who?" she exclaims excitedly.

"I'll tell you later. For now, go back to Jayson! I wouldn't want him to get distracted by anyone else."

Half true, half lie. I'm keeping my feelings for Ben close to the chest until I figure out what's going on in his mind...and mine.

"You're the best. By the way, thank you so much for being a good friend and trying to set me up with Jared. I've had many friends, but you've shown yourself to be a true one. The other girls would've chosen the guy over me. You're a good person."

She hugs me by surprise, squeezing me tight. I lean into the hug and squeeze her back just as hard. Wow, a true friend. One I've only ever had in Ben, and never a girl.

This is my opening to get closer with Shirley this summer before college. It'd be nice to have a girl best friend to talk to about womanly things instead of a boy who turns his nose up at it. I grin thinking of Ben's reaction whenever I talk about my period. His scrunched-up nose and spitting his tongue out dramatically is my favorite.

She wiggles her fingers playfully to say bye and walks back to the kitchen to resume her conversation with the cousin.

I return to the pool area, kick my shoes off and walk over to the side where I recognize some cross-country girls. Julie, Yuni, Kelly and Porter are sitting on a shelf in the pool in the deep end, lounging and laughing together. With an inhale so deep my ribs expand to the max, I pull my pant legs up to my mid shin and stick my feet in the water next to them, the icy cold water a lifesaver in calming my nerves.

"Hey guys," I say cheerily.

They all stop talking and smile up at me. That went better than my original fear. I half expected them to ignore me.

"Charlotte! Oh my gosh, I can't believe you're out and about. Look at you. You look great!"

I revel in their compliments and let it build a small amount of confidence. This isn't so scary after all. I should've done this sooner, should've tried sooner, been braver sooner.

"Aw, thanks so much, guys! You look good too. I promised Jared I'd come, so here I am. Are you all excited for the summer?"

As they excitedly tell me about their plans, regret buries into my chest. Regret that I never tried to make friends and settled with what was easy. I always had an excuse not to put in the effort. I think I've always feared rejection from them. Keeping them at an arm's length was the safest way to protect myself from hurt, but now looking at it, all it did was keep me isolated.

I always believed this was just how things were and that was that. Always telling myself they didn't want to be my friend for this reason or that reason but never trying to disprove that theory. I could've had so many more moments like this and now I won't.

My eyes begin to burn, and I bite my lip to keep the tears from rolling out. I *really* hate this window where the tears flow easier. *Ugh.*

"Hey, Charlotte. Since school's over and you cannot possibly tell us you're busy all the time, do you want to come to my bonfire next weekend? We're going to have a girl's only night and a sleepover. Although, you don't have to sleepover if you're not comfortable with it." Julie grins, her wet hair sticking on her shoulders so thickly it's as if she has a drenched animal on them.

Wow, I can't believe I'm getting invited to a sleepover! After constantly rejecting them, they're still trying and being so nice about it. I should have given these humans a chance much earlier than this, but this is my moment. I'm not going to mess up this opportunity. I'm going to be brave.

"I'll be there," I say brightly, leaning back on my palms and kicking my feet in the water.

"Yasss. Get your phone out so we can exchange numbers. That way I can send you my address." She rattles off her phone number and instructs me to text her, so she has my information.

This summer might be greater than I expected after all. Excitement bubbles under the surface of my chest. My life *can* be different than what I've had. I don't have to be a loner like my mother; I can have a social group.

It's sad I have to convince myself there's nothing wrong with having a collection of friends. For some reason, I've always looked down on groups of friends, as if they weren't strong enough to be by themselves and had to lean on other people. But that's not the case. Those people were strong to lean on multiple people and be vulnerable with their peers. There's no reason I can't become one of them now. Become someone who has that group, that collection of humans they can trust more than anyone. All I have to do is keep taking these small steps in putting myself out there.

I send her the text with my information and linger in the messages, staring at Ben's text line. Pausing, I hover for a second over it before clicking on his name and texting:

ME
Hey

A response pings through immediately.

BENNY BOY

Hey, you. How's the party?"

I love when he says, "hey, you". It always makes me feel so special.

ME

It's going well. I'm actually becoming better friends with some of the girls from the cross-country team. Julie even invited me over to a girl's only bonfire next weekend!

BENNY BOY

Oh, I see. Am I not enough anymore? You need to make other friends now? 😜

ME

You're right. I don't need them. So, let's talk about my period last month. It was KILLER. I mean the cramps were so bad

BENNY BOY

...... You got me there. You need more girlfriends.

I laugh out loud and send a silly face emoji back.

BENNY BOY

You seem better. I'm glad.

ME

Yeah, I am doing better. Thanks to you. I wish you were here though.

Shit.

Saying I wish you were here is much too forward too fast. He's going to suspect something.

Shit.

BENNY BOY

Oh, yeah? 😈

ME

Don't flatter yourself. It's only so I could make you more uncomfortable with period talk from three other girls including me. I love watching you squirm.

BENNY BOY

I'd put up with the talk just so I could sit with you there. I'm not afraid. I big strong man. Me no fear woman.

Falling back, I belly laugh out loud from hearing his caveman voice in my head. Not wanting to push my luck, I sit my phone down beside me and return to the conversation with the girls.

Of course, the biker boy on Xypher is what they're giggling about. But this time, I gladly participate in the conversation about how hot he is, while simultaneously shoving the knowledge down of what I do to myself during those videos, even though I'm mad at him right now. I wonder if any of them have either.

Yikes. Ew, too far. It's gross to think of these girls doing that. My graphic brain needs to chill.

Has he reached out to any of them as well? Is he just a player who stalks and randomly pursues all the girls who obsess over him? Most likely...

Fighting the small tinge of jealousy, I ignore my brain for a while and tune back into the party happening right in front of me.

The rest of the night flies by. The girls invite me to the humongous bathroom to change where we hang out and get dry before heading out to the bonfire setting up in the backyard.

They pull up a truck with loads of pallets tied to the back and lay ten pallets down in the middle with stacks of long wooden planks up along the sides. It's even bigger than the bonfires held at homecoming games. We have to stay back while they make a small sand barrier to make sure it won't spread.

The fire rages quickly, the searing heat stinging me from outside of the sand barrier. The girls and the rest of the guests start unfolding lawn chairs to relax and hang out by the fire.

Jared never told me to bring a chair, so I don't have one. I suppose I can sit on the ground, although I'll feel left out. I walk up next to Julie and stand there to make conversation in the meantime until I decide what to do.

"Do you have a chair, Charlie?" Julie asks.

"Oh, no. I didn't know I was suppos—"

Jared cuts me off mid-sentence. "Here's yours, Charlie."

He winks and sets a huge blue rocking lawn chair down in between Julie and his. He pats the seat inviting me to sit.

"Thanks, Jared." I force out a chuckle. Did he purposely plan on not telling me to bring a chair so he could make sure he set one up next to his?

His chair is incredibly close to mine, the plastic of the arm rests touching. If I move my arm too much to the left, his arm will graze mine. He doesn't seem bothered by it, so I try not to focus on it or care if we brush our arms, eventually settling into a constant position with them resting against each other. I shrug it off, figuring it's no big deal, and focus my attention back on Julie and Porter who's sitting beside her.

Time flies from the fun of girl talk with them. We discuss everything—periods, what sucks about being a girl, how boys have it so easy and even our home lives.

A couple hours later, a vibration in my pocket tickles my leg. I pull my phone out and see a text from Ben.

BENNY BOY

You still there?

I swipe up to reply but get distracted by Julie and Porter saying goodbye and getting up to go home. And no wonder. It's twelve-thirty in the morning. Matter of fact, almost everyone else has already left too. I was so engrossed in our conversation I didn't even notice how small the circle had gotten.

I stand up to leave as well but a hand on my arm holds me back.

"Wait. Hang out with me a bit more?" There's a small plea in Jared's voice. Why not? It's an innocent enough request.

A vibration in my hand, pulls my attention, delaying my response.

UNKNOWN

I'm going to come get your ass if you don't respond to me Charlotte. Either respond to me or GO HOME RIGHT NOW; Otherwise I'll be there within the hour. Don't play with me.

What the hell? Ok, this guy is getting a little scary...

An eerie chill drags down my spine, spreading goosebumps under my skin all over my body.

"Charlie?"

Should I call Ben and have him come pick me up?

"Charlie?"

"What?" I respond, still half distracted while anxiously chewing on my thumbnail.

"Will you hang out with me a bit more? Please?" His puppy dog eyes practically beg me in this second request.

With Jared here I should be safe. If the biker shows up, I'm sure he'll protect me. Then when it gets too late, I'll just call Ben and have him come get me or follow me home so I know I'm safe. I should confess what's been happening with the biker boy anyways to rid this minute amount of guilt that rises whenever I think of him when I'm around Ben. It's like I'm cheating on Ben, even though I know that's not the case.

"Sure. But just so you know, my social battery is nearing zero, so I'm not sure how much fun I'll be or how long I'll stay," I answer casually.

Jared doesn't need to know about my newfound stalker. It'll be on a need to know basis for him.

He laughs, "That's totally fine."

I sit back down and rock back and forth in the rocking lawn chair. A small tremble lingers under the surface from worry about if and when my previous obsession is going to show up. Soon after, the last group leaves, leaving just us two sitting in front of the now more conservative fire. It burned down fairly quickly; we can barely feel the heat of it outside of the sand barrier now.

"It's getting chillier out. Want to get closer to the fire?"

"Yeah, for sure."

I'm grateful he's cold too, because I'm *freezing*. I step closer to the fire, keeping myself a couple of arms' lengths away. The fire's crackling music fills the air around us as we watch the floating embers dance around the burning logs. One ember flies up particularly high, my eyes trailing it up to the beautiful stars shining brightly in the night sky.

The ember burns out and falls to my left onto Jared who's staring at me intently.

"What?" I shift on my feet, backing away out of instinct.

"I'm glad you came tonight. It was great seeing you having so much fun, although I do regret that we didn't spend more time together."

"Well, I'm sure there'll be other parties during the summer that we'll both go to. I'm going to attempt to be a socialite now so you may catch me out and about more," I say lightly, smiling.

"So, tell me, why exactly *were* you trying to set me up with Shirley tonight?" He sticks his hands in his back pants pockets and rocks back and forth on his heels.

I chuckle, meeting his gaze. "Shirley told me she's had a crush on you for ages and since me and you had gotten closer this last week, she wanted me to set her up with you. I promised her I would so that's what that whole situation was about earlier."

He furrows his brow at my answer, his lips tightening together. "You'd rather her be with me than you?"

"What do you mean?" I utter hesitantly. I know what he means. Another truth hiding in my brain surfaces, showing me how naïve I've been once again.

It's official. He does like me. He does want to be with me.

But that small part of me that did want to be with him, however briefly, is completely gone.

My gut instincts pull at me, telling me it's time to leave and now, but I'm unsure how to make my exit without making him feel bad. An eeriness settles over me as he moves closer, his steps slow but intentional. My feet take another step back on their own.

"Why didn't you wear a dress for me today like you have been all week?"

"I-I didn't wear the dresses at school for your attention. I randomly decided to wear them for myself," I stammer back, almost tripping backwards as I pick up speed to get away.

He's less than an arm's length away from me now. His scent wafts toward me in the breeze, the smokiness filling my nostrils.

"I think you did; you just didn't know it. You willingly rested your head on my shoulder in between classes and embraced me when my arm was around you. I told you we were going to be more than friends, Charlie. What didn't you get about that?"

He thrusts his arm out and grabs me by the left arm hard and pulls me roughly to him. Swinging his other arm around my waist, he positions my right arm, so it's pinned between us and looks down at me. I know I need to run, but I'm frozen. It doesn't matter anyways, he's holding me so tightly, it's a struggle to move. What the hell is he doing?

"Jared, please don't grab me like that. It hurts. Let me go." I wiggle to see if he'll release me, but he doesn't budge.

His eyes no longer look kind but instead are filled with a scary almost-black intensity, the only glow in them the reflection from the now simmering fire. "You know you want this, Charlie. We'd be great together. I guarantee it. Plus, no girl has ever *not* wanted to be with me, so just go with it, okay?"

He lowers his head, his lips puckered and in position to kiss me. My heart pounds in my chest, but the adrenaline provides no help. I squeeze my other arm up in between us and try to push away from him with both palms on his chest, but he doesn't budge. He's so much stronger than I realized. Not good. Not good at all. With nowhere to go, I scrunch my face and turn to the left just before he reaches my lips, positioning him to land on my cheek instead.

He moves his lips to my neck and kisses slowly up and down. His lips are so cold. Goosebumps trickle along my whole body, like little ants are crawling all over. I know they're not only from the cold of his lips, but the disgust with him and myself. I hate it. I hate this.

I continue pathetically struggling to wiggle out of his grip, but it's no use. My mind races along with my heart, my breathing stuttered and short.

I'm too weak.

Why am I so weak?

How did I let myself get into this situation?

How was I this naive?

I never thought Jared would do anything like this.

He kisses my neck harder, trying to keep me still so he can continue. In horror, I feel him exploring, moving down and grabbing my ass, pulling me roughly into his hardness.

The fight in me freezes at the intimate violation, my body going still. No one's ever touched me that way. I don't want my first intimate touches to be with Jared. Not like this.

Not like this.

Not like this.

The pleas fill my head, but my mouth stays shut, silent, like my body wants to betray me.

No.

Stop.

No, not like this.

He holds both my wrists in one hand as he brings his other to the front of my jeans and fumbles with the button. My voice balls up in my throat, straining as I push with everything to get a word out. But all I manage is a weak croak.

"Jared, no. Stop. Jared, I don't want this. You need to listen to me. P-please st-sto-stop," I plead, finally able to speak.

"Shut up, yes, you do," he growls.

With my pants now unbuttoned, he moves to his, flicking the belt off with ease and zipping down his pants.

Tears trickle down my cheeks. My body's giving up on the fight already.

Pathetic.

His pants fall down to his ankles revealing tight underwear that show his arousal at the situation.

Disgusting.

My stomach twists in knots, vomit surfacing in my throat. I squeeze my eyes shut. I don't want to see this. I can't watch this happen to me.

"Jared, please," I beg, tears pooling on my chest.

He ignores me, tugging my pants down hard, while keeping hold of my wrists.

A motorcycle roars behind me, getting louder and louder. I peek over my shoulder to see a bike speeding straight toward us, then go flying by without a rider on it right next to us as it skids on its side, tearing up the lawn.

Next thing I know, the biker's running at us, his feet thundering on the grass. In one swift movement he leaps at Jared. I stagger out of the way, finally free from his grip.

Jared shuffles backwards but not quick enough. The biker jumps in the air, cocks his arm back and with all his weight throws a punch at Jared on his way down, knocking him fully on his back before landing on his feet directly over him. He bends down, grabs his shirt collar and punches him one more time in the face. He shoves him hard back toward the ground, causing Jared's head to bounce as it hits the grass.

I stand at a distance, pulling my pants back up and buttoning them while debating whether I can safely run to my car or not without them noticing me. But my mind goes quiet when I hear my savior speak.

Ben's muffled voice screams from under the motorcycle helmet as Jared starts to get up, his pants still at his ankles.

"Stay the FUCK down, you piece of shit." His voice shakes with anger.

Jared's upper lip is cut, blood bubbling over his bottom lip and down his chin. More blood drips down the side of his face from under his left eye, most likely due to the silver rings always present on Ben's hand. Ben's hands are fisted as his side, shaking. He doesn't have motorcycle gloves on. He always wears them. Did he rush over here? How did he know what was going on? Ben starts walking backwards toward me, keeping his eyes on Jared.

Jared's chest heaves quickly up and down, his brain clearly calculating what to do next. He sits up quickly to make a move, but it's too late. Ben crouches down over him and lifts his visor, his helmet inches from Jared's face.

"If you do not stay the fuck down, I will beat you so hard that you *will* lose *everything*. Your life will be ruined because I'll make damn sure your legs won't work properly enough to run anymore. Your face will be so gruesome, you'll never be able to look at yourself in the mirror again, let alone get another woman. You'll be fucking lucky if you can ever grab anything with those disgusting hands of yours if you try me. I swear it, Jared. I will fucking destroy you." He raises his finger and points it in his face. "Don't you *ever* touch a woman when she says no. Don't you *ever* fucking push yourself on a woman. If I hear of you trying to pull this shit again on Char, I will *fucking* kill you! That's a promise," he threatens, his voice deep and loud.

Jared stays down, his teeth gritting in pain and fury and gives Ben the most vile look, as if he's going to find a way to take him down and make him regret it. Ben, with a look of rage, steps over Jared and runs toward me. He grabs my hand, pulling me to run next to him toward his bike that's still lying on its side in the grass.

The tread marks from where it skidded are deep, completely ruining that section of their yard.

I can't think. My brain can't process everything happening. How did he know where Jared lives? How did he know what Jared was doing to me? Whose bike is he riding? It's not his usual red or black one.

He picks up the bike, kicks it on and yells over the engine noise, "Get on!"

Without hesitation, I obey.

I wrap my arms around his waist as we speed off toward the front of the house. The wind's cold as ice as it dries my tears, but the coolness calms me enough to stop the crying. I close my eyes, embracing the sting, the rush of wind and noise of my brain being drowned out by the engine.

He stops in the valet lot where my car's the only one left and puts his feet on the ground to hold the bike steady for me to get off. My legs are unsteady, almost giving out when they hit the pavement, but with resolve they stay steady enough, enabling me to shakily walk to my car in a daze.

"I'll follow you home," he shouts over the sound of the bike, flipping his visor back down.

I nod, unable to speak and start up my car.

It's a torturous drive home. Scenarios of what could've happened haunt me in the silence. A staggering whiplash of emotions runs through in succession, mocking me. Anger the most prevalent. Anger at myself for getting in that situation. Anger at the piece of shit Jared turned out to be. Tears cloud my vision as the anger releases.

Has he done this to someone else before?

Was this what he planned to do all along to me? Damnit, I'm so naive.

I blink fast to clear my vision, the road becoming hard to see through the cloudiness of the tears.

The only thing keeping me sane is seeing Ben's headlight in my rearview mirror.

I'm unable to describe the feelings I want to express to him about what he's done for me tonight. I don't know how I'll ever make it up to him.

I park in the driveway and turn the car off. A second later, he pulls his bike up next to me, shuts it off, and sets his helmet on it. His face is unreadable, calm, steady.

I'm unable to look at myself in the rearview mirror. I must look like a pathetic mess, but I can't find the energy to care right now.

He says nothing but instead opens my car door and pulls me out into his arms. As he walks me to the door, I curl up into him, reveling in the safety of his embrace. I burrow into his chest and soft cloth hits my skin, instead of the expected scratchy leather.

That's right.

He isn't wearing his motorcycle jacket either. He must've left in a hurry because he never rides without all his gear on.

Whatever, I don't care. All I care about is that I'm out of that situation. It could've been so much worse. I froze in a moment when I needed to be strong the most. I can't believe I stopped fighting so quickly.

Pathetic.

He holds me tightly as I sob into his chest. He sets his head on mine and whispers over and over, "I know. It's okay. Let it out. You're safe. It's okay. I've got you."

My legs weaken, my crying now inconsolable. Whatever strength I have left is gone, causing me to slide down his sweatshirt as I start to collapse.

Noticing right away, he picks up my legs and carries me the rest of the way up to the house. He opens the door with his key and quietly shuts it before carrying me up the stairs.

I stay buried in his shoulder, wishing I could melt into him. I don't want to think. Don't want to see those images of what could have happened. Don't want to imagine how it could've ruined my future.

He quietly opens my bedroom door and sets me on the bed before going back and shutting it.

I lean over and rest my arms on my legs, trying to shrink myself up as much as possible. The bed dips underneath his weight as he places a gentle but firm hand on my back.

"Are you okay, Charlotte?"

"Don't use my full name to coddle me like my mother would," I snap in a congested tone from all the crying.

Guilt twists my stomach even more for snapping at him right now, but I don't know what to do with my emotions. The fear, guilt, rage and disgust are overwhelming and hearing my name out of pity from his mouth is unbearable.

"Sorry, Char."

"I feel so gross, Ben. I can't believe I was stupid enough to allow myself into a situation like that. I barely even put up a fight. It was pa-pa-thetic." I choke out the last word as more tears soak the skin on my arms before falling to the ground.

He moves off the bed and kneels in front of me, his hands gently resting on my shins. His hair slightly covers his left eye that peers deep inside me, begging me to hear the words he says next. I look away, ashamed.

His knuckle grazes my chin and gently lifts it, forcing me to meet his gaze again.

"Now, I want you to hear me, Char. You were *not* stupid to be caught in that situation. Jared is a fucking piece of shit to put you in a situation like that in the first place. You did absolutely nothing wrong. And you didn't stop fighting; your body was frozen. It's a trauma response. How could you expect yourself to handle a situation like that when you've never really been around guys." He pauses, his brows creasing. "If he had gotten any further, I would have fucking killed him. I swear it."

He drops his gaze and his knuckle and places his hands on his thighs, still kneeling.

"I heard rumors that he's done shit like this to girls at other schools, but I never saw or heard concrete proof, so I didn't think much of it. Then when I saw you guys getting closer and seemingly cozy, I started to be more cautious...to pay attention more. I wanted to keep a close eye on you guys to make sure he was behaving. I didn't want anything bad to happen to you."

He leans back and runs his fingers through his hair, a small amount of Jared's blood glimmering off the silver ring on his right hand in the moonlight coming in through my window. Taking a deep inhale, he studies me as if waiting for me to say something.

"How'd you know where Jared lived and why were you there and whose bike is that?" I ask more calmly. The tears slow down as I focus on him and wait for his answers. How *did* he know where I was? I guarantee he hasn't been to Jared's before. Was he following me?

"I kept checking in with you while you were there, because I had a bad feeling something was going to happen. My gut had this horrible tug in it the later the night got. So, when I texted you the last time and you didn't respond, I got worried. It was so late...By how you were texting me I was hoping you might give me a call or at the least text me when you got home."

We lock eyes for a fleeting moment before he shies away his gaze to the floor. I know he's referring to my text about wishing he was there. He's right. I would've called him on my way home.

"His family's rich, but they're still listed so I googled his address. I was originally planning on just driving by and seeing if your car was there and to check if the party was still going, but once I got there, I saw your car and no one else's, leading me to believe you guys were alone. As I drove further past, a light in the backyard caught my attention. I flipped my visor up and saw two shadows in front of a fire." He fidgets his hands together and clenches his jaw, scowling at the memory. "I....I wanted to get a closer look. When I started slowly driving toward the backyard and your shapes became clearer, I noticed you were in a defensive position and seemed to be writhing away from him. I knew immediately what was going on right then."

His breathing increases, lips tightening into a thin line. "It took everything in me not to ram him with my bike straight into the fucking fire, but I didn't want to take the chance of hitting you. So instead, I angled myself in a way where I could punch him and throw him to the ground in one shot so I could get you away from him." His knuckles are white, gripping each other as he grits his teeth.

"And the bike?" I whisper.

"It's my bike. I own it."

I had no idea he owned more than two bikes.

Words escape me on how to express my gratitude and how much what he did meant to me. My protector. My best friend.

It doesn't matter what's happened in our life, he always comes back for me.

"Thank you, so, so much Ben," I whisper, looking down at my feet. "I...I don't know what else to say besides that right now."

His boots scrape the floor as he crawls toward me. I don't move, allowing him to wrap his arms around me in a tight hug and give me a kiss on the top of my head. Heat and butterflies surge through my body, warming up the coldness from the night.

I let him hold me until a wave of tiredness overtakes me. He releases me from the hug as I move to lay on my side. A tug on my feet pulls my legs down softly.

He's taking my shoes off for me. Wow.

He places my feet up on the bed and walks away.

"Don't leave me," I whisper with my eyelids closed, afraid of his answer.

"I'll be right here, always," he whispers back, stroking his fingers through my hair. My lips upturn into a sleepy smile, and I drift off to sleep.

Chapter Eleven.

A soft knock on the door wakes me up from my deep sleep. My heavy eyelids slowly lift, my vision distorted while I try to remember where I am. A blurry picture of my mom appears in my room before flashes of last night rush back to me.

Ben!

I fling the covers off and look around in panic. He's going to get in so much trouble if he slept over, even if it was me who asked him to. But he's not here. It's just me and my mother in the room.

"It's noon so I wanted to check on you and make sure you were okay. You never sleep in this la—" she stops mid-sentence. "Charlotte, your eyes are so swollen. Were you crying? What happened? Are you okay?"

The pity in her voice angers me, but I can't explain why.

"Yeah, I'm fine. I was only crying because I was sad school's over," I say dismissively, running over to the window. His motorcycle's gone. I didn't even hear him leave.

An ache of loneliness cuts into me without him here. A lonely ache my mother's presence won't help.

"Charlotte, talk to me." Concern softens her eyes, her mouth down turning into a frown.

"I'm fine." I sigh in frustration. "I'm just going through a lot of emotions right now with school ending and all the changes going on. I even made some new girlfriends last night. They invited me to an all-girls sleepover next weekend." I plaster a fake grin on to console her.

All I want is for her to leave the room so I can call Ben. I refuse to tell her what happened. Matter of fact, I don't want to tell *anyone* what happened. I want to forget the whole thing.

I raise my arms to stretch and notice bruises where Jared had grabbed and held me. Fresh images of him trying to force my pants off and holding me by my wrists return to haunt me.

My stomach churns like I just got punched in the gut and the room starts to sway. I inconspicuously try to hide my arms under my comforter as to not draw her attention to the bruises, although she likely already saw them. Leaning on my computer desk, she watches me, analyzing my every move.

I hate this. What will it take for her to go away. What almost happened to me last night makes me unable to be in her presence out of shame. It's hard to explain but it's like I'm not her special daughter anymore. The more I debate telling her what happened, the more I can't find the words... Or courage.

"You know you can tell me anything, sweetheart. Right? I'm here for you."

Claustrophobia suffocates me as she moves closer.

"Yes. I'm fine. Can you just leave so I can get showered and dressed please?" I ask sternly.

A flash of hurt crosses her face, but she smiles, nonetheless. Great, now I feel even shittier.

I miss the old relationship with my parents. Will things ever be the same again or will it only be a memory?

She steps through the doorway and whispers without looking back, "I love you."

My eyes well up with tears. *Will the crying ever fucking stop?*

I examine myself more closely in the mirror after she shuts the door. My body appears okay except for the markings in the discernable shape of fingers—purple and blue bruises around my arms and wrists. A soreness is present as I rotate my wrists and watch how the coloring changes under my skin. I stare at the bruises, willing them to go away.

My phone's alarm sounds from somewhere in my room, pulling my attention away from my body. Where the heck is it? I scour between my blankets, sheets, pillow, and dresser, until finally I drop on my knees and find it under the bed. Why's my alarm going off at twelve-thirty in the afternoon on a Sunday? I never set my alarm for this late in the day. I pull it out from under my bed and see a note written for the alarm.

Aw, how cute of him to do this. I smile and swipe open my phone to text him, but it opens directly to my notes app, revealing a letter he wrote me when he must've set my alarm.

Char, I left before your parents woke up to make sure neither of us got in trouble. Things are strained enough with your parents right now, and I didn't want to be another reason to put any further tension on that. I'll make sure to walk my motorcycle a good amount away to ensure it doesn't wake them up or you, especially.
I cannot begin to express how pissed I am at Jared for the situation he put you in. Rage, so severe it's indescribable, hits me every time I think about what could've happened if I hadn't gotten there when I did.

Another flash of Jared's contorted face as he tried to unbutton my pants crosses my mind. I wipe the tears away and continue reading.

I will never let anyone do that to you again. Ever. I fucking swear it. I stayed awake the entire night because I wanted to make sure you felt safe... That no nightmares came to haunt you while I was there and if they did then I'd be awake and ready to fight them off with you.
Anyways, I'm not writing this note about last night. Be at the farm at four and meet me in the back barn. I have something I want to show you.

P.S. Did you know you whimper in your sleep? It's the most adorable thing...

Heat trickles through my cheeks at his last sentence, but my chest also tightens.

Grabbing my chest and rubbing the muscles to soothe it, I lean back on my bed and close my eyes. He didn't sleep because he wanted to make sure I didn't have bad dreams? I've always known Ben and I's friendship is something special but for him to act like this? To act this protective to this degree? He hasn't always been this way with me. This is new. I like it and I'm grateful for it, but I'm not sure what he wants or if I can deliver what he wants.

After last night, I'm not sure how I feel about being touched by a boy again for a while. Will he ask that of me? Does he even want something with me or am I overthinking this? Maybe I'm too tainted now.

My chest tightness worsens, a heaviness settling into it. I let out a deep sigh, keeping my tears in check.

Breathe. I need to Breathe.

In….1….2…3…Out…1….2….3.

By breath five, the heaviness dissipates, and the tears settle back into their ducts.

I've got this. I've got this.

I stare at myself in the mirror after my shower, disappointed that the bruises are still there like I could've somehow washed them off.

I don't got this.

How am I going to cover them? I don't own any foundation to conceal it.

Thunder cracks outside providing me a glorious solution to the problem. The weather forecast on my phone confirms colder weather at fifty-five degrees, scattered thunderstorms and cloudiness. Perfect. I'll wear a long-sleeved shirt and a sweatshirt to cover everything up. Easy peasy.

I painfully shrug on my favorite plain black, long sleeve shirt and a sweatshirt from my junior year of cross-country along with faded blue jeans and all white tennis shoes. To top off the casual look, I throw my hair up into a wadded bun. I look at myself one last time.

Atleast my eyes are less swollen now. I took the coldest shower known to man to reset my nervous system and to attempt to get the swelling in my face to go down.

Let's see if eyeliner does the trick to help me hide the residual puffiness. I grab the only pen of black eyeliner I own and angle my wrist to apply under my bottom lashes.

"Ouch!"

Ugh, bending my wrist upwards like that hurts.

Great.

Welp. This is as good as it's going to get. If anyone asks, I'll say my allergies are acting up or something.

Well, that only took an hour. I have no idea what I'm going to do until four.

I mosey to my desk and open my laptop. It's a problem Xypher is open every time I open my laptop, but then again how'd I forget my biker boy reached out to me last night? The me who was engulfed in him seemed like eons ago, but there he was... still posting new videos, thirst traps and new seductive dances with his bike in the background. Heat and wetness begin in my core as I watch his videos, relieving me of a fear. I was worried after last night I would be too broken to get turned on, totally screwing my future relationships. Thank God I have nothing to worry about on that account.

I scroll through his videos, dissociating to the various thoughts flying across my mind.

Who is this guy?

Did he ever show up last night after Ben saved me?

What's his life like and what he's been through?

Why does he seem so obsessed with me and how does he know me?

Is he our age or older?

Why hasn't he reached out since last night?

His aggressive texts did scare me last night, but I still wish I could meet him and ask him these questions. I'm magnetically pulled to him and his page like he's meant to be in my life, probably because of what I've done to myself late at night because of him…but deeper down I know there's something more to it.

I lean closer to the screen, searching for clues in his videos—for any hint that would give him away and tell me a little more about him. His bike, his muscles, his clothes, his body, the background... but nothing's striking a chord in me. I waste another half an hour on his page and then give up.

Screw it, I'm going to Ben's early. I have nothing else to do, and I'm not about to sit downstairs and endure an awkward, forced conversation with my parents.

I sneak down the stairs, grab my keys and get in my car. Flashbacks of driving home last night creep up as soon as I shut my car door. My damn brain's torturing me. Why won't it let me forget it ever happened? Cooperate with me, brain.

The tightness in my chest is unbearable. I close my eyes and massage the muscles across my chest to ease the tension, taking a few more deep breaths to settle my now racing heart. I need to be calm. I'm not going to let this experience haunt me. I'm going to face this and conquer it. Jared's actions will not hold power over me.

In...1...2...3.... Out...1....2...3.

I say my affirmations with the breathing exercises over and over again.

In...1...2...3.... Out...1....2...3.

I'm not going to let this experience haunt me. I'm going to face this and conquer it. Jared's actions will not hold power over me.

Finally, the images fade along with the tightness.

God. Fuck that guy and fuck this whole situation.

I angrily shove my keys in the ignition and drive over to Ben's farm, making sure I take deep breaths along the way. I just know being on the farm will help me. The countryside with barely anyone around, fresh air, animals, nothing to focus on but work...

A hopeful and happy feeling breaks through all the sadness and anger. I hold onto that feeling the rest of the drive, focusing only on the dusty fresh smell of crops in the summer, the smell of straw in the barn in the winter, and the smell of fresh dirt and dust from working the ground.

Rain splatters my windshield right as I park by the back barn and run into it to wait for the rain to stop.

The smell of fresh hay and cold rain fills my nostrils. I breathe it in and sink onto a haybale, savoring the feel of the alfalfa poking through my jeans. Right as I close my eyes and lean back, a loud boom sounds from behind me, making me squeal in surprise.

I whip around to see Ben walking through the side door that must have slammed open from the wind. My mouth gapes open, my body on fire as I behold his current state.

His hair's drenched from the rain, lost strands stuck to his face, and laying perfectly against his sharp jaw. Not to mention, his white T-shirt's completely soaked through, highlighting each dip in his chiseled abs. And God, stuck just above his pants that are weighed down perfectly enough to display his v-cut, are the rim of his boxers sliding on his olive skin. His jeans are a deep, dark blue from the rain, his work boots littered with mud. A throbbing heat sears between my thighs, making me tighten them and a ball settles in my chest.

What do I do? Do I hide? No. It would be even more embarrassing if he caught me trying to hide. How would I explain that? Sorry, you were so hot I had to hide because I couldn't handle my body's reaction to you?

He chucks an ax with a log stuck on it into the side of the barn and runs his fingers through his hair, clearing his face of the loose strands, and letting loose a deep sigh.

Luckily, he doesn't notice me at first, giving me enough time to rid myself of the drooling expression I know I have plastered on.

His shirt's half-way up in a sad effort to wipe his face dry when he finally notices me watching him.

"Char! Is it four already? It started raining out there right when I was finishing up cutting wood for the bonfire I was initially going to hold tonight. I'm fucking soaked."

Hesitantly, I sit still, waiting for flashbacks of the fire to come into my brain, but none do. It's quiet along with the rest of the world, the only sound being the pattering of rain on the aluminum roof of the barn. The only thing I see is Ben. Hot, soaked Ben.

It takes all my energy to fight the strong urge to look lower than his eyeline because I know he'll notice and give me shit for it. He drops his shirt, which barely moves down, sticking to his wet skin and wipes his hands on his pants.

"Uh, no, I uh, came early. I mean arrived early." *Oh my God, be more obvious, Charlotte.*

My cheeks singe with heat and my heart pitter patters in my chest, making me short of breath.

I want nothing more than for him to take his shirt off and come over and kiss me. I want to feel him against me, skin to skin to see if it feels different when he touches me instead of myself. He's not the only one soaked now... I pray he doesn't notice.

"Oh, yeah?" He smirks like he knows my current state.

Fuck.

He walks a few steps toward me, and winks, his tongue flicking out on his bottom lip.

"Do you want to help me get ready?"

My eyes betray me. Damn them. They trace down his stomach and linger on his pants, blatantly showing the dirty place my mind's stuck in. I bite my lip, barely holding myself back from being reckless and risking our entire friendship by placing my mouth on his and tasting him, experiencing him and his lush, full wet lips.

Wearing a cocky smirk, he closes the gap between us. He licks his lips and lifts my chin with his rough knuckle...*sigh*...farmer's hands.

God, I love them.

The skin's cracked and calloused on the outside but soft on the palms. Veins protrude on the back of his hands, going down his arm and into the part of his bicep not covered by his T-shirt.

I search each of his beautiful brown eyes, trying to figure out what he's thinking. My attention moves back to his lips and then his eyes on repeat, searching each crinkle of skin and each minute change in expression to see if he's feeling the same as me in this moment.

The rain's a distant drumming on the barn, yet barely an echo of sound can cut through the tension between us. The only thing I can clearly hear is him, his voice, his breathing and my own. I lick my lips and bite the inside of the lower one to be subtle about what I want, giving him permission to take that step if he wants. His breath hitches as his gaze dips to my mouth.

We lock eyes, his staring at me with intensity, mine begging him to make a move.

Do it, I will them to say. *Kiss me*.

A hint of a smile appears but then he backs away, his eyes softening. It feels like he broke a bond that was just forming between us but now has been ripped, catching my breath with it. The rain and wind appear again but slower than before. It must be about to clear up outside.

"How are you doing today, Char? You doing, okay?" he croaks, his throat bobbing. Is he breathless from the interaction between us like I am?

I lean back on the bale, the alfalfa sticking into my palms, grounding me.

"I don't want to talk about what happened last night. I'm over it. I promised myself I wasn't going to let that jack-ass ruin or control my mood and feelings. Fuck him and fuck that."

"That's my girl," he says proudly.

Butterflies flutter wildly in my stomach at being called his girl. I curl my lips in to hold my smile back and look away. "By the way, did you get any sleep last night at all? When did you even leave?" I ask, changing the conversation.

He rubs the back of his neck and looks down at his boots.

"Uh, no I didn't get any sleep. I left around four, I think?"

"Holy crap, four in the morning? And you didn't sleep? Why?" I know he told me already in his note, but I want him to tell me in person. I need to know he won't play games with me and will be direct and up front with his feelings. He shoves his hands in his pockets, visibly nervous.

"Well," he says exhaling forcefully, "I was too nervous to sleep in your room in case I didn't wake up in time and your parents found us. After the night you had, you didn't need any more drama. Plus, I wanted to be there in case you woke up and needed some comfort. I wasn't sure if you'd have nightmares and get scared if you woke up and were alone. I wanted to make sure you didn't feel alone in any capacity because I know how scary it can be to wake up like that."

I'm shook. He's had nights of feeling alone and scared? He's had nightmares that've haunted him? Why's he never told me any of this before?

I push my luck and press for more. "You've woken up scared before?"

"Mhmm..." He stops talking and forces a cough. "Oh, good the rain's about stopped...*which* is convenient, because I have a surprise for you, and we need to go to the other barn to get it."

My eyes widen. "A surprise? Y-you got me something? What is it?"

He grins broadly and grabs my hand, pulling me up and leading me out of the side door he came in through. His touch lights my whole body on fire until...

"Ouch."

He pulled too hard on my hand which triggered pain in my wrist, and I vocalized the pain before I could stop it which unfortunately made me out myself.

He whips his head around so fast I'm not able to pull my hand back in time before he pulls up my sweatshirt sleeve to look at my arm.

"I'm going to kill that fucking bastard," he snarls in a low guttural voice.

He drops my hand, allowing the sleeve to fall back down and angrily stalks to the barn where he keeps his motorcycles. I chase after him, panicked about what he might do.

"Ben! Ben, stop!" I grab his arm, but he angrily rips it away from me. "Ben! You can't do this; you need to leave it alone. You showed him what he did was wrong last night, you don't need to go back over there."

Tears cloud my vision and trail down my cheeks. Damnit, I'm so weak now. He faces me, a crazed look in his eye, one of anger resembling last night's only with more fire.

"He's a fucking piece of shit. I cannot believe he left marks on you. He needs to have his ass handed to him properly, and he needs to be reported for assault."

His chest heaves but he stays with me instead of turning back toward the barn. I need to buy more time and calm him down.

"Don't leave me, please. I'm asking you, for me, not to do this. Jared will get what's coming to him, but you going over there is only going to make things worse. I'll file a police report against him and let the authorities handle it if you want, but I do *not* want you risking your future for me on a guy who is the scum of the earth. Don't let Jared win. You let him win if you let your anger control you and end up in jail because of *his* actions. Plus...I—I need you right now. I don't want you to leave me alone right now."

His eyes search mine for any sign that I'm not okay and for answers on what he can do to make any lingering pain go away. I grab his arm and boldly put it around my waist. His breath catches at my touch, but his hand relaxes against my hip.

I wrap my arms around his waist, wetting my sweatshirt from the residual rain and sweat on his clothes. His shirt's cool against my skin, the dip in his back perfect for me to rest my arms in. I lay my cheek against his shirt and close my eyes, breathing him in. He stiffens, not hugging me back, instead letting me lead.

"I'm going to be okay, Ben. Because of you, I'm going to be okay. Please don't leave me right now. Don't leave and ruin your party. Let's celebrate you tonight and the wonderful life you're going to have. Let's not give Jared another moment of our time. We both know he'll get what's coming to him, eventually. So, please. Stay with me. I need you." My voice cracks at the end, sounding more like a whimper than a plea.

His body relaxes at these last words, his arms fully wrapping around me, his head resting on mine. He kisses the top of my head. Lightening shoots through to my toes, making me squeeze him tighter and nuzzle into him.

"I won't leave you, I promise. I'll let it go, but only because you've asked me to. But I swear, if anything like this happens again, I *will* kill him or whoever puts you in that situation and you won't stop me next time."

He kisses me again in the same spot and holds me tightly, smushing my face further into his chest. God, he smells *so* good. His sweat mixed with the rain melts together to create an earthy scent mixed with his usual leathery-mint cologne.

His protectiveness over me is turning me on, I'll admit, but I don't want him to follow through on any of those violent threats. I only want him to be safe.

"I need you too, Char," he whispers into my hair. He pauses then says, "By the way, risking my future for you is worth it, you know."

Butterflies fly into my breasts, tingling my nipples and almost exploding out of me. I lean back and meet his gaze.

"No, it's not. Not over something stupid like that," I scold him.

He nips my nose and gives me a kiss on the cheek. "We'll agree to disagree then."

"I do not agree to disagree," I retort, loosening my grip and stepping away.

He pulls me back and holds me there, his wet hair slightly falling over his face as he gazes down at me with a soft smile, but it quickly fades into something different, something that lights my soul on fire. Meeting his stare, I notice his focus moves down to my mouth. He slowly leans in, his eyelids beginning to close and my body sighs against his in anticipation.

"Charlotte! Hey! I see you came early to help us set up, huh?"

We release each other at the same time and awkwardly stand side by side, hands behind our backs. My cheeks blush from being caught in whatever we were doing. I don't know if he was actually going to kiss me this time, but I was hoping, praying he was.

His mom runs over, her pruning shears sticking out of the front of her jeans, dirt on her knees from whatever gardening she was doing and a long sleeve-flannel flowing in the breeze.

"Hi Joan! Yup, came over to help set up!" I say brightly, trying to act normal. I'm still attempting to catch my breath, my heart pounding from the adrenaline surging through me. Ben sheepishly shoves his hands into his back-pockets, his cheeks tinted a deep red.

"Good! Ben, did you finish cutting wood?"

"Nah, the rain washed me out, but since it's stopping, I'm going to finish up here in a minute. I was actually about to show Charlotte her gift in the barn."

"Oh! Well don't let me interrupt. Give that to her and then you finish up the wood-cutting and have Charlotte come find me. She can help me start setting up tables under the canopy Koa and I put up in case it starts raining again."

"Sure thing, Ma. Char, let's go."

Joan and I exchange smiles before she turns around and strolls back toward the house.

Chapter Twelve.

"She knows about my surprise? Now I'm extremely curious what you got me. It better not be something gross. The last time you said you got me something, it was roadkill stuffed into a bucket...."

He laughs loudly as the large, faded wooden barn comes into view. "I forgot about that."

I scowl at him from behind. Maybe I should trip him for revenge.

He opens the back barn doors and steps inside.

"Ben, it was disgusting. It smelled so bad, I almost vomited."

"We were ten. What else was I supposed to get you?"

"Candy?"

"Well, hopefully this'll make up for it. Come on."

I follow behind him, jittery down to the bone from anticipation. He walks to a workbench behind his red motorcycle that has what must be my present on top of it. An all-white motorcycle helmet with a pink bow on it. My mouth drops open in shock. I squeal, unable to contain my excitement and run over to it.

"You're going to let me ride your motorcycle?" I squeal excitedly, jumping up and down with the helmet and turning to him for confirmation. I can't believe it. I've been begging him since we were little kids to ride, but he's never let me. Well unless I'm getting sexually assaulted, I guess. I shake off the thought. No, this moment is too precious to be ruined.

When I first asked him to ride as kids, he said he didn't want cooties on his tyke bike. Even after I showed him the cootie shot on my hand and gave him one, so we were both protected, he wouldn't let me.

Then when he got his first automatic motorbike in our teens, he didn't let me ride with him because he said it was too dangerous. Plus, he said he didn't want to scare other chicks off because he didn't want them to think we were dating.

Then finally, when he got his last adult motorbike, I asked one last time and he said no it was too dangerous, point blank. So, then I gave up and haven't asked since. I got sick of the rejection.

He belly-laughs, watching me jump up and down and dart over to his classic red Ducati. The other motorcycle he saved me with last night isn't in the barn, but I don't give it much thought. I'm too excited to ride this one.

"I'm glad you like it." He crosses his arms and one leg over the other, goosebumps trickling all over his skin from the chilly air and being half wet. I admire the seat of the bike, gliding my fingers over the beautiful black leather as small resistances from friction catch on my skin.

"What changed? Why now?"

Even Tree never rode with him.

Oh my God, I'm going to be his first official backpack.

I don't know what to do with myself. An ease settles over me, giving my limbs a sort of lightness like I'm walking on air.

"Well, I wasn't ever allowed to have anyone on the bike because my parents wouldn't let me. I obeyed their rules and proved to them I could be a responsible rider all these years. I've shown I can handle a bike on my own just fine and am responsible enough to have someone on my bike if I want to. Now that I'm eighteen and going off to college, they've agreed to let me make my own decisions on the matter. So, I've decided you're my first."

"Good to know all your past excuses were fake," I laugh. "But seriously, I'm honored to pop your backpack cherry," I wink.

He bursts out laughing again. God, his smile is beautiful. That laugh will be the end of me.

I caress more of his bike in awe, the smooth plastic making my insides buzz and start to swing my leg over.

Time to ride.

"Woah, woah, woah. Not so fast, sparkplug."

Grimacing, I cross my arms in front of me. "Sparkplug? Really? That's what your dad calls me."

"Well, you're jumping the gun here a bit."

"But you said I could ride with you!"

My inner only child makes its entrance with my pouting. He chuckles and walks behind me. His hands cling onto me, grazing me right under my breasts and lifting up my shirt slightly as he heaves me the rest of the way onto the bike. I forgot how strong he is.

My desire for him heightens at the intimate touch, my whole body tingling. I suck both lips in, hiding my grin.

My feet swing back and forth, making me realize how high up it is when you're on the back of a bike. It doesn't seem that high until you're on it and the seat leans forward a bit to push you into the driver. The leather from the seat's cold and the shape's more uncomfortable than I expected.

He takes my brand-new helmet from me and sits it on the workbench.

"Why'd you take my helmet? I'm going to need it on our ride."

"Because we're not going on a ride today, Char. It was literally just raining. You never ride in the rain or when the road's wet. It's too easy to crash in these conditions. I'm only allowing you to backpack in perfect conditions, so I know you're safe."

I pout and slide up the seat as I scootch to the front of the bike, putting my hands on the handlebars. The main seat is much more comfortable.

I understand where he's coming from, but I'm still disappointed.

"As soon as it's clear out and the road's dry, I promise I'll take you out for a ride. Okay?"

I nod and rub my hands along the sleek bright red plastic of the bike. It's so smooth and clean; I can't help it. He watches me intently and then looks me dead in the face, his eyes shifting back to their mischievous aura.

"Man, I wish I was my bike right now," he says quietly with a smirk.

"Huh?" Then his words hit me. My mouth goes dry, my brain glitching from the direct implication.

He wishes my hands were running over him? I stop and move them to rest on my lap as my breath hitches, my mouth parting slightly as I try to gain my bearings.

He smiles at the realization on my face, licking his lips and flicking his tongue off the bottom one briefly. We lock eyes again but right when he takes a step toward me his dad walks in.

"Ben, I need help moving the last of the equipment out of the barn so we can put up the rest of the tables for food since it's supposed to start raining again tonight."

Damn his parents.

"Sure thing, Pop. Be there in a second."

Koa, realizing I'm here, beams at me and waves.

"Ah, I see you gave sparkplug her new helmet! She must be excited since she's already on the bike. But you're not going now, are ya?"

"Nope, too wet out. I know the rules, Dad. Don't worry. I'll make sure we're safe when we do go out, but yes, she is *way* too excited. I'm probably going to have to pry her off that bike to even go to the party."

I grin at them both and stick my tongue out at Ben. I love this family so much.

"Careful. Your face might get stuck like that," Koa chuckles, winking.

I stick my tongue out at him next and cross my eyes. He laughs and slaps his hand on the barn door.

"Alright I'll be in the west barn waiting on ya. Don't take too long."

As soon as he's gone, a strong hand grips my waist, and another hand lands under my chin pulling me upwards. Ben's face no longer shows humor, only a longing intensity.

I don't know if I'm breathless because I forgot to breathe or because of the desire in his smoldering expression. He nips me on the nose with his teeth, making me scrunch it, then dips down, pressing his lips gently on mine, pulling my body as much he can toward his.

My arms lay slack at my sides, my body completely frozen. I don't know what to do with my arms or my body. I'm in complete shock...and ecstasy. My body's on absolute fire, a burning desire quickly filling me up for him everywhere.

The world falls silent, my inner soul drawing a blank as I'm all consumed by this moment. I can't think. All I can do is stay still and let him lead.

He lingers on my lips for a second more before pulling back just enough to exchange glances and then crashes his mouth onto mine more intensely. He's as breathless as me. I watch him lean into me, eyes closed, his brows furrowing like it's almost painful.

He's so handsome and vulnerable. If I could frame that facial expression and look at it forever, I'd be happy. I sling my arms around his waist and wrap his shirt in my fists, embracing him back.

His kisses are so hard it's like I'm giving him life. Like if I pull back, he'll fall into a black abyss without air and never resurface until I come for him.

After a few more strong kisses, he loosens his grip and steps away, putting his hands in his back pockets. His v-cut and abs rise and lower in beautiful definition from his panting, like he just ran a few miles, while he stares me down.

"I'm sorry. I just had to. I've been wanting to do that for far too long, and I couldn't wait any longer." His mouth lays partly open, that expression of want still on his face like he's about to crash himself into me again.

"I-I-It's okay," I stutter just as breathlessly, my brain still empty of everything but him and that kiss.

"I wish I didn't have my party tonight. I don't care to spend the rest of the night with anyone but you."

The flush in my skin sets my temperature to feverish levels, sending the throbbing below into overdrive. I attempt to get off the bike and instead of gracefully landing on my feet, I plummet off the side as my foot gets stuck on who knows what, causing me to land on the concrete.

Oh. My. God. Kill me.

This is so embarrassing. I totally ruined the mood.

He rushes over. "Are you okay?"

I start laughing to play off the embarrassment even though my wrists and hips are killing me from the bruises already there that slammed into the concrete.

"Uh, yeah. I'm fine."

"I bet that didn't help your bruises, but I'd say ten outta ten landing for style," he laughs back, reaching down to help me.

I reach out for him to pull me up but he squats down and picks me up under my knees and arms instead, setting me up straight.

"You could've just pulled me up by the wrist, you know," I say brushing myself off, but totally swooning underneath the surface.

"I didn't want to hurt you. If I pulled you by your wrist that'd hurt you from... prior injuries," he says cautiously.

His concern's so attractive. I've never had anyone be this protective or caring over me. Yes, my parents protected and cared for me, but in a different way.

This. This is something entirely unknown to me. It feels more primal. More instinctive.

"Thank you."

My body moves on its own and wraps my arms around him. I stand on my tippy toes, nuzzle my nose against his and kiss him again, wanting more. He reciprocates, wrapping his arms around my waist and presses hard into me. His body's as hot as mine. Is he on fire inside too? It's like I've been lit up from the lightning shooting through me and I'm melting from the heat of it.

He pulls away quicker than I want him to.

Does he not enjoy it? Is he regretting it already?

"Stealing kisses, already huh?" He smirks, smoldering intensely.

"I...I'm sorry," I reply, feeling foolish.

He nips my nose again with his teeth. "Don't apologize. If I had it my way, I'd stay here and kiss you the rest of the day," he stops talking and kisses me on the cheek. "Here." He then grazes my neck with his fingers and rubs his thumb gently along the side before kissing me there, causing molten lava to stir in my core. "Here." Lastly, he kisses me on the mouth and bites my lower lip. "And here." He pulls away, keeping his palms on my cheeks. "But I gotta go help Dad in the barn. Plus, you're supposed to help my mom, remember? The party will be here before we know it. Don't worry though. I've got another surprise for you after the party if you're feeling up to it."

He tilts my chin down and kisses my forehead before taking a step back.

"Another surprise? Is *this* one a dead animal in a bucket?"

"Haha, no, but I think you'll like it. It's not as good of a surprise as the bike helmet, but it's pretty up there if I do say so myself."

"I mean, your kiss was better than the bike helmet," I mumble sheepishly. I can't believe I admitted that. I need a hole to hide in.

"Good to know you're not just using me for my bike."

"I've known you for years. If that was all I was after then I would be known as a champion of patience, and you know that's not true."

"True. True. Alright I'll catch up with you after a bit, Char." He winks.

With that, he walks out of the barn, the muscles in his back rippling with each step as he takes off to help his father.

I slap my palms over my mouth and shriek loudly, bouncing on my toes. I can't believe what's happening to me right now!

How the hell am I going to get through this party without grabbing him and kissing him every chance I get? How am I going to face his parents? Is he going to tell them about us?

A million questions swirl around now that the shock's wearing off.

I wish we could run away and spend the night together somewhere and just enjoy each other and figure out what this is.

"Okay, get a grip, Char," I say out loud, steeling myself. Don't let your lizard brain control your life right now.

I force myself out of the barn to find Joan and help her set up tables and food, trying but failing to ignore all the lustful thoughts flying through my brain.

Chapter Thirteen.

Time drags unbearably slow until the party. I catch glimpses of Ben here and there, but his parents keep us so busy that by the time the first car arrives, Ben is just getting in the shower to change. I end up sitting in the west barn, waiting for him by the food table and zoning out to the sound of sprinkling rain gently falling on the roof. This barn has music, food and decorations so I figure most people will hang out here instead of under the canopy.

I'm at the food table putting vegetables and dip on my plate when I get startled by a slap on the ass.

"Hey, you." Ben walks around and gives me a quick peck on the cheek.

His hair's gelled back, and his two silver rings are back on. Damn, he looks great in that tight black shirt, covered by a leather jacket and blue jeans. I want to rip it all off him while we hide in the east barn together and explore this new intimacy we've uncovered.

"You almost made me drop my plate!" I playfully shoulder bump him. I pause, debating whether to tell him how good he looks, but I can only be so brave. "You look...cleaned up."

"Is that your way of telling me I look good? If so, I'm flattered. You as always, are looking beautiful."

I beam brightly, soaking in every single handsome feature of his... the sultry brown eyes with small slices of golden yellow in them, his full lips which were pressed on mine just hours ago... I bite my bottom lip and look down at my plate, too shy to keep eye contact.

He inhales sharply and his mouth brushes my ear as he whispers, "Careful biting that lower lip or I'm not going to be able to do anything else but steal you away and kiss you the rest of the night."

"I'd be okay with that," I bravely whisper back. I set my plate down at the table to sit down and eat but he grabs my hand before I can.

"Bring that with you. Let's go socialize."

"Do I have to? It's *your* party." I'm serious. I don't know most of his friends and I've only met a few relatives in his small family. I'd rather sit by myself and melt into the background until we can be alone again.

"No, you don't have to. But I'd like you too." He smiles down at me, his eyes softening.

"Alright, fine, but only because you asked me nicely."

I squeeze his hand, feeling the rough callouses from earlier softened by the lotion he must've put on after his shower. Holding my plate in one hand, I let him lead me out the door with the other while he holds an umbrella over us. We go under the canopy where I have to set my plate down because he introduces me to so many people.

He doesn't release his hand from mine the entire night and if he does let go for a minute, he makes sure to keep at least one hand on my low back.

I feel so safe and secure and flattered that he doesn't care if people see us acting like this. I'm so happy, I don't want the night to end.

The rain doesn't let up all evening, turning the farm into a muddy mess. As the light fades, we all transfer back to the west barn and settle in with a mix of country music and alternative rock blasting in the background. Sounds of kids running around, people playing games and idle conversations fill the room.

The atmosphere's euphoric.

Ben and I sit down with an uncle of his when a group of four guys walk in. They all dress similarly to Ben's style and seem like they're around our age.

"Heyyyyyyyy. Happy graduation my man!" The first guy sporting a brown leather jacket, blue jeans and a white T-shirt and his short brown hair speckled with raindrops greets Ben first.

"Paul! What's up, man?" Ben stands up excitedly and gives him a handshake with a one arm hug as a greeting. He goes through the rest of the guys just as enthusiastically while I get up and wait nervously for an introduction. I've never seen them around school before.

Ben hugs the last guy and turns back to me, grabbing my low back and bringing me forward.

"This is Charlotte, my childhood best friend. Charlotte, this is Paul, Jake, Troy and Isaac," he points as he calls out each of their names, "these guys are part of my riding posse."

All of them crack up, punching him in the shoulder and trying to ruffle his hair.

"Hey, easy, easy, it took me hours to get my hair to look this good!"

"Who said your hair looked good?" Jake jokes before turning his attention to me. "We're not part of his *posse*, per say, but we *are* just a bunch of dudes who like riding together. Nice to meet ya, finally." He reaches out his hand to shake mine. His hands are as rough as Ben's.

"Very cool. It's nice to meet you all," I say brightly, rocking on my feet to expel some of the nervous energy. "And finally?" My focus flies to Ben. "So, you've talked about me to them, huh?"

He smiles sheepishly. "Only to tell them what a pain in my ass you've been all these years."

I stick my tongue out and turn back to the group. "How did you all start riding together? Ben's never mentioned any of you before."

How come he has this close group of guy friends and never mentioned it to me before? Why's he keeping big parts of his life from me? 'Course maybe they all linked up when him and Tree got together after he cut me out of his life.

My core tenses and teeth clench in jealousy. More parts of him I don't know...another piece of him that Tree might've known that I didn't.

"We met last year at a gas station actually," says the short guy with blonde hair named Troy.

"A gas station? That's random."

"Gas stations are actually a common place to meet other bikers," Ben says to me.

"Really? Why?"

"It's a common place where bikers go to film content, either for Xypher or for their other social media pages. Plus, we all gotta get gas and they're great places to take a rest if you've been riding for a while."

"I didn't realize that was even a thing."

Biker boy pops in my head, but instead of getting turned on, guilt and shame rises in me. It's like a betrayal to Ben to think of him now. Maybe I should tell him tonight after the party about my mysterious stalker who I used to be obsessed with. Although, my curiosity gets the better of me...

"Do you guys know who the viral biker boy is on Xypher?"

Ben stiffens next to me, his palm flattening and stick still against my back. The rest of the guys exchange glances at each other before they burst out laughing hysterically.

"No, we don't know him. We call him the thirst trap king though. It's really weird and no one does that shit on social media but him. We do keep a lookout for him when we're out riding, but no one's ever seen him in action. Dude's like a ghost. We can't figure out who he is," Isaac says, shrugging.

Ben exhales a chuckle out and loosens up. What an interesting reaction. Does *he* know who the mysterious biker is? Will that harm our new, fragile bond we've just found?

"Ah. I see."

"Why so interested? Are you one of his fans?"

My skin prickles with heat. Damnit, that's going to be a dead giveaway.

"No, I was just curious. A bunch of the girls on my track team are obsessed with him, so I was curious if he was well known in the bike community too."

Isaac seems unconvinced but doesn't ask further questions. Paul raises his eyebrow but stays silent as well.

"Alright, since we can't go riding tonight, let's play some games, shall we?"

I let out a breath, thankful for Ben changing the conversation.

"Ayyeeee. I'm down," says Paul.

We walk over to the nearest table and start playing a variety of card games and board games that we picked up off the side table.

Chapter Fourteen.

We spend the rest of the evening laughing, sheltering from the wind and the rain, our fun moments only broken up by random interruptions when Ben has to greet other guests that arrive. Another reason why I love being here is the chill vibes. No fancy expectations, no nuance of rules, only real people, real memories and wholesome moments.

By eleven, the rain has stopped, and all the guests are gone besides Ben's friend group of bikers. Even his parents go inside to start cleaning up.

Ben glances at his phone and then at his buddies. "It's about time we wrap this up, gentlemen. I'll see you on Thursday at the meetup, right?"

"Kicking us out, man? Not cool. It's your graduation! We should be celebrating all night!" Paul says, stretching his arms and yawning.

"You sure about that grandpa? By that yawn, I don't think you can handle the whole night."

Paul chuckles, yawning again. "I suppose you're right. Well, hey, congrats on graduating, man. We'll see ya Thursday. Love ya."

One by one they grab his hand and pull it into their chest as they embrace in a hug with the other arm. Surprisingly, they all give me hugs too.

When they walk out of the barn into the cool night, I wonder if it's time for me to go too.

But when I turn to ask him, his expression catches me off guard. He's staring at me dreamily, like he's never seen me before. Warmth bubbles inside me, shooing away the damp cold around us.

"I suppose I should get going?" I say bashfully, trying to initiate the conversation to see if he actually wants me to leave or not. I hope he doesn't want me to leave. I want more affection, more kisses, more of him...

"Absolutely not. You still have your other surprise." His eyes light up. "Sit. Don't move until I tell you to, okay?"

I nod, relieved, and obey. He starts rummaging around somewhere outside the side of the barn where I can't see him. I have no idea what he's up to. He grunts right outside the door at the same time another door slams shut. What the heck's he doing out there?

I stand to check it out, my heart hammering in anticipation. But when I reach for the side door handle, it pulls away from my grip.

"Impatient, are we?"

"Well, all I could hear was you causing a ruckus out here, so I was coming to investigate. What're you doing?"

"Let's go. I'll show you."

His cold fingers wrap around mine as he leads me out to the back pasture. The back pasture used to be where they'd keep cattle but since they built a new pasture for grass-fed beef, they just use this one to store pallets, equipment, wood, and other various things they don't have room for in the other barns.

Our breaths swirl in the cold air as we walk in tune with each other, the mud squishing noisily beneath our feet. I definitely wore the wrong shoes for this. I can already feel my feet getting wet through them. They're going to be soaked if we don't get out of the mud soon.

When he leads me left, a large wooden pallet covered in blankets with pillows and a small radio next to it comes into view.

"Surprise!" He throws his arm out and dramatically points to it.

"I can't believe you did this," I laugh, pleasantly surprised. "This is awesome! Although it's a bit cold to be doing this, isn't it?"

"That's what the blankets are for." He winks.

Man, this brings me back. When we were younger, we would play back here all the time, past dusk into the night and sometimes sit on the pallets and talk about our futures and dreams...the things we wanted, people we hated, random things we saw on TV that week. As time went on and we got busier, we outgrew it.

Back then, we'd just freeze our butts off on a wooden pallet with no blankets and only go inside when we couldn't take the shivering anymore. I'm glad we won't have to do that tonight.

I'm excited. *And* nervous.

Is he expecting something from me? It doesn't sound like something Ben would do, but I've never entertained anything from him in a romantic way until tonight. Does he like to move fast?

My legs feel heavy, and it's not from the mud pulling my shoes down as he leads me the rest of the way to the pallet. I take my shoes off, step on it, not looking at him, and sit down.

"Holy crap. It's so soft. Did you put a mattress under here?"

His eyebrows rise in delight. "Something like that. We had a few unopened memory foam pads, so I used those up and put them under the blankets. I'm glad you find it comfortable. Here, lay down and get under the blanket so we can keep the heat trapped."

Oh God. Is this it? Am I ready for this?

No, I'm not...but I know him. He won't push me to do something like this so soon, especially after last night, right?

The moment with Jared last night whirls around in my brain sending my heart racing. My breathing becomes faster, coiling up in smoke above me as I gaze at the stars, trying to calm down.

"Hey," he says gently. "Are you okay?"

"I-I just...I've never done anything like this, and I wasn't sure what you were expecting, and then Jared forcing me last night popped in my head and I don't know. I'm a mess. I'm sorry," I blurt out way too fast. I pull the blankets over my face to hide, embarrassed and self-conscious at my honest outburst.

He doesn't respond for what seems like an eternity. I keep my eyes closed with the blanket over me to feel safe, praying he doesn't kick me out and send me home.

"I...I'm so sorry you're feeling uncomfortable. I promise there are no expectations. I'm not wanting or demanding anything like that from you tonight. I just figured since we started this tradition as kids it'd be fun to end it as adults. I do *not* want to push you or put you in any situation you're uncomfortable with. Char, I apologize if this seemed to push your boundaries. I'm so stupid for not considering what you went through last night and to think after our kiss where your head might be at. We can totally go inside and hangout, or if you'd like, you can head h-home." *Home* catches in his throat and comes out as a stutter.

I take a deep breath to steady my nerves. He's right. I do know him. I've known him forever. He would never expect anything like that from me or force me to do anything I don't want to do. He saved me last night, and he's been so great and kind and protective since. I need to trust him.

I pull the covers back under my chin and turn on my side to face him. His eyes are wide and filled with worry. I wonder what he's thinking. I feel terrible I made him feel like he did something wrong.

"I don't want to go home."

He releases a breath I don't think he realizes he was holding.

"I'm sorry it even crossed my mind that you'd do anything to push my boundaries. Last night scared me, and I'm trying to navigate it. You're my safe place, right now. My guardian. I know you wouldn't do anything I'm not comfortable with, and I'm sorry I thought you meant any ill intentions. My brain's just... off right now."

"You lead, Char. Whatever you're comfortable with, I'm game for. Well, mostly game for," he chuckles, back to his cool, laid-back self.

He flips on his back, as do I, and we lay in silence together, looking up at the stars. The night sky is always so clear after a long rainstorm. You can never see the stars like this in the city, but in the country, they're endless, flowing through the sky forever.

Electricity sparks between us in the unspoken silence, a magnetic energy actively drawing me toward him.

I zone out, noticing how soft the bottom blanket under us is. Without thinking, I glide my fingers across it, feeling the plushness against my skin.

I continue running my hand along the fabric until it bumps into his. That small touch is all it takes for my body to go wild. His finger twitches as if reaching out toward mine, but he doesn't pursue it. He's true to his word, not pressuring me and letting me drive this at my comfort level.

With courage, my hand creeps closer until our fingers intertwine and his thumb rests over top, lazily stroking it back and forth on top of my thumbs knuckle. My stomach leaps, butterflies fluttering rapidly into my breasts.

This time my breathing pace picks up from adrenaline, excitement. I start to get too hot under the covers as his touch sets me on fire, so I pull the top blanket down under my boobs and rest my other arm outside the blanket.

"So, what are your plans now? For college and your career, I mean."

We've talked randomly about things we wanted to achieve over the years but never seriously. Since he'd been with Tree so often the last year, I hadn't had an opportunity to ask him what he now plans for his life.

"Well..." He shifts his body so it's right up against mine, our intertwined hands resting on his stomach.

The heat between my legs is going to sear me if it keeps up at this rate. Even when touching myself, I never have this intense build-up of anticipation, of want, of *need* arise. I shift my focus to his voice and the cool night air instead of the dirty, dirty images rolling through my imagination.

"I actually want to get into coding."

That isn't the answer I expect. The last time we talked, he was between helping his father on the farm, eventually taking over while majoring in business or majoring in chemistry and getting into research.

"Coding? What would you do with that, exactly?"

"Well, my ultimate goal is to get into the CIA or FBI and help with cybersecurity or cyber terrorism."

My eyebrows raise at him in surprise. He doesn't notice but instead smiles, his gaze excitedly focusing on the sky.

"That's so freaking cool, Ben. Wow. I never knew you were interested in anything like that."

Another unexpected pang hits me. Did Tree know this dream of his too when I didn't?

"Yeah, I'm very excited about it. I've been taking college classes after school and on the weekends to learn more about coding and computer software and to get a jump start on school, so I don't have to attend the full four years."

Damn, he's so smart. He's handsome, intelligent, motivated... Why has he stuck with me all these years? Why does he seem to want me now? I'm not at all on his level.

"What are you going to do, Char?" He squeezes my hand, encouraging me to speak now.

"Well, I didn't get into any forensics programs. So instead, I'm going to major in chemistry at Charle's since they don't have a specific program for forensics. Hopefully I can find an internship in my third year or so, to get some experience. After that? I have no idea. I've thought about working in a forensics lab, but I'm not set in stone on my dreams like you seem to be. Luckily graduation's four years away so I have time to figure it out."

"You need to stop being so hard on yourself."

I look over to see him staring at me, his expression unreadable.

"You're smart, funny, and beautiful, and you'll do great at whatever you set out to achieve. College admissions are a sham. They want the gems in every pack but not every single person can be a rare gem. If I didn't have to go to college, I wouldn't. The idea of going through more school kills me. I don't want to be in debt from it, and I don't want to have to listen to these professors judge my intelligence based off the 'normal' guidelines. It's a ridiculous, mandated waste of time."

His attention fixes back on the sky, his brows furrowing in annoyance, and his teeth chewing on the inside of his cheek.

"For someone who wants to work for the man, you sure do seem to hate the man."

He laughs so hard, so full of life. "This is why I'm glad I have you around. You lighten the mood when I need it. Sometimes I get too serious. I need someone who can ground me and bring me back to the fun in life."

"Me? Fun? You know I'm a homebody who barely does anything. I'm not special or fun at all."

He rolls on his side, facing me. "Come here, you."

His hand glides to my lower back and pulls me into him, our hips and legs pressing against each other now. I avoid his gaze even though I can feel it intensely on me. The steam of our breath dances in the air together. We're so close the tips of our noses are almost touching.

"I've thought about this for so long," he whispers.

Shivers radiate down my spine and I have a feeling it has nothing to do with the chill in the night air.

"Thought about what?" I whisper back breathlessly, the tension between us about to snap explosively.

"Holding you... kissing you... being with you..."

I can't catch my breath. I can't speak. The tension between us is too great—the want, the need overwhelms me. I look in one eye, then the other and finally to his lips.

"I love it when you look at me like that," he whispers onto my lips. "Can I kiss you?" he whispers so quietly it's barely audible.

"Yes," I say panting, begging him silently.

He kisses me, soft at first and then more passionately. I open my eyes to catch an almost pained expression on his face, his eyebrows drawn together as if in concentration. I pull back.

"You okay?"

"Hm?" he responds out of breath, his eyes still closed.

"You look like you're in pain when we're kissing..."

He opens his eyes. "I'm just trying to hold myself back and go at your pace."

"You have to hold yourself back?"

"If last night hadn't happened and if I knew that this wasn't your first time being with a guy then I would've already started having my way with you. It's taking everything in me not to rip every single piece of clothing off you, spread your legs and be inside you."

I can't breathe and by the sounds of it, neither can he. I'm beyond happy he wants me this badly. I want him too. God, do I want to fulfill this sexual tension more than anything, but I'm not sure how my body and mental state will handle it. My emotions keep hitting me out of nowhere and I don't want to ruin this moment.

"I... I don't know how to do anything."

His confident smile puts me at ease.

My legs clench together and my hips twitch on their own. I'm literally pooling between my thighs. Am I going to seep onto the blanket? Will that turn him off? Even when masturbating, I never get this wet.

"Don't worry. I'll teach you." His voice is so low it's almost animalistic. He pulls me back into his lips and separates mine with his tongue. His tongue scrapes my teeth before our tongues connect, his lightly playing with mine while his fingers dance on my back. A whimpered moan escapes my lips.

Oh God.

I pull away out of embarrassment.

"I'm sorry. I-I couldn't help it," I whisper, tilting my head back to look at him.

His mouth is gaped open, panting, and his eyelids are heavy. He licks his bottom lip, staring at me hungrily. "That was so fucking hot," is all he gets out before he crashes his mouth into mine, pushing his tongue deeper as our chins lightly scrape together. Another moan slips out of my mouth which triggers a small moan from him. He's right. That is fucking hot to hear.

I open my eyes again, curiously watching the emotions on his face as he kisses me. He's so handsome, I can barely stand it. The concentration on his face burns me hotter, somehow. How's it possible to feel this sexually turned on?

He opens his now, catching me red-handed as he rotates his head to kiss me deeper. He smiles against my lips, simultaneously pulling away and nipping my nose.

"Stop staring at me, creeper."

Shit.

Did watching him turn him off? Are you not supposed to do that?

He continues grinning, his cheeks as flushed as mine have to be based on how hot they feel.

"Is it really creepy?" I shrink back; afraid I've ruined everything.

"No, I'm just kidding with you. But proper kissing etiquette is closing your eyes and enjoying the moment. Closing them pulls you further into your senses and helps you enjoy the experience. It heightens your pleasure sensors."

"You would phrase it like that," I chuckle, nipping his nose back.

He doesn't respond but instead kisses me hard, showing me how to move my tongue to fit his style of kissing and what would feel good for both of us.

"If you ever feel uncomfortable at any point, tap me anywhere three times and I'll stop, okay?" he whispers breathlessly between kisses.

I nod, too out of breath to answer out loud.

"I need you to say it out loud." He pulls back, staring me in the eyes.

"I'll tap three times if I feel uncomfortable and want us to stop."

"Good girl," he whispers in a low voice, shoving his tongue back down my throat.

Good God, that tone's going to get me in loads of trouble.

Soon after our agreement, his hand begins exploring, first at my waist and then slowly working its way under my shirt, his soft callouses scraping against my skin, sending goosebumps down my arms and legs. His touch is firm on my skin, but gentle, feeling every small part of me he's never touched before. He takes his time as if he knows exactly how much time a new space needs before I'm comfortable and he can move on.

But I want him to move faster. I need more of him. I can't get enough, fast enough.

He leans up on his elbow, gripping the base of the back of my neck in his hand and gently pulls my hair to move me in whatever direction he desires. Just as he moves me to the left to search deeper into my mouth, he grasps my breast. Soft at first, then harder and back to soft again. Again, testing the waters and seeing what I like and don't like. What a gentleman.

I don't have to talk. My body tells him everything he needs to know as my hips move of their own accord. He smiles against my lips before thrusting his tongue into me again.

He abandons my breasts and skims lower, slowly, lazily as if he has all the time in the world.

He reaches my waistband and pauses. Then one by one he crawls his fingers just under, my essence tingling in anticipation. I'm dying to know if it'll feel better when he pleasures me than when I pleasure myself.

I grab his forearm and shove his hand down to feel me. My anxiety that he'd think I was too wet and be disgusted is pushed out of my mind from the eagerness to feel him touching inside of me.

"Easy, Char. No need to rush," he rumbles, jerking his hand back so he doesn't touch me yet. I whimper in protest, but even as he said that he unbuttons my jeans making his way easier.

A realization hits me. He's been touching me, but I haven't touched him at all. It's not that I don't want to, but I'm nervous. I've never seen that part of a boy, let alone touched one. Do I go for it?

He feels around above my apex, making circles and allowing me to get used to him touching there when I make the bold choice to move my arm and reach for him. He immediately stops.

"Don't worry about me. All I want is to feel *you* right now. Let me please you first. *Please*," he begs.

He pries my lips apart with his tongue at the same time he dips his finger into me for the very first time. I grip his back and crumple his shirt in my fist, the other gripping for dear life on his forearm.

My eyes roll back, a louder moan escaping into the night as my back arches and my nails dig into the skin on his forearm. I don't even know what's up or down at this point. All I know is him and this pleasure, this amazing pleasure sending my body into tingles and flames all at once.

He kisses my neck, his tongue sliding up it and licking the beads of sweat off my skin. His moan in my ear drives me crazy, sending a deep throbbing ache below for more of him. Sweat coats my body under the blanket but the extra heat adds to my experience, boiling me in pleasure.

Another finger slides in. God, I can barely take the ecstasy. It's so far out of this world. I've never felt anything as good as this.

He flattens his palm and surges deeper, just how I like it. Just how I discovered I liked it with myself earlier in the week.

Fuck.

Fuck.

Fuck.

Fuck.

I moan at the stars; I'm going to scream from this ecstasy that needs to get out somehow. He hushes me with his mouth, stifling me.

Damn, that's hot.

I lift up his shirt, needing his skin on mine and move closer. A soft moan escapes him when our skin touches. I smirk and start to watch what he's doing to me.

I'm on the edge and so, so close to that blissful release. My hips grind on his hand as my nails pulse on his forearm keeping him in place, urging him to keep going. His fingers pulse in rhythm with my hips, each plunge more aggressive.

"You're close aren't you, Char? Are you going to come for me?"

I can't speak between the moans and labored breaths. I'm completely engulfed in pleasure, in him, in what he's doing to me. All I can do is whimper and nod.

"You're never going to want to come for yourself after you come for me. Come for me, Char."

Release hits me as my name echoes on his voice. My entire body convulses, moving in rhythm with his until I completely finish. He drags his fingers out of me, once again taking his time. I lay there panting and catch him staring at me with a lazy, satisfied grin.

"You never answered me before on who made you come. You've only made yourself orgasm, haven't you?"

I nod, keeping eye contact, exhausted and unable to speak, still coming down from the high. But then I'm thrown from the high into a small panic as I remember who I used to come to. The biker boy. Should I tell Ben now? Would I ruin everything by doing so?

"Good," he says, kissing my neck and cheek. His arm moves and I catch him wiping me off on his skin.

"I'm sorry if that's gross. You can wipe it off on me if you want."

"You have a lot to learn. It's hot having you on me. I want you and your smell all over me."

Empowerment in myself surges like it did when I masturbated for the first time, shoving the biker boy out of the forefront of my mind for the time being. Pride and satisfaction replace the anxiousness present before. Pride in that he finds me this hot and wants to taste me, smell like me and enjoy me and satisfaction that I can make him feel this way.

Apparently, I do have a lot to learn about what gross means for guys.

"So...I smell?" I ask curiously.

He pulls me completely flush against him and takes a deep breath. "Mhmm. I can smell you every time you get...excited. You smell *so fuckin good*."

"Wait...what? That's a thing?" *Oh my God, he knew this whole time how I was feeling...?*

"Oh yeah. Your excitement smelled so strong earlier. It took pure willpower not to throw you over my shoulder, pin you behind the barn and take my time exploring you and feeling you and kissing you all over. All night I've been getting waves of you but nothing like how you've been under the blanket tonight. It's flattering you want me as badly as I want you and insanely hot how wet you get for me." He pauses for a minute, a shyness taking over his demeanor. "I'll admit I was worried you wouldn't want me."

"Ben," I huff. "Everyone wants you. You're hot, smart, everyone thinks you're cool, and you're good at everything *and* you ride a motorcycle. If someone didn't want you, they'd be crazy."

He moves his bicep under my arm and holds me to his torso, his shirt mildly soaked with sweat.

"I don't care what everyone else thinks. I only care what you think. I never knew if you ever saw me as anything more than a friend. With graduation coming up and the unknown of how much longer we'd have with each other, I decided it was time. I wanted to make my feelings known and push the boundaries to see if you felt the same way about me or if you'd push me away. I...." He hesitates and for a moment, all I can hear is his breathing. His chest rises and falls up against me as he rests his head against mine, keeping me as close as possible.

"I've wanted this for years, Char. I've had a crush on you since the seventh grade, but I never knew how to approach you. You're incredibly hard to read."

My body stiffens and I press away, looking up at him in shock. "What?"

My brain glitches, unable to compute what he just said. He's known how he's felt about me for *this* many years and has never said anything? Why? We've had so much lost time. My life could've been so different. *Our* life could've been so different.

All the emotions surface at once. I'm so happy he decided to pursue me finally, but I'm also confused, sad and angry.

My anger subsides quickly when he gives me a few more pecks on the lips. He was right to wait. It wasn't until Tree that I even had a flickering thought about him in a non-friend way. Even if he approached me in junior high or early high school, I don't know if I would've ever gone for him or tried anything. I was so inexperienced and so shy. So unsure of myself. I most likely would've sabotaged the whole thing.

"But if you knew you wanted me, why'd you date Tree?"

He rolls onto his back away from me, leaving me vulnerable under the blankets and completely aware of what we had just been doing. He sighs and ruffles his hair, his silver rings shining in the light given off by the low barn lights. The rings that have the residual of me on them.

"Because I was dumb. Tree came onto me, strong, mind you. She was the girl everyone wanted, so I figured why not. Why not try it. I wasn't getting you anytime soon, so I figured I'd use her to learn. I'd never been with a girl—"

A rush of envy hits me at the remembrance he'd been with her and done things with her I hadn't. I cut him off, unable to take it.

"I don't want to hear anymore."

"Why?"

"Because I'm so fucking jealous, I can't stand it!"

He turns his attention over to me, his arms under his head, his biceps pressing against his T-shirt so hard the sleeves look like they might burst.

"So, you *were* jealous. You never admitted it to me."

"Why would I? You were with her and wouldn't talk to me. I didn't think you wanted anything to do with me. You gave me no other reason to believe otherwise, especially since you cut me off."

"I wish I could take that back, Char. I really do. I was dumb. She was giving me sex and for a while it was all I could think about. I'm a man and I gave into my lust at the time. As I told you, she said if I didn't stop talking to you that she was going to withhold it, and I wasn't ready to give it up yet."

I scoff and focus on the stars, needing to look away from him.

"I'm not proud of it. I'm sorry, Char. I really am. I-I know it's no excuse, but it's not easy being a man at my age. We give into our lust easily."

"Why didn't you pursue me earlier than the other day then?"

"I did start to, didn't I? But the day I was going to ask you out; you started getting attention from Jared and then it seemed like I was nothing to you. You wore those dresses for him, he had his arm around you in the hallways, and you guys were together constantly."

Anger shakes his voice. His biceps flex as his hands ball up before relaxing as he takes a deep breath.

"I only did that to make you jealous because I was pissed from our fight the night before. But after a while you still weren't speaking to me, so I figured I'd give him a shot, because why not. You seemed done with me. I didn't know what else to do..."

Saying Jared's name lobs a rock into my stomach.

"Fuck that guy. He's a piece of shit. He only gave you attention because he obviously only wanted one thing from you. I hope he gets karma for all the shit he's done to women and especially for what he tried to do to you."

"Yeah, fuck him right in the asshole."

He chortles. There's a pause present allowing a free moment for the anxiousness to resurface. I need to tell him or else I won't be able to relax the rest of the night.

"Ben, I have to tell you something."

My serious tone catches his focus quickly, his brows frowning.

"Okay. What's up?"

Inhaling to dig up some courage, I ask, "So, you know the biker boy on Xypher right?"

Was that a twitch of his mouth upwards for a split second?

"Yeah."

"Well..." Oh, God. Why is this so hard to say?

"I don't want to hear about it."

"Huh? But I think it's important to tell y-"

"Nah. I don't want to hear it."

Well, what the fuck? He won't even hear me out?

"So, Char. Tell me the moment you knew you liked me." He moves over and kisses me on the cheek, changing the conversation.

I adjust my head on the pillow and face him, crossing my arms and pouting because he wouldn't let me speak.

Well...I tried to be honest with him. When he does find out who I masturbated to and was contacted by, he can't get mad at me for it.

"Why?" I retort shortly.

"Because. I want to know." He squeezes my abdomen, egging me on.

"So nosey." I poke him in the stomach back, loosening up, my annoyance quickly dissipating as I ponder over his question.

"Tell me."

"Well, I think I've liked you for a long time, but I didn't realize it until I heard you and Tree were dating. I'd never been jealous before but now I realize that's what I was feeling at the time. Then when I heard you guys had sex from the other girls in the locker room, I broke down and cried to my mom all night. That's when it really hit me that I wanted you as more than a friend."

His mouth is a tightline, his eyebrows drawn-down and nose wrinkling, displaying a sign of hurt.

"I'm sorry, I hurt you like that, Char. I will never, ever hurt you again and I promise, I don't care about other girls anymore. You're the only one I want. You're mine now… If you want to be, that is."

"Are you asking me to be your girlfriend?"

A rush of adrenaline surges through me. I can't believe he's asking me this right now. I curl my toes and fists to keep my composure but all I want to do is scream and shout it to anyone who'll listen.

"Mhmm." He nods, keeping his eyes on mine.

I bite down on my lower lip to hide my smile.

"Yes, of course I'll be your girlfriend!" I kiss him hard and lean over him, my hair draping next to him and off his shoulder. My grin is so wide it's about to split my skin. We stare at each other as I stay above him. He caresses my face gently, searching for something in it, but what, I don't know.

"What?"

"I'm just so fucking happy right now." He leans up and slams his mouth to mine. We make out for a while again, our body heat misting out from under the blanket.

"One thing," I interrupt.

He stops; his hand still tangled in my hair.

"Hmm…?"

"Can we use different terms other than boyfriend and girlfriend? I hate the way they sound. I don't know why, but they make me cringe."

He laughs softly. "Whatever you want, babe."

Ooof, *babe*. That makes me feel some type a way.

"What do you want us to call each other, instead?"

I lick my lips in concentration. "How about we just say we're each other's person? Or you're my man and I'm your woman?"

"Hm. I like the sound of you're my woman. It sounds great. Better be prepared though…if someone asks what we are, I'm going to say you're my woman and if they get offended and think I'm anti-feminist, it's your fault."

I smile down at my man. *Ah! My man!*

"I'll take the heat for it. I don't care." I give him an eskimo kiss.

Butterflies explode inside me. I officially have a man, and he's my best friend. I never would've predicted this. Getting to be with him used to seem like a far-fetched dream and now he's mine. *All mine*.

I study him, running my fingers over his cheeks, his eyebrows, his chin, admiring every part of him. He lets me explore while looking at me like I'm the most precious thing in the world, a small smile permanently set on his face.

My fingers reach his chest and I notice his shirt's still pulled up, his v-cut clearly sticking out, his belly rising and falling with his breaths. And then... and then there's him, his hardness, pressing against his jeans, forming a huge outline.

My body reacts quickly. The rebound rate on me still surprises me but I'm not complaining about it. He clearly notices the change in me as his eyes glaze over, his lips now parting, tongue dancing slowly in his mouth as it lies in wait for my next move. His breathing picks up in sync with mine.

Feeling bold, I lean down, kissing him fiercely and explore his face, his neck, his chest and finally his v-cut and the creases in his abs.

Our tongues dance, his body trembling with each light touch I trace on his skin. I can feel him pulsing beneath his jeans on my leg which isn't helping how wet I already am.

He can't tell me what to do. I want to see what it feels like. I'm going for it.

I move my leg off him, making room for me to travel my hand along his skin, savoring every ripple until I run over the button on his jeans. He doesn't stop me. I reach down and drag my palm over him on the outside of his pants. His thickness takes up most of my palm, the length longer than I expected.

When I reach the end of it, I drag my palm down again and apply a small amount of pressure. His hips buck and his eyes roll back as I rub my palm harder on him, slowly grinding up and down.

"Fuck, Char. *Fuck*," he moans. I revel in his reaction, soaking in the control of his pleasure that makes me feel powerful.

"Even though I was forbidden from touching you, bet you're glad I did, huh?"

"You brat," he smirks mischievously.

In one move he hooks his arm around my leg, flips me on my back and climbs on top of me. He inches both my legs apart with his knees and lays himself on top of me.

Nervousness arises but I swallow it. There's no need to be nervous. I trust him. Plus, I'm having fun, and I am *really* enjoying this.

I want to keep experiencing this pleasure and giving him pleasure back. This is how couples are supposed to be.

Ahhh, I love that we're a couple.

He rests his hands next to my ears, the veins popping out from the strength it takes to hold himself up over me.

"Tap if you need to," he pants.

He lowers, his full weight dropping on me before he begins grinding into me. Hard.

Up and down.

Up and down.

He drops to his forearms and places his other arm under my head, grabbing my hair, his bicep pressing into my neck. He's fully back in control. I let him lead me, closing my eyes as previously instructed and soak into the moment, my hands clinging for dear life on his belt loops.

"Do you feel how hard you get me?" he pants into my ear.

"Yes," I moan softly, followed by another higher pitched moan.

"Grind into me harder. Please," I beg.

I needed more.

I let go of the belt loops and latch onto his sides, my grip easily gliding from the sweat.

"Fuck." He lifts my hips up to press himself harder into me.

Slowly up.

Slowly down.

Harder and harder and harder.

I open my eyes, hoping his are still shut so he doesn't catch me peeking at him. Sweat drips off his brow onto my face, the muscles in his arm holding my waist up totally flexed and the head of his shaft peeking out of his pants. The head is *huge* and dripping onto my stomach where my pants are still unbuttoned.

A strong desire to bend down and lick him and clean it up takes over me and I let it. I reach down, unbuttoning his pants before he can stop me and cup my hand over his boxers and the tip of his head. It's so soft. Much softer than I expected.

"I'm going to come if you keep doing that, baby."

Baby sets my world on fire. These pet names are going to be the death of me.

"Do you want me to lick you instead?" I whimper boldly.

He opens his eyes and meets mine, surprise on his face before warm liquid squirts on my hand and stomach as he twitches, groaning to the final finish. He lowers my hips and continues to hold himself over me, panting. I pull my hand up refusing to fight the other urge that hits me. I stare straight into his eyes as I lick his cum off my palm. He tastes so good, like pineapples.

"You're going to drive me crazy doing shit like that."

I smirk, feeling accomplished in my ability to drive him crazy.

"Good," I lean up and kiss him.

"Now let's get you taken care of."

Before I realized what he said, he flips me over on my stomach and tugs my pants down.

"I'm not doing anything different. I just want to finger you from this angle so I can stare at that beautiful ass of yours."

He thrusts his fingers inside me, twirling them, and pulsing them while marginally lifting my hips as he plays maestro. I come again more quickly this time, my moans stifled by the pillow I shove my face into. After my last twitch, he pulls my pants back up, flips me over and situates me by his side like a ragdoll, tossing me and laying me where he wills. He buttons his pants back up and snuggles into me.

Disappointment riddles throughout me.

"Is that all? No more?"

"Greedy girl," he chuckles as his fingers stroke through my hair. "There's no rush, babe. I'm going to do this the right way or at least do my best to try to do this the right way. For now, let's just talk and cuddle. We have plenty of time to explore more of each other in the future."

"Hmph," I protest.

He holds me so tight I barely have any room to move. I feel so safe. I love it. He pulls the blanket all the way up to our necks and starts massaging my back as my thumb strokes back and forth on his bicep lying across his stomach.

"I love how impatient you are to have me, Char. Believe me, it's unbearable for me right now to stop, but I think it's best. I don't want you to have any regrets about us. So as much as I can manage it, I'm going to take my time with you. But, if I happen to slip up and rush, forgive me. I have a feeling that after tonight it's going to be near impossible to control myself around you."

With this last declaration, he gives me a kiss and starts a conversation back up about the farm.

Chapter Fifteen.

It was hands-down the best night of my life. I keep fearing it'll disappear, that it isn't real.

I thought I knew Ben, but last night showed me I only knew a fraction of the man he is. I can't believe he chose me, that he's wanted me, let alone, wanted me for so long and was patient enough to wait to pursue me until he felt we'd be ready for each other.

He walks me to my car around four in the morning. I want to stay there with him all night, but he's right, my parents will kill me if I don't come home now, especially if I tell them I was with a boy all hours of the night.

He opens my car door, gives me a kiss and helps me in. I almost cry. It doesn't feel right to leave him. I feel so close to him that without being right next to him, loneliness consumes me. The magnetism between us is something I've only read about in stories.

I love him. I know it and I'm not going to fight that feeling. I love him, and I want to be with him always.

The love I've always had for him as friends blossoms into a deeper one after last night. From the intimate physical moments to the intimate emotional moments. I feel seen, my soul bared naked before him which he accepts fully and reciprocates.

I force myself to look forward as I drive away, afraid that if I look back, I'll stop and run back to him, begging him to let me stay.

My knuckles turn white from gripping the steering wheel with all the strength I have.

Get a grip.

I need to be an adult about this and not be crazy. I'm probably overdoing it if I can't stand to be away from him at all. That can't be normal, can it?

I certainly can't tell him I love him this early. Not until he tells me he reciprocates my love. What if he doesn't feel the same way? I worry that after everything he showed and told me last night that it's just a phase.

I pull in at home and have no idea how I got there. Sleep finally comes knocking on the door of my mind, my eyelids barely staying open as I open the front door and stumble up the stairs. I succumb to it, laying down on my bed fully clothed and pass out.

My eyelids are so heavy I can barely open them. Where am I?

God, it's so hot in here. My clothes are soaked.

I rub my eyelids, forcing them open. My vision, blurry at first, slowly clears until my room comes into view.

That's right. I'm home.

I turn over, my jeans rubbing harshly on my sticky skin. No wonder I'm sweating like crazy. I forgot I'm still in my sweatshirt and jeans.

Ugh, I don't want to move to take my sweatshirt off, but I have to or else I won't be able to go back to sleep. I sit up and struggle to pull it off before laying back down, hitting my head on my phone.

"Ouch."

I must've been holding it when I passed out. I turn it over to check the time and see a text from my man. Elation at his text instantly wakes me up. I click on the message sent two hours ago at ten in the morning.

BENNY BOY

Will you come over later? I miss you. I need to see you.

"Eeek!" I fall back, kicking my legs in giddy fashion.

I miss him too. I'm so glad last night wasn't a fluke. I'm so happy and surprised he texted me already to hangout again. I roll over and instantly text back.

ME

Absolutely :). I miss you too, babe. What time should I come over?

My phone dings right away.

BENNY BOY

Oooh. Babe? Now would be good :).

I smile down at my phone, so unbelievably happy, I don't know how to hold it all in.

ME

I just woke up, so let me shower and eat something, then I'll be over. :)

BENNY BOY

Ok. See you in a bit, baby. :)

"Eeeekkkk!" I hop around my room and dance a nerdy jig, my hips and arms uncoordinatedly swinging side to side. How is the word baby when used as a pet name such a damn turn on? I can't hide my joy when he calls me that. Every time he uses it, I fall harder for him.

Shrugging, I dart to the shower so I can get to his place as quickly as possible. I can't stop thinking about

Ben, can't stop smiling, can't stop wondering what we're going to do tonight.

The memory of his fingers inside me and the tip of his length keeps getting me so hot that I have to masturbate in the shower just to curb it until I can get to him.

I throw on a deep red dress, one that I haven't ever worn to school, curl my hair and make my way down to the kitchen to get something to eat. Mom and Dad sit at the kitchen table, writing and chatting with each other, but go silent as I enter the room.

"You were out late," Dad says, perturbed, biting the inside of his cheek.

"Yeah, Ben's graduation party was a lot of fun. Everyone hung out all night since we're not sure when we'll all be able to once graduation is over," I nonchalantly lie through my teeth.

No guilt surfaces as I blatantly lie to my father's face. I'm not sure if that's a good or bad development.

"I see. And when Ben was in your room late the other night...were you two behaving?"

Don't get hot in the face. Don't get hot in the face. Think of sticking your head in an ice bucket, feel the cold rush of water stinging your skin.

"Yes, of course. We're just friends."

Not a complete lie, I suppose.

"Good. Just make sure you're being smart, Charlotte," he says sternly, looking back at his computer. Scolded once again... I hate it.

"I know, Dad. I will be. I'm an adult and you raised me right. I can take care of myself. Don't worry."

"Even if you *can* take care of yourself, I don't want you to ruin your future," he says, avoiding my gaze. My mother glances anxiously from him to me, her mouth opening and closing, obviously debating whether to intervene or not.

"I'm not dumb. I promise I'm being smart in all my choices. Why do you not trust me? What have I ever done to break your trust?"

He doesn't respond, but continues typing, his mouth twitching as if biting his tongue, holding back what he really wants to say.

I scoff and turn to the kitchen. I grab a protein bar and a sandwich out of the refrigerator and strut toward the front door.

"Where you going now?" he yells into the hallway.

"Ben's," I say shortly and slam the door behind me, not waiting for his response.

Don't cry. Don't cry. Don't cry.

I fight the tears burning my eyes. Don't ruin my makeup or the excitement of going to Ben's. Everything's fine. Dad and I are just adjusting to our new way of life. Things will be okay.

After a deep breath, I get in my car. I take my sandwich out of the Ziploc bag and bite into the crust. I'm too hungry to wait until Ben's to eat, but I refuse to eat it in the house with my parents. If I ate inside, more questions would surface causing further anger, crying and shouting and I don't want to deal with it. Not right now. Not with the happiness I'm feeling with Ben.

I shove down the rest of the cold cut turkey sandwich and protein bar and leave for my man's house.

Ben is outside the barn, working on his red Ducati when I pull in. His shirt's off, his skin dripping with sweat, and his jeans are held up by his belt that's glimmering in the sunlight.

Fuck, he's so hot.

And he's all mine.

I park my car by his and walk over, playfully walking on my toes and casually approaching him. He doesn't notice me, too ingrained in what he's doing.

How do I want to play this? Do I sneak up on him and hug him? Give him a kiss? Will that be too obvious with his parents around? I opt for giving him a swift quick kick in the butt, almost knocking him forward into his motorcycle where he squats.

"Hey, you!"

He jumps up, grabs my chin and tilts it up to kiss me.

Swoon.

"Hi," I say out of breath from being swept off my feet. "What're you doing to your bike?"

"Ah," he says, wiping his brow, smearing black fluid on his forehead. "Just maintenance. She needed an oil change, and the chains needed lubricating and all that. Just basic stuff you have to do every once in a while, to keep her purring."

"Her?" I giggle.

"Yes. You must adhere to calling her by her name if you're going to ride her."

I laugh but his expression's dead serious.

"So, you're getting her ready for me to ride her?" Oof, that sounds dirty. "What's her name then?" I chuckle, nervously playing with the folds in my dress.

"Yes, I am. She's got to be in top shape for my first backpack. And by the way, her name's Dalia."

"Huh. Dalia. I like it." I affectionately stroke the shiny red plastic on the tank.

"How'd you come up with that name?"

"She was my first adult bike, so I called her Dalia since she was a version of my first flower." He lovingly gazes at the bike currently held up on jacks.

"Should I leave you two alone?" I joke, crossing my arms.

"Such a sassy attitude from my girl today. I love it."

I stick my tongue out. He goes to grab it, but I jump back out of range.

"Ew! Your hand has oil all over it, don't touch my tongue!"

"Don't stick your tongue out at me and I won't." He winks.

Our laughs mesh together, echoing into the fields. The sun shines brightly outside and in my heart as well, the fight with my father long gone from the forefront of my mind.

Footsteps crunch on the stone driveway behind us. I turn around to be greeted by his parents. Do they know about us already? I hope they didn't hear us last night or have any idea of what we were up to on their property...

"It's about time you two started dating," Joan says cheerfully, hugging me.

Koa, unable to help himself, chimes in his two cents. "Yeah, we've been betting on this for years. If you guys waited much longer, I'd have lost the bet, and no one wants that."

Relief sweeps over me. They're being so cool about it. Which also means there's no way they know how physical we were last night.

Phew.

Ben drapes his arm around my shoulder and kisses my forehead. I blush, nervous about being so open with our PDA in front of his parents and fold my hands in front of me.

My brain replays Koa's comment. They thought we should've gotten together for years, and they actually bet on it? How am I the only one who had no idea how Ben felt about me all this time?

Probably because he was screwing another girl.

I clench my jaw together and tighten my lips at the thought of him and Tree. To distract my mind, I ask his dad what he would've had to do if he lost the bet.

"I'd have to wear Joan's dress for an entire day while we ran all sorts of errands to the other farmers."

I bend over and burst out laughing. "Oh my God, that's hilarious. Now I wish we would've waited longer just so I could have witnessed that."

We all laugh together and then continue chatting about the upcoming graduation and Ben and I's plans for dinner. They want me to stay and eat with them tonight—steaks on the grill, green beans, potatoes, cottage cheese and salad.

I politely accept, giving them both hugs before they return to the fields and turn back to Ben who's already bent down, working on his bike again. I've always felt at home here, but now, I feel even more a part of their family. It makes me never want to go back to my home again. This feels right, natural, easy. Unlike my house which is quickly turning into Vietnam.

"I see your bruises are looking better today," he says as he wrenches something off his bike.

"Oh...yeah."

I actually forgot all about them. My fingertips lightly brush along them, their presence now back in my attention. They're still raised but healing nicely, already turning yellow.

Shit. I bet his parents noticed them though. I didn't even think about covering them and they're clearly noticeable in this dress.

Shit.

"Did you tell your parents what happened?"

He continues working, still focusing on what he's doing to his bike and not me.

"Nah. But I doubt they noticed the ones on your arm, because if they did, they definitely would've said something. They noticed mine though."

He flexes his hand toward me, the blue and purple coloring clearly popping out on three of his knuckles.

"I told them when I was taking my bike apart, I messed up and smashed my hand. So, that's what they think these bruises are from."

"Oh, Ben. I didn't even notice the bruises on your hand yesterday. I'm so sorry you got hurt too."

I bend over and grab his dirty, grease slicked hand and raise it up to my mouth, gently kissing each knuckle.

"You're too adorable. That does help..."

His arm holding the wrench drops and rests on his thigh while he stays squatted down. A mischievous expression washes over his face.

"I have bruises in other places that could use some attention too."

I smirk and drop his hand to stand up, setting my hands on my hips for a sassier effect, not caring I just smeared oil onto my dress from them.

"Oh yeah? Where exactly are these other bruises and how did you get them? I only remember you throwing one punch and then dipping out."

"I threw three, mind you, and it was all done to protect you. That's an important detail." He winks.

I blocked out to the moment when he punched Jared square in the face, practically flying off his motorcycle to come save me. That *was* pretty hot.

"Have I left you speechless, baby?"

Heat sears in my core at his tone change and being called baby. I curl my toes, forgetting I'm wearing sandals.

He lights up in delight when he notices my feets reaction. "Good girl," he utters roughly.

I bite my lip, a small whimper escaping as I continue getting utterly wet from this electric banter.

He drops his tools and squats up just enough, so his shoulder dips down. With one quick movement, he grabs the back of my knees and throws me over his shoulder, his arm holding my dress down as he carries me away.

"Ben! Ben! What are you doing?"

I squirm and kick my feet in the air, his shoulder digging into my stomach.

"Stay still," he demands, giving me a sharp spank on my ass to shut me up.

He puts me down behind the back barn where we're out of sight and immediately throws his hand up, pinning me to the cool metal siding, his other hand clinging roughly to my low back pulling me into him, *hard*.

"If you want me to stop at any point, tell me a word..." he pants.

I blink, confused, not sure what he means.

"What word do you want to use if I need to stop? Tell me now."

My eyes widen in understanding and from intimidation at how intensely he's staring at me, even with his half-gelled hair falling over his eyes. I cower underneath him but not from fear of him, but from fear of how turned on I am. He breathes heavily, his hand flexing against my back, making it seem like it's taking everything in him to stop from pouncing on me. Fuck, what word do I use. I blurt out the first word I think of.

"Barn."

The word barely leaves my lips before he crashes his mouth onto mine, kissing me passionately, our tongues intertwining with each other. I allow the moans to freely escape, tearing at his pants, pulling on his belt to undo it. My fingers fumble as I struggle to get it undone. Damn, I'm so clumsy.

He grabs my fingers to help me and aggressively whips the belt off all the way. He flips me around, pushing me against the siding with one arm, and spanks me with his folded belt. A sharp sting shoots through from my limbs and into my toes and fingertips, a residual throbbing lingering on my ass.

Another whimper escapes, but I stay still. I'm not afraid. I trust him with everything. And damn, mixing pain with pleasure is good. Count me in for future spankings.

He whips me back around, his eyes on fire as he picks my legs up by the thighs and presses me up, settling my legs on his shoulders. His hard biceps press into the underside of my thighs while his hands grip the tops of them, his fingers digging roughly into my skin. He doesn't shake. Doesn't waver at all. He's so fucking strong.

Oh my God, is he doing what I think he's doing?

His hands flex on my skin, gripping me into place, my back pressed fully against the cold metal of the barn. His brown eyes are so beautiful, gazing into mine. He raises his eyebrows up and down once and gives me an amused smirk before dipping his head under my dress, gently kissing the inside of my thighs, inching closer and closer to my center that I can feel dripping down me.

I struggle to catch my breath and flip my dress up so I can grab onto his hair because honestly, the anticipation is unbearable. I don't know what else to do with my hands, my body, my mind. Each kiss gets closer, lingering at each spot longer. This is torture.

"Babe, *please*," I beg quietly, unable to bear it any longer.

He smiles against my leg and finally, my thong slides to the side as his teeth lightly scrape against my skin. He slides his warm tongue into me and nips me gently. I jerk, inhaling sharply, the thin strings of my dress falling off my shoulders.

He dives in, growling into me, sending reverberations down my entire body, licking me up and down, fully ravaging me. His hands grip onto me so tightly it prevents me from what my body naturally wants to do right now—writhe my hips on his face.

His grip on my thighs becomes painful, and the small pain still on my ass is melding with the pain on my thighs and the pleasure he's giving me. I could get used to this.

Unable to do anything else, I grab his hair harder and hold on for the ride.

He doesn't relent, continuing to suck and lick for what feels like hours. I can't take much more. I'm right on the edge. My moans are loud, too loud, I know it, but I can't hold them in. It's like we're the only two people in this world and I need him to hear how much he satisfies me.

My legs start to shake and the sweat from him holding me and eating me out causes things to get slippery.

He stops for one breath and instructs me. "Come for me, baby."

That's it. That's all I need. I clasp my palm over my mouth in a sad attempt to stifle myself and climax, my eyes rolling so far back that I don't even know where I am anymore.

In relaxed bliss, I feel myself lowering, my hair sliding down the barn wall until my feet hit the ground. My legs shake, feeling as though they're about to give out, but he holds me up with his strong arm around my waist. I look up at him and find a triumphant grin shining as he wipes his face of me.

"That's my good girl," he says, nipping my nose and kissing it.

My brain is dead. I have no thoughts, no words. All I know is pleasure and all I want is more of it from him. I move to grab for him, but he gently moves my hand away, wrapping it in his.

"Come. Let's get cleaned up."

I pout, pushing my bottom lip out, but let him lead me, my ass still stinging with each step, giving me a reminder of what we just did practically out in the open.

Hopefully no one saw us, but a larger part of me doesn't care. I'm one happy camper, well mostly.

He takes me inside to the bathroom and lifts me up on the counter.

"Spread 'em babe."

"Again?" I exclaim hopefully.

"So greedy," he chuckles, kissing me. "No, I'm going to clean you up."

He places a washcloth under hot water, pulls up my dress and begins cleaning me. The hot water feels amazing.

God, I love him.

"So, where did you learn all this? I mean, damn, it's all so amazing but where did you learn to talk dirty and do all the amazing sexual things you do to me? I feel very inexperienced."

"Don't sell yourself short. You're doing amazing. I'm not some sex master like you make me out to be. How I'm acting with you and what I'm doing to you isn't from experience."

"Oh?" Elation and relief wash over me. Knowing he didn't do these things with Tree makes me feel even closer to him.

"Yeah."

He finishes cleaning me up and pecks me on the lips, pulling me off the counter.

"*Soooo*, you didn't do any of this with Tree?"

"You are not subtle, you know that?" he chuckles.

He brushes his fingers through his hair and takes a deep breath as he puts a new washcloth to his face, cleaning himself off.

"Nope."

He dries his face and throws the towel in the laundry basket before leaning on the counter next to me and folding his arms.

"When Tree and I messed around it was pretty vanilla."

"Vanilla?"

"You're so innocent, it's adorable. Vanilla means straightforward things like the standard moves with sex, missionary etc. When we finally had sex, she was the dominant one and wouldn't let me lead. I mean it still felt good, but it wasn't my cup of tea."

I scrunch my nose and fake gag.

"Nothing felt as good with her as it does with you, baby. Don't worry." He kisses me reassuringly. "She basically emasculated me and wouldn't let me be the man in the bedroom. To be honest, I let her do whatever at that point because I got sick of fighting with her, and the more I fought with her the less sex she'd give me. The ecstasy of sex didn't last long though. So, once the sex wasn't fulfilling me anymore, I went online and discovered more of what fit my...tastes."

"Online, like porn online?"

"Mhmm. Some of the guys I hang around gave me some sites to check out and once my world was opened, I never went back."

He pulls me close and looks down, his nose pressing gently against mine.

"When I would watch those videos, the only person who popped up in my head was you. I became addicted to getting off while watching those videos and imagining you were the one I was doing those things to."

Thinking of him getting off to me is so fucking hot.

Damn. Wet, wet again. This is going to be my constant state if we keep this up.

He presses his lips on mine and grabs my ass, pulling me into his hardness.

"Come on, babe. We need to get back outside."

"*Or*, we could play more? From the feel of it, you're as ready as I am."

"Oh, believe me, I am. *But* I have a feeling if we do more right now, I'm not going to stop and then we'll be inside the rest of the day and my parents will definitely notice we're up to something nefarious."

I whimper in protest and pout my lips.

"My greedy, greedy girl. I lo—" he stops, looking thunderstruck.

Was he just about to...?

"Uh, let's go. We need to help my parents out." He walks out the door, leaving me dumbfounded and calls me from the kitchen where I find him putting his boots back on, cheeks flushed and eyes down.

The rest of the night is filled with laughter, a delicious home cooked meal, and helping him and his dad put equipment away in the barns.

Alas, the time to leave arrives too soon as it nears eleven o'clock. I don't want to push my parents' boundaries any further so as we leave the barns, I bring up the conversation that I have to go. He looks sad but reluctantly agrees it's probably best and squeezes my hand.

He closes my car door after we pry ourselves apart from each other, the familiar feeling of magnets trying to pull us together surfacing. It's torture leaving him, but we already made plans for the next three days on the farm, so it's not like I don't know when I'm going to see him next. I have a love/hate relationship with this feeling.

Watching him wave goodbye in the rearview mirror as I pull out of the stone driveway tugs hard on my heart. One hand waves in the air, while the other squeezes the back of his neck in discomfort. Does he feel this way too? The pull to never leave each other's side, the constant pain when we're not near one another?

Butterflies flutter in my stomach in the hopes he might feel as strongly about me as I feel about him.

My parents are already in bed, making me regret coming home early. I toss and turn in my bed, but I can't get comfortable no matter what I try.

All I want is for Ben to be here with me. It's as if my body and mind are in pain without him. Is this what love is supposed to feel like or is this just pathetic behavior? I exhale roughly into my pillow in agony.

Who would've thought my life would've turned into this at the end of the school year? I never saw myself experiencing love, especially with Ben, nor saw myself having a sexual awakening or almost getting sexually assaulted.

Life's crazy.

Finally, after what feels like hours have passed, I find a comfortable spot on my bed in an odd position of an arm and a leg laying off to the side and pass out while dreamily thinking of Ben and how my first experience with oral went.

Chapter Sixteen.

Every day is bliss with Ben.

I wake up, shower, eat, try to look as cute as possible then go over to Ben's to spend the day. So far, we've had just enough alone time to get in a quick session of making out and him playing with me, but we haven't gone any further and he hasn't gone down on me since he held me up against the barn. He *does* make sure to grab my ass and boobs whenever he gets a chance, and I make sure to tease him by sneaking in a feel through his work jeans, but I'm dying for more.

I zone out, enveloped in memories about our escapades, as we walk side by side to the next field to help his dad unhook the wagon he's using to pick up wood that fell off dead trees around the farm and the backwoods. It's pretty much full now.

The week flies by and Thursday night is here before I know it.

After we finish eating dinner with his parents, he grabs my hand and escorts me to his bedroom. We haven't hung out in there since we started our relationship. Is tonight the night things will progress further?

I've been dying to feel him, skin to skin and see what it fully looks like. Plus, I want to repay the favor. He makes me feel so good. I want to make him feel good too. I might even be ready to have sex. I think...? I don't know how you ever know if you're truly ready for sex.

Either way, I've done my best to prep myself. I've taken birth control for years because my periods have always sucked, which works out because I hear that it feels better for the guy if he doesn't use condoms, so we don't have to worry about that. I also researched blowjob techniques yesterday which provided... interesting results to say the least. Badgirlsbible definitely earned itself a bookmark on my private tabs to look at more in depth later.

I even braved a quick trip to the store to grab lingerie making sure I went to one an hour away from home so I didn't chance running into anyone I knew. The lingerie store accentuated my self-consciousness. I wish I had a best girlfriend who would've been able to have this experience with me. That would've been much more fun.

The lady who measured my bra size was nice enough though and tried to bolster up my confidence. She gave me recommendations on what would fit me and what would look good. I bought several new lacey thongs, a v-string and two full outfits equipped with stockings that went up my legs while the rest of the outfit was either tied together or closed with clips.

I pray he likes everything. I hope I didn't go too overboard.

Thankfully, I had enough money saved up from summer jobs over the years and from helping Ben and his family that I could use cash to buy everything so it wouldn't show up on my parents' card. I do *not* want to have a conversation with them ever over that purchase if at all possible.

He shuts his bedroom door and walks over to the bed, pulling me down with him and holding me against him tightly. He inhales deeply, smelling my hair.

"Your smell is so addicting, babe. I need you to give me some of your perfume so I can spray my pillow. I can barely sleep these days without you. I need something that smells like you so I can relax at night."

My heart leaps, beyond happy he feels the same way I do.

"I can do that, but I'm honestly having the same problem. You'll have to give me yours too. I wish we could sleep together instead of swapping perfumes."

He buries his head in my neck. "Oh yeah?" he chuckles.

"Not like that," I snap, jokingly

"I did think of a plan to address that problem."

"Oh?" Butterflies race to my chest.

"We'd risk getting in trouble with both our parents though, so it's up to you if you want to try it."

He rubs my stomach lightly, caressing the skin under my shirt, his other hand firmly holding me in place against him.

"If you'd stop that, I could concentrate on what you were actually saying."

My brain always stops working when he touches me and gets me all worked up.

He kisses the back of my neck, making my problem worse. "Sorry, babe."

Shivers run down my spine from another light peck on the neck, and another, and another.

Damnit, I'm soaked. She's so easy down there. I wish I could scold my own body part to chill out.

"So, what's your plan?" I reach back and run my fingers through his hair.

"I want to stay with you tonight. I'll ride my bike over after your parents are asleep and park down the street like last time, that way no one will hear it. Then you let me in when I get there so I don't wake anyone up by using the key. I'll set an alarm on my phone to make sure I'm out by like four in the morning before anyone gets up for the day. It'll be like I was never there."

Exhilaration rushes through me at the danger of getting caught *and* of us sleeping together in the same bed. Will he try anything? I tug on his hair behind me to pull him closer even though it's not possible.

"Absolutely. Let's do it."

I turn over to his smiling face full of happiness that matches my own huge grin.

"I need sleep. I've never been this uncomfortable in my life. It's like my body hates being alone now that it knows what being next to you feels like."

"Mhmm. It's as if every time you leave a piece of me goes with you, leaving me in a void until you come back and fill in that missing piece. I...." His brows furrow. "I.... don't want to be apart from you."

I kiss him softly. "Me either, baby."

Just when I think we're about to start messing around, he grabs me and pulls me flush on his chest as he flips on his back. He sighs loudly, rubbing his hand along my back in calming strokes.

"Wait, weren't you supposed to go out riding with the guys tonight?"

"Yeah, but I cancelled. Didn't I just say I didn't want to be apart from you?"

He kisses me on the nose, making me scrunch it. I lay my head back down on his chest and close my eyes, listening to his steady heartbeat.

"I can't believe graduation is in two days. Are you excited?"

I completely forgot about graduation...

"Not really. I don't really care about it to be honest."

My stomach sinks.

Shit.

I'll have to see Jared. My muscles tense and I start picking at my nails. His lips press against the top of my head, sensing my shift into anxiety.

"Don't worry. Jared won't do anything in public. Plus, if he says anything to you, I'll be there and I'm not afraid to kick his ass in front of everybody and expose him."

"I don't want you getting in trouble for protecting me, either. If Jared says anything let's just ignore it, okay?"

"No promises, but I'll try."

I grab his nose and tug.

"Ouch! Fine...I'll *really* try not to hit him."

I raise my head up and rest it on my folded arms.

"Ben. I'm serious."

He gently brushes his hand along my cheek, moving my hair behind my ear. I playfully bite his finger.

"Fine, Char. I promise."

I reach up and kiss him in thanks, lingering there to stare into his beautiful, beautiful eyes.

"Unless he pushes it too much," he whispers on my lips.

"Be—"

He cuts me off by thrusting his tongue into my mouth, kissing me deeply and wrapping his arms around me so hard I'm pinned to him, unable to move at all. I melt into him and let him have this win. I'll make sure to revisit the issue later.

"So, you'll be over around eleven-thirty? My parents are usually in bed by ten-thirty."

"Yup. Can't wait."

He blows me a kiss, winks and shuts my car door.

The tension to leave him is still present but lessened by the fact I'll be seeing him in a short two hours.

I can barely sit still. As soon as I arrive home, I run around my room like a mad woman, cleaning up anything that looks out of place. I can't believe he's going to stay the night.

Eeek!

Finally, the time comes and he texts me he's on his way.

Okay, the last thing I need to do is pick out pajamas. What am I going to wear to bed? Am I going to wear the new lingerie I got?

No, that might look like I was asking for it or trying too hard. I don't want to push him to have sex if he's not ready for it either. Alright, oversized T-shirt and boy-short underwear it is. That'll be cute enough, right?

Ben's message lights up my phone:

BENNY BOY

I'm here.

I quietly open my door and take a quick peek down into the hall to make sure my parents' bedroom door is closed. Perfect, I can hear my dad snoring from here.

I tiptoe down the stairs, avoiding the third creaky step, twist the lock on the front door as slow as humanly possible, praying the click of the deadbolt won't wake my parents and creak open the door.

Wow. How did I get so lucky?

Ben stands there smirking at me, looking devilishly handsome in his motorcycle jacket, pants and boots with his black motorcycle helmet clutched under his arm.

"Hey, you."

"Hey, you," I whisper back.

I step aside to let him in.

The walk upstairs feels like it takes years, but my dad's continued snores still echo in the hallway, confirming we're safe.

I shut my bedroom door, anticipation pulsing through me, and my core, setting my body on fire just watching him make himself at home in my room.

I sit on my bed and watch him shrug off his jacket, setting it on the back of my computer chair. I turn my box fan on for the night, so we'll have more of a noise buffer in case one of us accidently makes a sound. Next, he takes his shirt and pants off, his black boxers gleaming in the light of the computer, and lays everything neatly folded on my computer chair. The shadows dance in the dips of his abdomen and v-cut, perfectly displaying his chiseled body to me. I can't stand how deeply I ache for him in this moment. How's it possible to feel so far away from him when he's right in front of me? I can't get enough of this guy. Finally, he sets his rings down with a small *clink* on my desk and tiptoes over to me.

"You look hot," he whispers, bending down over me and jumping onto the side of the bed closest to the wall.

"So do you," I whisper back.

"I know. I saw you drooling over me."

I smack him in the dark, unsure of where I hit him.

"Ow! Hey, it's not like you were the only one drooling. Having you open the door only wearing an oversized T-shirt and underwear where I had to follow your ass just barely peeking out all the way up the stairs was torture. I got hard instantly."

"I was dripping as soon as you took your pants off."

"Fuck, babe. You drive me so fucking crazy. But...we have to behave tonight."

I pout in the dark. He's *got* to be kidding.

"Why?"

"Because I want to be with *you*, not just with your body and I don't want to chance making any noise. Plus, we really need to get some sleep. I promise we'll have plenty of nights where we don't get sleep because we can't keep our hands off each other. For tonight, all I want to do is hold you and drift to sleep. I want the sound of your breathing to sing me a lullaby and be surrounded by the scent of your hair embracing me in an inescapable aroma."

He's so romantic, and sweet and caring. He's proving time and time again my body isn't what he's after. It's all of me that he wants. I feel like a fool for only thinking about sex.

"Come here, you," he whispers, pulling me to lay on top of him in our usual snuggle position and running his fingers gently through my hair.

Comfort instantly finds me. My eyelids close on their own accord from the heaviness of lack of sleep this past week. This comfort is indescribable, as if I've been placed in an environment where I know nothing can get me and I'll never have to escape if I don't want to.

His fingers stay the same rhythm, starting at my scalp and finding their way to my ends. The perfect metronome. God, how I love this man.

I wake up at three-forty-five to his phone vibrating on the bed. Surprisingly, he's already getting ready to leave, putting his clothes on and donning his helmet. Pain aches deep in me. I hate to see him go.

"I'll see you tonight, babe. I'm glad you slept well."

He gives me a hug, letting the cool plastic of his helmet rest on my cheek.

"Did you sleep okay?" I mumble against his chest.

"Best I have in a long time, baby."

He squeezes me tightly, but instead of going back to sleep, I walk him downstairs and see him out. I want as much time with him as possible, even if it's just for another couple of minutes. I watch him walk to his bike resting behind the bush near our mailbox, pick it up and start walking off with it down the street.

He turns around for one last look. I wave goodbye. He waves back and blows me a kiss. I catch it and send one back. My heart can't handle how precious he is.

I close the front door as slow as humanly possible once again and scurry back up the stairs. At least my bed still smells like him.

Mmmmm.

I snuggle into the side of the bed he used and put a reminder in my phone to give him my perfume for his own room. Then I drift back to sleep comforted by his residual scent on my pillow.

Chapter Seventeen.

Nerves consume me as we approach the school for graduation. My parents spent the morning fussing over me as we made sure my hat and gown were situated right and had our tickets and information for seating.

Ben stayed again, but last night's sleep was... different from the first night. He kept grinding against me in his sleep and saying how bad he wanted to feel inside me which made it rather difficult not to start something. After being woken up like that all night and not getting pleasured, my body wouldn't calm down enough to let me sleep.

I could've pleasured myself, but I held back because I didn't *want* to do it myself. I wanted him to get me off. Plus, it would've been weird to masturbate right next to him. So instead, I showered, got ready and cooked my parents and I's breakfast.

My father was his normal self at breakfast, joking around and eating the eggs and bacon I prepared. My mom on the other hand, held back tears the entire morning while constantly reminiscing on my childhood and how proud she was of me.

I wasn't sure which was worse. It's uncomfortable to be around either of them anymore. I haven't told them about Ben, nor have I wanted to. The secrets I have continue piling up every day as of late to the point I worry one might spill out if I make a wrong move or they ask the wrong question, triggering its premature release.

So, I did what I had to do. I faked my emotions, acting like my old self around them in the meantime so I could get through the day until I was reunited with Ben. Minute shame lay under the surface for not caring I may hurt them, but I felt how I felt.

Parking, as expected, is a nightmare so they drop me off with the rest of the graduates at the front door of the school. Ben finds me immediately in the crowd and grabs my hand, leading me to where we can stand so we get seats together.

He pulls a chair out for me and kisses my cheek quickly before sitting down beside me and intertwining his fingers in mine. My cheeks burn at the looks from everyone watching us. Not to mention, Tree's glaring at me like she's about to tackle me in front of the entire school. Triumph rages inside me like I've won some competition, but a small voice tells me to keep my guard up and to stay vigilant against any attacks she may throw my way.

My heart's full as Ben keeps his hand in mine the entire ceremony, stroking his thumb on mine and caressing each finger to pass the time.

The best part so far is that we haven't seen Jared at all. The worst part is the rushes of adrenaline when any guy with blonde hair gets in my line of sight.

I look around for my parents during the speech segment of the ceremony, completely forgetting they have no idea Ben and I are a thing. Once I find them, I wish I hadn't. My dad stares daggers at me, and I know it's because I'm holding Ben's hand, the guy who he's known since he was a kid and who broke his trust only recently. Thankfully, mom seems to remain oblivious and watches the speeches unphased.

A ball sinks in my chest, deflating the happiness. I turn forward, avoiding my father's glare. I wish I didn't have to speak to him after we get our diplomas. I don't know how much time I need away from him, but I can't seem to face him and this new tense relationship we've entered.

Ben's thumb casually strokes mine, his rings pressing in on my fingers when suddenly his hand tightens, gripping mine so hard it's painful. I open my mouth to ask him what's going on but see his rageful expression and his eyes following something like a hawk. I chase his gaze and land on Jared who's pompously walking up on stage to give a speech. The ball stuck in my chest sinks to the pit of my stomach, pulling all the breath in my lungs with it.

I hold firm and stare at him as well, fighting the fear beneath the surface to look away and cower. I narrow my gaze, searching his facial features. You can't see it if you aren't looking for it, but a small outline of a cut under his right eye, obviously covered by makeup, where Ben decked him faintly shows. I guarantee there's significant bruising being covered too.

Good.

I sit up straighter.

I have to conquer this fear of seeing him. I refuse to let him control me.

He looks out at the crowd beaming proudly, acting as if nothing happened and he didn't try to take advantage of me just last week. What a joke.

Ben's lips sit in a straight line, his jaw clenched, and his back stick straight, not taking his focus off Jared for a second. I squeeze Ben's hand twice to let him know I'm okay and to calm down. I take a deep breath and try to stomach Jared's words as each one grates my ears like knives scratching a dinner plate.

"Living in a world where there is no pain is impossible, but we can choose what we do with that pain. We can use it to prosper, or we can flee from it and drown. Use your choices to your advantage. Remember, you have the ability to change your life at the drop of a hat. Choose to use your pain to your benefit and chase that future you've always longed for. It won't be easy, but the pain will be worth it. Stay strong, stay resilient and chase those dreams."

Was his speech written that way because he feels regret from what he tried to do to me and all the other women he's harassed? Doubtful...but I hope so.

After Jared's speech, we're called up to the stage one by one to receive our diplomas. Then finally, two grueling hours later we're able to perform our group celebration of throwing our hats in the air.

I don't bother finding mine in the crowd and instead walk with Ben over to his parents who... oh God, they're talking to my parents.

My feet quickly fill with lead. If Ben wasn't holding my hand and leading me over to them, I would've stopped and run the other way. He gives it a squeeze in assurance that everything's going to be okay like I did with him before. Unfortunately, as we get closer, I'm not so sure.

My dad spots us out of the corner of his eye, his face flashing with anger for a second before returning to normal as he turns back toward Ben's dad.

"Ben!"

Joan and Koa rush over giving him a big hug and then follow suit with me. My parents stand behind them awkwardly and obviously uncomfortable.

"Congratulations, you two! We're so proud of you!"

"Thank you so much, Joan and Koa," I sheepishly reply, trying not to sound too connected to them.

"Thanks Ma and Pop. Love you guys."

Joan kisses Ben on the cheek while Koa pats him on the back. I step behind them and slowly approach my parents, dread stirring in my gut. My dad's expression is back to being unreadable, my mom's uncomfortable. I try to take a calming breath but a heaviness in my lungs restricts me from it, so I settle for the shallow inhale and throw on a fake smile.

"Hi, guys. I did it." I shyly lift up my diploma and point, trying to get them to talk.

"Congratulations, Charlotte", my dad responds in a flat tone.

"Yes, congratulations, honey."

Mom's tears travel slowly down her cheeks as she gives me a hug, taking my diploma from me and stepping back. The hug feels cold, unfamiliar.

Ben walks up from behind me and places a comforting hand on my back. He throws his other hand out for my dad to shake while keeping the other one pressed against me.

"Mr. Windsor, how are ya?"

Dad shakes it back hesitantly.

"Mrs. Windsor, glad to see ya!" He nods at my mom in acknowledgement, ignoring the tense handshake and looks from my father.

"So, your parents just informed us that you two have been dating for the last week?"

Annddd there it is.

I need to hide. I *cannot* deal with whatever's about to go down. I search around for an escape, but the crowd's already parting. Maybe I can fit under one of the chairs...

"Yes, sir."

He shoves me under his arm, proudly displaying me as his. I find something incredibly interesting to look at on the floor, unable to meet my father's gaze. I'm not sure if Ben notices my reaction, but he begins to speak again as if to save me from speaking myself.

"It was unexpected and new, but we did have plans to tell y'all this weekend."

Lies, but I'm grateful for his cover story. We had no plans to tell my parents that I was aware of.

"I see," my father says in a stony tone.

"Well, congratulations!" my mom says brightly.

I look up, surprised to see a kind expression on her face as she leans in and hugs us both. I hug her back speechless, peeking at my father over her shoulder.

Yikes.

He, on the other hand, is fiercely scowling at me. I've never seen that look in his eyes before. They're cold and empty and resemble nothing I've ever known from my father. I shift my gaze away, too scared to continue looking at him. What's he going to do? What's he going to say? I really hope he doesn't make a scene.

Mom releases us after a too long hug and resumes talking with Ben's parents.

"Did you all want to come over to the farm later for celebrations now that we've officially got two grads on our hands?" Koa says excitedly, his eyes brimming with pride.

"No," my dad says sternly, stunning everyone into silence. "Charlotte will be coming home with us. We have some things we need to discuss."

Tears well up as I chew anxiously on the inside of my cheek. This is so embarrassing. Ben squeezes my shoulder, pulling me into him tighter.

"Charlotte! Oh my gosh—hi!"

Shirley runs up to me from behind my father and gives me a hug, interrupting the horrible situation he just created. Thank God. I have no idea if he was about to rip me away from everyone and yell at me or jump Ben.

I slap on a smile the best I can and hug her back. "Hi Shirley, congratulations."

"You too!" She steps back and takes me by the hand, leading me away. "I'm just gonna borrow her for a quick sec," she shouts to everyone.

Her hair, pinned up with curls flowing around her shoulders, bounces as she pulls me toward the stand. She looks so happy.

"*Girl*! Are you and Ben dating? I saw you two holding hands, and he's like all over you! What happened to your thing with Jared?"

Rage overwhelms me at the mention of Jared. "Jared's an asshole. Stay away from him Shirl." I take a deep breath and relax my tone, reminding myself she's not the one I'm mad at. "But yes, Ben and I are together."

"Eeek!" She bounces on her toes excitedly.

"How'd it happen? Oh my gosh, you have to tell me *everything*. And also, what did Jared do that made you change your mind about him? What'd he do to make you so angry? Why do I have to stay away from him?"

I frown, debating how much to divulge in the public setting. I don't want to start any drama. Graduation day's really not turning into a great day. All I want is to hole up with Ben in a bedroom, mess around and go to sleep.

"I don't really want to talk about Jared right now, Shirley. All you need to know is that he should not be around women. Promise you won't try to date him anymore?"

Her expression turns serious. "Yeah. Yeah, of course. He rejected me at his party anyways and I hit it off with his cousin, so I gave up on him that night. Plus, you never talk bad about people so to warn me about him means he must really be shitty on the inside. But hey, at least you got a biker now, eh? Even though it's not the biker boy on Xypher, next best thing is a biker that you know.

Right?" She elbows me and winks, wearing a playful smirk.

Wow, I haven't thought about Xypher or the biker boy since I tried bringing it up to Ben last Sunday. Masturbating to him feels like a fever dream from another lifetime.

"Yeah, I guess." I awkwardly rub my left arm. "Hey, you should do some investigating and see if you can get ahold of the biker boy and date him before the summer's over."

"Girl, believe me, I've tried. I've DM'd him so many times but never got a response. He's not very interactive with his fans."

I can't believe she actually reached out to him. I can't believe he actually reached out to me and threatened to find me and take me. If she knew, she'd probably flip; or be extremely jealous that I had both Jared and the biker boy after me. Probably best not to tell her that minute detail.

The desire to discover who he is, is long gone, replaced by my deep love and new infatuation for Ben. Small bits of guilt still linger from not telling Ben about him, but it's not like I didn't try. Each time I start to bring up the conversation, Ben interrupts me and refuses to listen. So, I gave up.

"Well, you'll find someone. But honestly, you should forget about boys. Just enjoy the summer and live it up! Boys make everything too complicated anyways."

"True that," she chuckles. "Can we hang out sometime soon?"

"Yeah," I say, smiling sincerely this time.

First an all-girls bonfire and now plans with Shirley? The rest of the summer is looking to be my best yet. Friends...boyfriend...riding motorcycles....

A soft tap on my shoulder catches my attention.

"Your father says it's time to go."

Dread radiates, embedding itself as tension in my muscles and making it hard to move. I do *not* want to find out what's in store for me at home.

"Shirl, I'll text you, okay?"

She looks at my mom and then me, confused, but says okay and gives me one last hug, her curls bouncing playfully as she darts off into the dwindling crowd of students and parents.

"We have to leave graduation already? Can't I just talk to you guys later?"

"No. Your father's extremely upset and wants to talk to you now, but he doesn't want to do it in public."

I roll my eyes and follow her to the exit until I spot Ben talking to one of the teachers.

"I'm going to run over and say bye to Ben really quick."

"Okay, but Dad's waiting in the car. Don't be long or I'm afraid he might come back inside and make a scene."

"What's his problem? What's the big deal with Ben and I dating?"

"I think it's just a lot for him to process all at once. It's overwhelming, especially finding out the way we did. We'll talk at home and sort it all out. Go say bye to Ben and meet us at the car, okay?"

Without another word I run over to Ben, hoping I can steal his comfort somehow and bottle it up to take it with me for this conversation.

"Ben!"

Ben says goodbye to Mr. Henley and turns around, brows furrowing in concern.

"Are you okay? I've never seen your dad look so angry. I always thought he liked me so I didn't think us dating would be that big of a deal."

"No, I'm not okay. I have no idea what his problem is. They're making me leave right now to go home to have a *discussion*, and I'm absolutely dreading it."

"What the fuck?" He brushes his fingers through his hair. "I can go with you, if you want? I can try and provide a buffer?"

"As much as I want you there, I think that'd only make things worse."

He forcefully exhales and fists my gown, pulling me into him. I know he feels as helpless right now as I do about the situation.

"Yeah, probably. Call me when you guys are done talking and I'll either come over to your place or you can come back to the farm, okay?"

"Okay, I lo—" I stop, my eyes wide, my body stiff as a board. I cannot believe I almost said I love you here, now, before he said it *and* in public.

Holy shit.

"Gotta go! I'll text you!" I give him a quick peck on the lips and run away.

"Char! Wait, Char!" he yells as I run away.

I don't dare look back, afraid if I do, I may see something I don't like, and I can't bear his rejection right now with the storm I'm heading into at home.

The ride home is completely silent, the tension between us all unbearable. Once in the house, dad utters two words and points.

"Living room."

I proceed to follow him and my mother, my head down. What the hell is wrong with him? He's acting like I've committed an unforgivable crime.

He motions for me to sit on the couch next to my mother then stands in front of us, in an intentional authoritative stance, his arms folded, and legs spread apart.

"It's like we don't even know you anymore, Charlotte," he sharply scolds.

Oh good, he's digging right in. The pacing begins right away with stern glares at me as he continues his unfair berating.

"You've barely been home the last week, not telling us anything about what you're doing or where you're going and *now*, we find out from his parents you're dating Ben? You've been extremely disrespectful to your mother and I with how you've spoken to us. You've bailed on our family time and game nights together, and you've been sneaking around with some boy. You're like a completely different person. You've lost our trust, Charlotte."

"He's not just some boy. He's Ben, you *know* him. Plus, I haven't done anything wrong. I'm an adul—"

"You still live under our roof, young lady. You have got to communicate with us. Are you and Ben being safe?" The last word catches in his throat like it's painful.

"Oh my God, yes. We're not even doing anything," I lie, embarrassed he would even ask me that. "I'm not an idiot. You guys raised me right."

"Don't call us 'guys' and do *not* talk down to us like that." His nostrils flare and a redness overtakes his skin traveling from his face down past his neck. What's making him so mad?

"I wasn't eve—"

"From now on, curfew. Every night you must be home by eleven. *No exceptions*."

I shoot up, outraged. "That's not fair! This is ridiculous! What'd I even do?" I exasperate, flailing my arms dramatically.

He continues spouting rules, ignoring me. "Your phone will be kept downstairs after eleven and you will not be able to have it in your room. You are only allowed to see Ben under supervision max three days a week."

"Honey..." my mom cuts in gently. She stands up and reaches for his arm, but he jerks it away violently.

"Absolutely not. These rules are extremely unfair. I'm not some child who needs to be disciplined. I've done *nothing* wrong! Bailing on one game night shouldn't make you lose your trust. That doesn't even make any sense! And I've never had to tell you where I've been before. Why are you being like this?"

"Until you learn to respect yourself and your mother and I, this is how it's going to be."

God, I want to fucking deck him. A pounding in my ears drowns out external noises, followed by a high-pitched ringing. My heart beats so hard it shakes my body with every beat. The rage at my father nears to the point of hating him. I refuse to adhere to these rules. I'm not going to be his prisoner just because he can't accept that I'm growing up.

Before I can lead my feet, they lead me, taking me away from him and up the stairs. My brain and body work on their own agenda.

I stomp each foot onto each step up the stairs, savoring the sting reverberating into my bones.

"Where do you think you're going, young lady. We are not done here," he shouts into the hall from the living room, his voice getting closer as he chases me. My mother's no help, pathetically turtle shelling, providing no barrier between him or I.

I ignore him, continuing up the stairs and grab a suitcase out of the hallway closet. Flinging it open on the bed, I throw my computer, clothes, and anything else I may need into it.

My father's stomps up the stairs are almost as loud as his shouts. "Charlotte Rose Windsor, what do you think you're doing?"

I can't stand to look at him, so I keep my back turned, ignoring him. "I'm leaving. I'm not dealing with this. I don't deserve to be treated like a prisoner in my own home. I've done *nothing* wrong."

I continue packing, this time grabbing a few things out of my closet. He takes hold of my bicep and whips me around, his grip painfully tight and pinching the skin between his fingernails. Flashbacks of Jared and the bonfire flood my mind triggering fear and further anger.

In a low voice I growl, "Do not *ever* touch me like that again."

I death glare at him and rip my arm out of his grip, fighting every urge in me to physically push him away.

"You are not leaving this house, Charlotte. I forbid it."

"Get out of my way!" I lug the suitcase past him and struggle out the front door. Mom's standing at the top of the stairs, tears rolling down her cheeks.

"Thanks for not helping at all," I spit at her, daring her to say something to defend herself.

She says nothing and looks down at her feet. I shake my head in disgust.

The suitcase behind me stumbles on the front steps but I keep it as a barrier between me and my father who's still following behind me.

"Where do you think you're going?"

"Don't worry about it."

"You are not allowed to leave this house, Charlotte."

"I'm eighteen. I'm doing what I want. Do *not* follow me or you'll regret it," I snarl viciously, gritting my teeth.

The heavy words sink in. He takes a step away from me and shuts up, keeping some distance at last.

I throw my suitcase in the front seat, jump in and slam my car in reverse. My mother's nowhere to be found. Only my dad can be seen standing on the front doorstep huffing and puffing in rage, his fists curled tightly at his sides, knuckles stark white. His eyes look crazed, untamed and terrifying like someone who would murder you in a second if you looked at them the wrong way.

Tears roll down my cheeks, my breath already catching in my throat as I try my hardest to hold back the violent sobs shaking my throat. I shouldn't have done it, but I glance behind me as I back out of the place that used to be my safe space to stare at the man I used to know. That man is not the man who raised me. I don't know who that is or what happened to make him this way in such a short time.

I drive toward the farm, leaving the people who used to be my everything in the rearview mirror, and praying Ben will be the haven I need right now because I don't know where else to go.

Chapter Eighteen.

I don't feel anything. My mind becomes a black void of nothingness, leaving me numb, and in a daze. Is this even real? Am I dreaming?

I can't remember how I got here, and the world is spinning.

I lean forward in my car, resting my forehead on my fingers gripping the steering wheel and let it all out, sobbing so hard I can't breathe. My heart breaks into pieces. It's shredding and ripping itself apart and there's nothing I can do to stop it. So, I let my body do what it needs to as I continue to cry, heaving and gagging from my stomach twisting so viciously in between my gasping breaths.

A voice in the distance calls my name, echoing onto the walls of my heart while it tries to hold whatever pieces are left together. Arms wrap around my shoulders and stay there, holding me as I release all the emotions I've been keeping down about my parents and our now deteriorated relationship.

"Come here, baby," Ben voices from somewhere far away. Arms curl underneath my knees and around my ribs as he lifts me out of the car. I bury my neck into his, wetting his shirt with my tears and trying to escape into his scent.

He carries me into the house straight to his bedroom, shutting the door with his foot and lays me down on his bed, holding me as the little spoon until I calm down.

I inhale deeply, soaking him in. Bit by bit, his cologne calms me, peace slowly wandering its way through my body, getting the shaking to dwindle.

"Do you want to talk about it?" Ben whispers, kissing the top of my head.

"My father was treating me like a prisoner. He told me I had a curfew of eleven, that I wasn't allowed to have my phone after that time, and I was only allowed to see you max three times a week *and* those visits had to be supervised. So, I packed a bag and left. I couldn't stand the feeling of being treated like that. I'm eighteen. I've graduated. I believe I have a right to my own freedom especially since I don't think I've done anything wrong." I pause, second guessing myself. "You should've seen my father's face, Ben. He looked at me like I committed some heinous crime. I-I just can't figure out what I did to make him so angry because his reasonings didn't make any sense. Did I do something wrong? Did I deserve all that?"

He squeezes me tightly, stroking my hair and lightly brushing his fingertips over my back. "No, you haven't done anything wrong, baby. He was being extremely unfair. Ever since I've known your dad he's been the most laid-back guy ever. This is very out of character for him. What did your mom say? Did she agree with him?"

"Pfftt..." I scoff into his warm chest. "There was only one time she tried to stand up for me, but she backed down immediately. Otherwise, she did absolutely nothing. She just fucking stood there. I know she loves my dad but to see her be a complete pushover disgusted me. She's supposed to protect me and instead she did nothing." Small sobs resurface. "I don't know what I'm going to do, Ben," I whisper, barely audible.

"Well, obviously, you're going to stay here... with me," he says so confident and sure about his spontaneous plan.

I came here with nowhere else to go, not even thinking about my next steps. I was scared he'd turn me away. That he'd be uncomfortable with me coming to him with this heavy drama, but I should've known better.

I tilt my neck back and look at him. "Really?"

"Absolutely." He smiles brightly.

"I'm gonna take care of you. Don't worry about it. You can stay here as long as you need to." He presses a soft kiss on my lips and brushes his nose against mine affectionately.

"Don't you need to ask your parents?"

"I actually already asked them last week. I obviously had no idea something like this would happen, but I asked them if you could start staying overnight here after graduation and they said 'Sure, as long as we're responsible.'" He winks, waggling his eyebrows.

I'm floored. He had the balls to ask his parents if I could stay over before this all happened? Well, it was probably because he was sick of getting up at four in the morning every day, but still. What an amazing human and boyfriend. He must really like me. The small strings of my heart vibrate as they start connecting in hopes they can meld back together.

"I don't know what to say. I'm...I'm very grateful, but that wasn't an agreement for me to basically live here. I'll talk to your parents and double check an extended stay is okay."

He kisses me hard, lingering there for a few seconds before pulling away.

"Figured you would. No rush though, they'll be busy for a while. They're out in the fields and have things to fix in the shop when they get back, so we can walk out there whenever you're ready."

"Okay," I say, snuggling back into him and closing my eyes.

We lay there for I don't even know how long. I steal some kisses, as does he, but mostly he holds me as I stroke my fingers along his back.

I don't want to move out of this safe place. I'm scared if I move then all those emotions will come rushing back and I'll crumble all over again.

Ben starts to pull away from me, but I cling onto his shirt to hold him there.

"I had a thought..." he pauses.

"Yeah?"

He presses his forehead to mine. "Wanna go for a ride?"

We knock heads from me shooting upright so quickly.

"Ouch!" he cries out laughing, holding his forehead.

I hold my forehead to stop the stinging and squeal, "I'm so sorry! Are you okay? I'm so in. Let's go! I can't wait to wear my helmet and backpack you!"

"Okay, well giving the driver a concussion before you go on the road is not a good start," he chuckles, smacking me in the ass.

"You're tough, you can handle it," I joke, running to the bathroom to pee. This is exactly what I need.

Oof.

I shouldn't have looked in the mirror. Puffy eyes stare back at me and red blotches cover my skin in an extremely unattractive way. If only I could hide, but that would do me no good. Ben's been looking at me in this state since I got here. I splash cold water on my skin, hoping for a miracle and avoid the mirror on my way out.

I flick the bathroom light off but stop in my tracks when I step back into the bedroom. Ben's plump member is outlined perfectly in his underwear, his leather biker pants surrounding his waist but not yet zipped. My eyes widen, lips parting in lust.

"Eyes up here, Char."

Shit, of course he can see where I'm staring. He winks, smirking at me like he knows I'm wrapped around his finger.

"Your biker pants are on the bed."

"What? You mean you bought me biker clothes too?" I exclaim excitedly, running over to the bed.

"Of course. I wasn't joking about safety. Your riding jacket is next to your helmet in the barn as well."

This is absolutely the pick-up I needed. He knows me so well.

I pick up the pants, admiring them, and caress the cool leather, feeling the bumps and the pads on the knees and thighs for protection. They're all black except for a double white stripe that goes across each thigh.

I hoist them on under my graduation dress. Damn they're tight. I have to jump and pull up hard at the same time several times to get them up all the way while sucking in my stomach to button them.

"Damn, I'm not *this* skinny!" I pant from the effort it took to slide them on.

"They're meant to be tight, silly," he chuckles.

I run over and embrace him, giving him a big kiss. "Whatever you say, Captain. Let's go!"

I turn to go out the door, but he grabs my arm, holding me back.

"Okay, there's no way you'll be able to fit your dress under the jacket. Here—" he throws a tight black T-shirt at me in my size.

"Put that on."

"Okay, you really didn't have to buy me all this stuff. I could've bought myself this gear if you would've told me what I needed."

"I know, but I wanted to. Plus, if I told you, then you'd know when I was giving you a ride and I wanted to surprise you."

"Well, thank you. I'm grateful..."

He nods in appreciation then goes quiet, blatantly staring at my breasts, waiting for me to take my dress off and change.

"Turn around," I sass, placing my hands on my hips.

He pouts, and mimics me by placing his hands on his hips too.

"Why?"

God, he's so fucking hot.

"*Because.*" I smile, barely able to contain the joy in my heart. "If you see me take off my dress, we won't leave the bedroom and go for a ride."

He throws his head back and laughs then turns around. "Yeah, you're one hundred percent right, Char."

I throw my dress on the floor and pull the shirt on. A perfect fit. Will going braless be a problem? Hopefully it doesn't get too bumpy or cold on the ride, because I don't feel like searching for a bra in my bags right now. I just want to get on the bike already.

"Okay, done."

My breasts get assaulted aggressively as he squeezes and fondles them. "Good God, baby, how am I going to ride if you don't have a bra on. I'm already getting so fucking hard looking at your nipples pressed against your shirt."

Feverish heat flushes under my skin stemming from where his warm touch caresses my breasts.

Seconds. It only takes seconds for me to be completely out of breath, and on the verge of succumbing to him, but I have to stop this. There'll be time for this later. As much as I want this now, I need to ride. I swear that bike is calling to my soul, and I can't put it off anymore.

Only one word is able to escape at a time as he massages my breasts and caresses my neck with his kisses, totally scrambling my brain.

"We. Can. Do. This. Later," I breathlessly whisper.

It takes everything in me to step away from him. I cross my arms over my chest to hide the goodies from his view and back away until I hit the doorway. His cheeks are flushed, and his hands are at his sides while his chest rises and falls deeply with each breath.

"Okay," he says with a straight face and proceeds to follow me out of the room. His cool demeanor returns shortly after and he makes sure to smack my ass every five steps until we hit the barn as punishment. I'll have to misbehave more often for these "punishments".

He pulls the barn door open, revealing my helmet and jacket right beside his. I love that. My grin spreads from ear to ear.

"Hey, where's your other bike? I just realized it's not in here."

"It's in the other barn with my other bikes."

"Bikes? How many bikes do you have?

"More than I should," he says rubbing the back of his neck and smiling awkwardly.

Why's he being so secretive about it? Whatever. It doesn't matter. I let it go and strut toward my new riding jacket.

I unhook the jacket off the wall and admire it like everything else he's given me. I love that he color coordinated this. My new jacket is all black with white stripes on the arms, matching the pants. Thick leather padding is on the elbows, and the pockets are zippered with gold. It's beautiful.

The zipper's easy to glide up. It's tight but not as tight as the pants, thank God. I shove my helmet on and jump up and down like a little kid next to the bike, my vizor still up, but threatening to slam down from the movement.

"You goofball," he chortles. Ben clips his helmet on and joins me by the bike, pulling out little bars near the back.

"What are those?" I point to the silver bars now sticking out.

"Rear pegs. They're what you're going to rest your feet on while we're riding."

"Cool!" I raise my leg up to set it on one of the pegs, but he grabs the bottom of my helmet and rips the nose of it against his, throwing me off balance.

"Not so fast, sparkplug." *Ew, not his dad's nickname again.* "We have to go over the rules first."

"Rules?" I whine, impatient and annoyed.

He lets go of my helmet and crosses his arms, taking a wide stance. My knees weaken at the sight of him standing there dominantly. His brown eyes stare at me playfully under his helmet, his visor still up, giving him a mysterious aura as he starts his speech. He holds up one gloved finger.

"First rule. Don't *ever* take your feet off the rear pegs."

He holds up a second finger, then a third and fourth as he counts the rules out for me.

"Second. Keep your hands around my waist at all times. Third. If you want me to slow down, tap my chest twice. Fourth. If you're having pain or discomfort at any point and want me to stop, tap me three times. Lastly, riding motorcycles is extremely dangerous. God forbid we get hit, you need to let go of me immediately and tuck and roll. You want to protect your appendages and use the padding on your gear. Got it?"

"Yes, sir."

"Good."

He relaxes his stance and mounts the bike, turning it on. The sound's electric. The pure power thunders into my soul, vibrating my bones and flaming a newfound fire of passion.

"Take my hand," he yells over the sound, throwing out his left hand, palm up to hold onto while I get on the bike.

The leather on the palm and fingers scratches mine.

"Grab my shoulder with the other hand if you need too, and step one foot on the rear peg while swinging the other leg over."

I do as instructed, finding it much easier than when I tried to get on last time and embarrassed myself.

Woah.

The vibrations surge through me, its power trembling every part of my body. The power emanating from Dalia's intimidating.

He reaches back and taps my thigh then grips back on the handle, kicks the kickstand up and walks the bike backwards out of the barn.

He drives slowly down the gravel driveway, easing me into the ride. He's so careful with me on here. The sweetness of this man is going to give me diabetes.

When we reach the end of the driveway, he puts his foot down, turns to me and slaps my vizor down as well as his.

"Hold on, baby."

I obey, wrapping my arms tightly around his waist and gripping the seat with my thighs with all my might.

He takes off. The acceleration nearly knocks me back, causing me to loosen my grip. I readjust my hands quickly to secure myself again. I can't see the odometer, but it feels like we're going impossibly fast.

Not to mention the rumble of the engine under my seat's so intense I fear it's going to trigger an orgasm.

God, this rush would be easy to get addicted to, although I have a feeling I'm already there. I'm completely in the present moment, leaving the worries of the real world far behind us. Everything blurs past, the fields, other cars, stores, lights. It's like we're sitting still, and the entire world moves around us, giving us a glimpse of its beauty in quick flashes.

Right as I think I never want it to end, we slow down. Ben pulls over onto the side of the road and turns the bike off.

"What's wrong?" I ask, releasing my grip and shaking out my hands to relax them. The adrenaline must have masked the pain in my hands and back during the ride because now a stiff pain settles in both. I'll get used to it; I assure myself.

"Nothing. I just wanted to check on you. How you doing? Are you okay? How do you like the ride?"

"Oh my God, Ben. That's why you stopped? Baby, this is the best experience of my life!"

"Oh, really? Even better than when I ate you out behind the barn?" I smack the back of his helmet. He smacks my thigh in return, as muffled laughs fill my soul up even more.

"I could ride forever, babe. I *love* this feeling. If we did this every day for the rest of our lives, I'd be a happy camper." I wrap my arms back around him signaling I'm ready to keep going.

"Alright babe. You call the shots."

The motorcycle roars back to life, throwing me right back into bliss.

Though, as much as I was in bliss, after a couple hours the pain in my hands and back could no longer be ignored. I unwillingly tapped his chest three times. He responded that it was getting dark anyways and we should get back regardless.

We arrive at the farm just as the sun sets. I couldn't have asked for a more beautiful end to my first real ride.

Ben lets me off by the house to stretch as I walk beside him to the barn to put the bike away. My ass cramped up during the last mile of the ride, so I need to loosen up my legs. He quite enjoyed watching me waddle next to him like a cowboy trying to duel someone because my legs were stuck in the straddle position. I had to smack him in the helmet just to get him to stop laughing so hard because he was bent over the bike and stopped moving.

I hang my jacket and helmet up next to Ben's once we're in the barn and wait by the entrance for him. My face feels stuffy from the helmet and my hair's frizzy as all get out, but it was worth it. Hopefully the helmet's compression helped the swelling in my face from my cry earlier too, so his parents don't suspect anything.

Ben, of course, looks perfect. His hair's slicked down with sweat, his cheeks are rosy red, and his abs are outlined in his tight T-shirt. God, he's immaculate.

He comes up to me and picks me up by my ass, making me throw my legs around his waist and leaving my arms resting on his shoulders.

"Let's eat. Eh?" he says kissing me, beginning the walk toward his house. I lazily kiss him on his cheek, his neck and his shoulder, teasing him playfully since I know we can't mess around just yet and he'll have to wait to have me.

"Oh wait," I say as we get near the front door.

"I have to get my suitcase out of the car."

He sets me down on the porch and pecks a kiss to my forehead. "I got it. Go on inside."

"You treat me way too good, you know," I mumble to his back.

"Lies. You deserve the world and thus I treat you accordingly," he yells already almost to my car, not looking back.

Joan and Koa are in the kitchen finishing up dinner when I walk in. I sheepishly cover my breasts to hide the fact I'm not wearing a bra, hoping courage will come on its own to ask them if I can stay here for a while, but right as I open my mouth, Ben cuts in.

The suitcase slams on the floor next to me.

"Charlotte's going to be staying with us for a while, is that alright?"

"Fine with me," Joan says, smiling brightly.

"Same with me," says Koa, smiling at us for a second before his expression turns serious. His chin tilts down, and he stares at us seriously through his eyelashes.

"As long as you two promise to be safe and behave. Don't break the trust we're putting in you. You're under our roof, remember."

Oof. Awkward.

"Yes, absolutely. Thank you so much. Both of you," I say gratefully, bowing my head.

I'll have to make sure I behave myself here. If we want to mess around, we'll have to do it outside so we're not under their roof.

Hello, loophole.

Ben kisses my cheek and sits at the table, pulling out a chair next to his for me. He slaps his hands on his knees.

"What we having?"

By midnight I'm exhausted and ready for bed. I kept dozing off during the movie we watched with his parents, until Ben woke me up at the end to say goodnight to everyone and go to bed.

I don't bother wearing the lingerie outfit I packed because all I intend to do is sleep. We put our PJs on with our backs turned, with the exception of once when Ben peeked, making his punishment an immediate whipping with my shirt.

He shuts the light off and crawls into bed next to me, his warmth already rocking me to sleep. I turn over to snuggle him, my hands resting on his back, while his arms wrap around my waist. I'm almost asleep when I feel him move, then hear his breathing pick up. His fingertips skim softly against my skin, almost tickling me, as they slowly work their way up to my breast under my shirt.

"Nuh-uh. We promised we'd behave," I whisper sleepily, grabbing his hand, stilling it.

"Nuh-uh. *You* promised. I kept my mouth shut on purpose."

I just know he's grinning mischievously at me in the dark at his cleverness.

"You're right. *I* did. Someone has to hold us accountable." I seize his wrist, but not with much gusto.

He abandons my breast and dips below my shorts into my underwear, making me freeze. My brain blanks at his touch. He quickly inserts one finger into me, making circles with it, teasing me.

"You sure are wet for someone who's wanting to behave," he whispers against my ear, kissing my cheek as I nuzzle into his neck.

I don't respond. I can't. Damnit, I'm so weak. I cave so easily, but to be honest, I don't really care. Now all I can think about is how much more of him I want right now.

"That's what I thought," he whispers gutturally.

He inserts another finger, flattening his palm above my essence and pulses in and out. When he inserts a third finger, it sends me bucking and arching my back from the pleasure.

In a moment of courage, I slide my hand to his pants and immediately find his hardness under my palm. I moan louder than I mean to at the sheer size of him.

"Shhh," he breathlessly whispers.

I stroke him up and down like I did before over his pants before diving straight in under his waistband. Damn. It's so incredibly soft. I grip him harder at the base and feel a large vein rolling under my palm on his erection as I stroke upwards. An audible moan escapes from him.

"Shhh," I whisper in retaliation.

I stroke up and down, unsure if I'm doing it right. Too scared to ask, I grip him tighter then looser, going faster and faster as I inch closer to climax. My rhythm's erratic as I try different methods to please him.

"Here. Let me show you, baby." He places his hand over mine, stopping me.

"I'm sorry." I remove my hand like it's on fire, feeling immediately dejected and embarrassed.

"Babe, it's okay. Please, don't apologize. It felt good, but I want to teach you how I like it. How else are you going to know how I like it unless I show you?" He kisses me, pushing his tongue into my mouth and grabs my hand, pulling it down with his.

He grips his hand around mine, placing it around his cock. He moves them up and down his shaft slowly, gripping tighter at the top and swiveling our palms before going back down slighlly looser. He shows me for a few more strokes, while never removing his mouth off mine. Finally ready to take the lead, I jerk my neck back, and bring my hand to my mouth, licking my palm a few times before going back down.

"*Fuckkk* yes, baby," he moans onto my skin, his cheek now resting on mine.

Keeping his pace when I'm about to come is next to impossible, but I'm determined to make him feel as good as I do.

"I want you to come when I do," I groan.

"How close are you?"

"Really close."

"Me too," he grunts roughly, his hot breath tickling my skin.

His rough moan pushes me over the edge, and I finish all over his fingers. Hard. He follows me over getting my wrist and belly wet while our hips writhe toward each other in pleasure. I shove my face into the pillow to stifle the moans that won't stop coming out of me. He pushes his face into my shirt between my breasts to quiet his.

"Fuck, babe. You instructing me when you wanted me to come was so fucking hot. You keep surprising me and showing me things I never expected out of you. I fucking love it."

I search for his lips in the dark, desperate for his mouth and to feel his tongue on mine. There's a different tension between us now. A deeper connection, like our souls are reaching for each other and pulling us even closer together. Our tongues glide together slowly as we take our time, holding each other tightly and kissing as deeply as we can manage.

The words *I love you* are on the tip of my tongue, trying to force their way out.

No, not yet.

I force the words back down.

Not yet.

"I'm glad you like my surprises," I whisper instead.

"I hope you like the surprises I've had for you too, because I have another one for you tomorrow."

"Oh yeah?"

"Yup. I'm taking you somewhere secret tomorrow."

Butterflies and a quick thrill shoot through me.

"I can't wait," I whisper, nestling my head into his chest. After a while, his soft breaths lull me to sleep while my dreams take guesses at his surprise.

Chapter Nineteen.

Given the horrible circumstances of why I'm at Ben's initially, it feels amazing to wake up next to him without worrying about hiding. We take our time waking up and lay there enjoying each other, stroking each other's backs and kissing softly and lazily like we have all the time in the world. Eventually, we can't hide the hunger grumbling in our stomachs and venture out for some breakfast.

My curiosity about the surprise for the day gets the better of me. I can't help but try to get him to slip up and tell me his plans.

Any chance I get, I ask him what we're doing or offer up a massage in exchange for any hint of what the evening might hold. He's a stone wall, never breaking no matter how much I pound against it. Even the pouty-face he calls irresistible doesn't work, although it does get me extra kisses.

"You ready?" he walks up smiling.

"It's time?" I bob excitedly.

"Yes, but please put down those wire cutters when you're jumping," he laughs.

Oops.

I forgot I was holding them. His dad recruited me to help him cut old fencing so they could take the posts out and expand the field with new ones.

"I'll text you the address to meet me at."

"We're not going together?"

"No. You're going to meet me there." His eyes shine with mischief as his eyebrows bounce up and down playfully.

What's he planning that requires us to drive separately?

He pulls his phone out of his back pocket and types something. A second later, my phone vibrates.

BENNY BOY

90 Lenny St. Walk to the stone drive and follow until it ends, then turn left. Meet me at 8 PM.

"Eight o'clock? But that's so far away!" I cross my arms and pout, pushing my bottom lip out. "Plus, having me park on some random stone drive and walk? You're not going to murder me, are you?"

"Why on earth would I murder you? If I did that, I'd have no one to pick on whenever I wanted."

I stick my tongue out at him, dramatically. He blows me a kiss and winks, walking away from me up to the house.

"See you then, babe!"

His tight jeans accentuate his perfect ass, sticking to him like glue with each step.

Damn. I'm one hundred percent going to bite into that later.

By the time Koa and I finish working on the fence, Ben's already back outside.

I'm too tired to find more work to do so I have a quick bite to eat, shower and pick out my hairstyle and outfit for the surprise.

I frown upon hearing a motorcycle roar out of the driveway.

He's leaving already? My phone lights up to show me it's only six-thirty. How far away is this place?

I plug the address into my GPS which shows an arrival time of six-forty-five. Why's he leaving so early if it's only fifteen minutes away? Is it going to take him *this* long to set something up?

I'll leave around seven-thirty then to make sure I have time to walk to wherever the destination is since I have no idea how long the "stone drive" is.

Feeling gutsy, I wear an all-black tight fitting bodycon dress with no underwear or bra. I assume wherever he's taking me means we'll be alone, and I want him drooling over me, and begging to touch me. I want him to want me so bad he can't take it anymore and takes me fully.

I straighten my hair in the mirror and choose a lighter make-up style with a darker lip liner, gloss and eyeliner with mascara. Simple and sweet, exactly how he likes it with just an added touch of spice to hopefully floor him.

Right as I put on my shoes, my alarm beeps, signaling it's time to go. I haven't heard from Ben since he left, which isn't helping ease my nerves that are already on edge from the daring look I chose mixed with a surprise in the middle of nowhere.

I stop by the west barn to admire my motorcycle helmet and jacket one more time before leaving, but they aren't there. Dalia's still parked here too. Did he take the bike he drove to Jared's?

My second alarm reminder beeps. Well, guess I'll find out what bike he rode when I get to the location.

The stone drive's creepy, especially since it's already dark. My headlights cast an eerie light, making the tree shadows lurch out dramatically. Sucking in a breath of courage, I park off to the side of the road as instructed, hoping I'm not about to get murdered and get out. Woods ominously line each side of the stone drive where it leads down into darkness with no visible ending.

What the hell's he getting me into? The only thing I hear are my black and white converse slipping on the stones and a few birds that are still out, otherwise it's dead quiet. I check my phone.

Seven-fifty-five.

I pick up my pace to a half-run, unsure of how much farther I need to go.

Finally, after what feels like forever, music sounds to my left which is a good thing because a line of trees blocks the way in front of me, leaving me nowhere else to go. Looks like this is the end. I follow the music through a thicket of brush, cursing Ben's name. I can't believe he knew I'd be walking through this thicket and didn't tell me to dress accordingly. I'm going to give him so much shit for this. If my dress tears and burrs stick all over my clothes, hair and face, I'm going to be a mess. God, that'll be a real attractive sight. It'll be like a human-sized bigfoot roaming the woods and trying to seduce him.

I stop dead in my tracks as the thicket clears. My stomach drops down to my feet and my legs start shaking, feeling as though they're about to give out.

There's a concrete lot in front of me with a tripod set up in front of a bike and...

Holy.

Fucking.

Shit.

It's him. The dancing biker.

Holy fucking shit.

I bolt behind a tree just outside the thicket, frozen, and afraid to be seen.

Did I take a wrong turn? Is there another stone drive I was supposed to go down? Where the hell is Ben and why is *he* here?

I peek back around the tree that barely hides me and watch him dance to the music, ending the move in a handstand and a front flip. He walks to the tripod, his chest heaving vigorously from exertion and presses a button on the phone, stopping the recording.

My body begins doing what it's been trained to do when it sees him. My core is getting soaked, and I know it's only a matter of time before I'm dripping down my leg from no underwear. The urge to touch myself, to envelope myself in its pleasure is strong as the pulse below strengthens.

Last time it felt wrong when I was with Ben, so why doesn't it feel wrong right now?

I step away from the tree back toward the thicket to see if I made a wrong turn when my foot steps on a large stick, breaking it, and sending a loud *crack* into the quiet woods, giving my position away. And that's when a whistle sounds from behind me.

I slowly turn around in shock, still frozen in my sneaky position, my arms out wide. He looks right at me beneath the helmet, cocks his head and without saying anything lifts his gloved hand up and motions me to come toward him with two fingers. If I thought my legs were going to give out before, that is nothing to how weak they feel now caught red-handed by my biker obsession.

Embarrassed to no end, I wobble toward him. He stalks his way toward me with steady, dominant steps. Shit, I don't know what to say.

What do I say?

Should I call Ben and have him come get me?

Shit, I left my phone in the car. I just *had* to wear the tightest dress on earth with no pockets.

The biker boy quickens his pace and runs at me. I stop and back pedal, now getting scared, but he's too fast. Is he going to attack me?

Without slowing down, he wraps his arms around my waist and pulls me up, his leather gloves scratching the skin on my bare thighs as he lifts and swaddles them around his waist. I squirm trying to get away and raise my hand to smack at the helmet when he speaks.

"Baby, stop! Baby, it's me!"

Oh.

My.

God.

"Ben?"

I flip up the vizor of the helmet to reveal his big, beautiful brown eyes smiling at me.

"Hi baby."

"Hi! Jesus, you scared me." I pause, my brain short circuiting as it tries to tie the truth together. "H-how? Wh-what?" My head shakes in disbelief. "I-I can't believe you're him. I can't believe you're the viral faceless biker..."

Ben's the biker boy... This is unbelievable.

But how is this possible?

I take his helmet off and rest my arms around his shoulders, holding his all-white helmet in my hands behind his head as I try to find the right words to say.

I am *not* prepared to face this situation.

"Wow, you look fucking gorgeous, baby. *My God,* I'm a lucky guy." He presses his lips to mine and squeezes my ass hard with both hands.

"I never would've guessed the viral biker was you. You've never been a big fan of social media nor told me that you could dance or liked to dance or...but...you-you...you do thirst traps!"

I can barely put proper sentences together, continuing to ramble from shock, until my brain clears and pegs one question now burning to be asked.

"Why? Why do you do it?"

"Well," he exhales forcefully, setting me down and running his fingers through his sweat soaked hair. "Basically, it comes down to wanting to make some extra money."

"But you're loaded. Why do you need more money?"

"*I'm* not loaded," he says sternly. "My parents are loaded, *not* me. None of that's *my* money. I want to be able to support myself, especially since I'll be leaving home soon. My parents have done enough. I don't want to ask more from them than I need to."

I stay silent for a moment, admiring the man I call mine. He wants to build his own wealth, not rely on his parents and he's taking concrete steps to achieve it. He has such a good head on his shoulders.

He interlaces his fingers in mine and walks me over to the tripod, reminding me of who was just revealed to be the face behind the mask.

"Your face is really red, Char," he chuckles, folding his arms and leaning on his bike. "Something wrong?"

"No," I blurt out a little too defensively. "Like I said, I just had no idea you could dance, let alone be the dancing biker everyone's obsessed with."

"So, were you one of my obsessed fans then?" A wicked smile flashes across his face as his gloved palms grip his biceps. More heat singes my cheeks, and my fingers fidget with themselves out of nervous energy. "Come here, you." He motions between his legs and throws his gloves on the ground.

I walk over, saying nothing. He roughly grabs my ass and kisses along my neck, his hands immediately wandering as small moans exit him.

Wait...

Waitwaitwaitwaitwait.

He pulls away from my neck as I stiffen, his eyebrows furrowing in concern. "What's wrong?" He brushes his nose against mine.

I push off him and back away, feeling furious, violated and embarrassed.

My head's spinning from trying to process how to handle the fact he watched me masturbate and then texted me pretending to be someone I didn't know. I need space to breathe for a minute.

"How." I whisper, short of breath from shock and anger. "How did you watch me masturbate to you? And why did you text me from an unknown number pretending to be someone else. And why did you not tell me it was you this whole time and lead me on! What game were you playing?" My shouts get louder with every statement of truth, my fists trembling at my sides.

He drops his hands to his sides, defeated and desperate. "I'm sorry, Char. I-I... Fuck. I didn't think you'd react like this."

"How the hell am I supposed to react, Ben?" I throw my hands up in exasperation.

"I don't know, honestly. I thought that if I told you after we were together, you'd be into it. Of course, you felt violated and confused instead. I'm such an asshole for thinking otherwise. I'm so sorry." He rubs his hands through his hair and down the back of his neck. "Listen, part of my coding internship focuses on hacking techniques. Obviously, we weren't supposed to be doing anything nefarious with those skills, but I couldn't help myself. You weren't talking to me, and I wanted to know what you were doing. Plus, I just couldn't stand the thought of you possibly being with Jared." He pauses, watching me intently, his eyes wide and brows curved from emotional pain.

Raising an eyebrow, I cross my arms and stick my leg out while tapping my foot. "Continue."

"When I saw you were getting off to me… I-I couldn't help myself. I couldn't stop watching. I was desperate." He takes a long, slow breath. "I figured if you weren't talking to me…maybe you'd talk to him. And when I was him, I could finally talk to you how I always wanted. I could finally flirt with you openly and give you what you were looking for. With how much you seemed to like the biker guy, I figured you may go for him. Then I figured it'd be easier to reveal myself to you once you fell for him. I don't know. I was desperate, Char. I-I had to have you and I resorted to any measure to get you. Fuck that sounds so wrong. I'm so sorry, baby. I'm such a fucking asshole."

I stand there observing him, deciding what to do as he stares at me with those big brown puppy dog eyes that practically beg me for forgiveness. He puts his hands in his pockets and stays where he is, respecting my distance.

"Baby, the only reason I got aggressive the last times I texted you as him was because I was desperate. I just knew Jared was going to try to pull some shit and I was doing anything I could think of to get you home and out of that possible threatening situation. This... This is why I didn't want to have that conversation you kept trying to bring up about the biker boy. Because I had plans all along to tell you and I wanted to wait for the right moment. But I guess that was all stupid and selfish of me. My ego got in the way. My fucking ego didn't even think of how violated you may feel. Baby, please forgive me."

He grabs me by the ass, pulling me completely into him. I rest my hands flat on his chest and stare up into his eyes.

This man has been my best friend forever and has now loved me so well as a girlfriend... Yes, he has his dumb moments and slip ups, but he really does care about me. And it is hot to think he wanted me so bad he tried to make me fall for him twice. The shock begins to wear off, settling more into a mixture of bratty anger and flattery.

"Answer me this." He nods his chin ever so slightly, awaiting my question. "Did you touch yourself while watching me get off to you?"

His eyes bulge and his neck jerks back the slightest amount. I can practically see the wheels turning in overdrive as he debates what to say.

He clasps his hands together on top of his head and rests them there, his biceps popping against his tight black shirt, and his v-cut clearly peeking above his grey sweatpants. This time, he's the one that takes a few steps back to create some distance.

"Yes."

"How many times?"

"I masturbated until you were done."

"How many times did you come?"

"Why does that matter?"

"Because I want to know. I'm the one whose privacy was violated and who was being stalked by their best friend. Shouldn't I get to know the details of what you did that night too as repentance? Or did you watch me the other nights too?"

His chest rises as he exhales out, "I watched you every time after I mistakenly caught you that first time. I set up a trigger to alarm me whenever you hopped onto my page."

Knowing he was timing his schedule to watch me masturbate sent my temperature skyrocketing to feverish levels.

"Answer the question then. How many times did you come when watching me get off to you?"

"Usually three..."

Okay, that's sending me over the edge. Picturing him sitting in his chair, fisting himself, watching me get off while touching myself to some stranger that turned out to be him... Dear God. I'm soaked thinking about it.

"Char, I shouldn't have—"

"Shut up," I sternly say, cutting him off.

"Excuse me?"

"I *said*, shut up."

He's before me in four quick steps, his hard chest now pressed up right against mine. He pulls my hair firmly, jerking my head back and forcing me to look him in the eyes. His lips softly caress mine.

"Listen. I'm sorry, Char," he says breathlessly. "I'm so sorry that I crossed a boundary, but you can't tell me to shut up and expect me not to do anything about it."

He pulls my waist with his other hand, pressing me aggressively into his hardness. "It gets me *so* riled up when you give me attitude. I can't resist touching you when you snap at me," he growls, nipping my nose, and then biting my bottom lip.

I gently unclasp his grip from my hair and press my hands on his chest, guiding him backwards toward his bike. His heavy lidded eyes never leave mine as he pants below my fingertips, desire so thick it's radiating off him. We come to a stop when the bike won't let us move anymore due to the kickstand holding it up at an angle.

I make quick work of untying the drawstrings on his sweatpants.

"Char, what are you-?"

"I'm assuming this whole thing was my surprise. But now that I've got my surprise, I want to give you yours."

My knees spread as I squat down forcing my bodycon dress to roll up above my ass, leaving it hanging out bare.

"Fuck, you don't have any underwear on. And this view, *holy shit*, baby."

I rip down his sweatpants in one move. He's so hard it looks like it's going to bust out of his underwear.

I'm nervous to see it for the first time. I have no idea what to expect.

My fingers clasp onto his underwear and tug them down, revealing him to me fully for the first time. I'm unsure how to do this or how to fit all of him in my mouth, but I'm sure as hell going to give it my best shot.

I think of watermelon to get my mouth to salivate like I read to do online and set my lips on him. His hips buck immediately, almost sending him too deep into my throat too quickly.

Fighting the gag reflux, I move one hand on his shaft to cover the distance I can't get yet while I run my lips and tongue over the rest. My other hand explores adventurously between his abs and balls to see which get him to moan loader.

His breathing increases with small moans of "fuck" escaping in between.

Good, I must be doing this right.

He bends down to ball my hair up and keep it out of the way. Or so I thought until my head motions without intentional movement. I let him guide me, but he's getting too deep. I gag, forcing him out of my mouth.

"I'm sorry. I just can't take you all in," I cough as I wipe the drool dripping down my chin. "You're too big."

Breathing heavy but not saying anything, he grabs my left hand and pinches me hard in the soft part between my thumb and index finger. He holds it for ten seconds and then drops it.

"Try now," he pants as he stares at me through his lower lashes, licking his bottom lip in anticipation.

His eyes are glazed over and full of nothing but want and need for me. It makes me feel invincible. He fists my hair again but waits patiently for me to be ready to take him in. I open my mouth, signaling I'm good to go as he guides me deeper and deeper and deeper. Slowly moving me fully down his shaft until it goes past the back of my throat.

Holy shit. My gag reflex is completely gone. I have no idea how he did that, but I'm not going to worry about it now.

He moans with each thrust, increasing his speed and the strength with which he grips my hair.

"Fuck, babe, I'm so close," he breathes, his thrusts quickening as he holds me still.

Soon after he releases a loud grunt, signaling climax, his fingers tense and release multiple times in my hair. My eyes water but I let the pulsating pressure sit in my mouth as I choke what I can down my throat, the rest falling out the sides of my mouth.

Releasing my hair, he leans back on his bike to catch his breath. I swallow and wipe the residual cum off, savoring the salty taste and look up at him through my eyelashes, admiring the perfection of his body. His abs deeply flex with each breath. Small beads of sweat form and drip down his skin and the muscles in his arms are still fully tense.

"How was it?" I ask sheepishly, not bothering to move my dress down as I stand up, letting my ass hang out and the dress rest at my waist.

"That was the best blowjob I've ever fucking had. I swear to God. I do not know how you knew how to do that so well, but I'm one fucking lucky guy."

"Good," I say proudly, kissing him. "By the way, how'd you get me to stop gagging?"

A know-it-all grin appears. "I read once about a nerve tied to your gag reflex in your hand at that spot. If you hold it down for five to ten seconds, it's supposed to relieve you of the sensation. Figured it was worth a shot." He shrugs and bounces his eyebrows.

"Glad to know you use your smarts for fun and not just to spy on and stalk people."

He chuckles, slowly eyeing me up and down, his expression turning feral. I suddenly become fully aware of my body, the cold breeze rushing against my exposed skin accentuating the goosebumps already present from the heat of his stare.

He skirts off his pants and underwear from his ankles without breaking eye contact.

"Remember the safe word?" he breathes.

"Barn," I whisper.

"Good."

He throws me against the bike, not letting me rest one second before he picks me up and flips me over, smacking my bare ass and bending me over the seat. His strong grip glides along my thighs, adjusting my right leg onto the rear peg and my left leg on the front foot peg. Without warning he slams all three of his fingers inside of me, holding me down with his other hand on my lower back to keep me still.

"Fuck, you're so fucking wet for me, Char."

"Yes," I moan, the pleasure instantly building.

"What do you want, Char? What do you want me to do to you?"

I try to string words together, but my mind is glitching out from the pleasure. "I want you to go all the way," I manage to get out in between moans as my hips writhe on his fingers and palm.

His fingers stop, creating a silence only broken by our heavy breaths.

"Are you sure?"

"Yes. Please. I'm begging you. Please. I want to feel what it's like and I want my first time to be with you. Please, Ben. Give me this."

"*Fuck*. Ok, baby."

His one hand grips my hip while the other guides him into me. I practically scream from pleasure, forgetting we aren't in a bubble and people might be able to hear me. I stare down at my hands death gripping the leather seat and focus on the sensation of our bodies intertwining as he slowly gets deeper, letting me adjust to his girth and length inch by inch.

He begins to pull out and thrust back in again but instead of pleasure a sharp pain zaps through me, making me tear up and almost vomit.

"Ow!" I yelp.

He quickly pulls out and rushes to the other side of the bike, squatting down so he's at my level.

"Are you okay? I'm so sorry if I was too rough too quickly." Concern covers his face as he brushes my hair out of the way and delicately cups my cheeks, caressing his thumbs over them gently.

"I...I don't know. It felt amazing until that quick shot of pain." I don't move, afraid if I do the pain will come back.

"That must've been your hymen. You just lost your virginity, baby. It can hurt sometimes for women on their first time, but that should be all the pain you feel." He pauses, looking conflicted. "Do you want to stop? We can just talk and relax instead."

"No," I state defiantly.

I am *not* going to stop. I've wanted this for a while now. Plus, I don't want to let him down and ruin our first time together. He said it shouldn't hurt anymore so I should be good. I'm doing this.

"Are you sure, baby?"

"Yes. Get back in me, *now*," I order him reassuringly.

He kisses me and bites my bottom lip. "If it hurts again tell me and we'll stop, okay?"

I nod, pushing my knees apart and looking down, signaling I'm ready for round two of the ride.

He walks back behind me, caressing my skin for a moment before gently and slowly putting himself back inside me.

Good, God.

The pleasure's better than the first time. A soft whimpered moan escapes my lips.

"Are you okay? How's it feel?"

"So, so, so good. Don't stop," I plead.

"Good," he says gruffly, picking up the pace.

My fingers dig into the leather to hold on because each thrust threatens to push me off the seat. My body urges to arch back but my position on the bike stops it. The pleasure becomes unbearable, devouring me completely. It's too much. It's building and building to the point where I know I'm going to die from this ecstasy.

A brief moment of clarity surfaces. "I want you to finish inside me."

"What?"

His thrusts become erratic, faster then slower, then faster again. His grunts are deep and spur me on more, creating a beautiful duet with my higher pitched moans. Sweat drips all over my backside, cooling my hot skin and making it easier for us to glide into each other.

"I want you to come inside me. Please, Ben."

"Fuck, babe. God, I want to so bad, but I want us to be safe. I shouldn't. God, as much as I want to, I shouldn't," he pants.

His nails grip into my sides even harder as he fights the desire I could hear in his response.

"I've been on birth control for years. It's safe," I breathily moan, desperate for him to give me everything.

Seconds later, his loud moans match his throbbing finish inside me as he easily gives in to my request. His hand settles on mine and becomes still as he rests his forehead on my back, still inside me and panting. I revel in the closeness of how he's holding me and what we've just done.

"I've never come inside a girl before," he whispers onto my back and kisses where he's laying. "That was the most amazing feeling ever. You're so amazing, baby. Damn."

I rest my chin on my hands and smile. Happiness radiates through me in knowing we shared this first milestone together.

"Wait, you didn't finish," he says, a realization that must've just occurred to him.

"No, but that's okay," I say, still vibing off the high and totally content.

"Nope. Unacceptable."

A cool breeze chills my skin now that his warmth's gone, giving me goosebumps. I hoist myself down off the bike and turn around to him fully naked and putting on his helmet.

"What are you doing?"

He picks me up and wraps my legs around him, which quickly begin sliding down his sweat slicked skin.

"Put your elbows on the seat," he commands under the helmet as he lifts me over the bike seat once more. I obey, extremely curious as to what he has planned.

"Ben. What are you *doing*?"

His hand barely fits around himself as he grabs it, guiding into me again. As soon as he breaks through, I buck from pleasure, now understanding why I needed my elbows down. Leaning on one elbow for leverage, I reach to lift his tinted visor so I can see his eyes, but he knocks my hand away.

"I'm keeping the vizor down. I've watched you, remember? I know you like to watch yourself. You like to admire and study how your body reacts to the adrenaline and ecstasy coursing through you. To enjoy how powerful you are when you're vulnerable and exposed. You've seen how you make you feel. Now I want you to see the beautiful mess I make of you."

He thrusts hard inside to the hilt. I moan loudly, skipping the build-up and already tense in my core, preparing for a release.

"Keep your eyes open and watch yourself, baby," he grunts in between each thrust.

I open my eyes and stare into the tinted visor, obeying him.

"This is what I saw when I watched you touch yourself. This is how fucking beautiful you are. Now watch how good I make you feel, baby. Watch how much better your body likes my dick than your fingers, baby."

My heavy-lidded eyes are frosted over in a glazed, intense way. There's a remnant of the aftereffects of what I saw when I looked in the mirror at myself but nothing like this. My lips purse in between breaths and the moans make my eyebrows furrow together in pleasure. My cheeks and neck are completely splotched red, and there's sweat sticking my hair to the edges of my face.

"I want you to finish for me, Char. Come for your man, baby."

"Yes, sir," I whimper, loving the way he's commanding me through everything.

"Sir? Fuck." He rams into me harder.

I'm screaming from the pleasure filling my entire body, spreading into each limb all the way to my toes and fingertips.

I'm on the edge. Tingles set in, the sensitivity almost too much as he pinches my nipples.

I'm close.

So close.

"Don't stop. Don't stop," I squeal, trembling all over as my head rocks back.

"Don't look away, baby. You have yet to see the most beautiful part."

With what little control I have left of my body, I grab hold of him and move myself up so I can see me again.

One more thrust.

"Baby."

Another.

"I'm almost there," I whimper in a high-pitched moan, my muscles so tense I can barely move.

One last hard stroke causes me to burst.

His moans match mine as he comes too, our hips melding together, grinding frantically as we enjoy the last vibrations of the ecstasy.

He takes his helmet off and hangs it on the handlebar of the bike. His hair and face are slicked with sweat, but instead of seeing pure happiness, his expression resembles something like painful satisfaction.

"What's wrong?" I caress his cheek with my thumb, worrying I did something wrong.

He lifts me up, keeping himself inside me and holds me close. We're at eye-level with my arms wrapped around his shoulders and my back arched, giving him a place to rest his arms.

"I love you, Charlotte Windsor," he declares, staring deep into my eyes.

Lightning radiates from my stomach into my chest at the words, making me feel light as air. I'm so unbelievably happy. So unbelievably happy he feels the same way I've been feeling toward him this whole time.

"I love you too, Ben." I kiss him hard and nip his nose like he always does to me. But when I pull back, it's to watery eyes and trembling lips.

"Why are you upset? What's wrong, babe?" I say, running my fingers through his hair and down his cheek.

"I just—I was afraid I'd scare you off by telling you how I truly felt so soon. But I couldn't hold it in any longer. I needed you to know that I love you so much and so deeply that I am physically in pain when you're not around. I know we only got together like a week ago but the thought of losing you is unbearable. I don't know how I'd get through it. I can't lose you, baby. Ever."

I gently wipe away the tear that falls and kiss him, ever so softly.

"Well, you don't have to worry about that because I love you, Ben. I love you so much that I don't even know how to feel all the love I hold for you. Like, the happiness that you give me is indescribable. And you love me so well, Ben. I'm so lucky. I can't believe this all has happened, and I get to be with you. I can't believe you're mine."

He parts my mouth with his tongue, kissing me with immense care to show the words he's unable to express. The kisses continue until he sets me down on a nearby blanket behind his motorcycle. This time, he doesn't rush making love to me, pressing his lips on every inch of my skin with whispers of "I love you" along the way.

We lay there completely naked in each other's arms after we finish while he strokes his fingers through my hair and down my back, holding me so tightly it's like he's still scared I'm going to run away.

A chill breeze blows through the woods, sending shivers down my spine, making me remember we're still naked and out in the open.

"Should we get dressed? I'm suddenly aware of how naked we are and what we've been doing practically in public."

He kisses my forehead mid-chuckle. "Don't worry. I've been coming out here for the last year and have never seen anyone. I even checked the land records which state its public property, so I don't think anyone else knows about this place."

"Oh. Well either way, I'm starting to get cold now that our sweat is drying. I probably need to put something on, even though I don't want to so I can keep laying here naked with you."

I stand and brush myself off before beginning to walk over to my dress that's on the ground by his rear tire.

"Actually, hold up."

He comes up next to me and pulls out my gear and helmet out of the two backpacks on the ground.

"But I drove my car..."

"We can pick it up tomorrow. I want to ride with you tonight. I want to feel you holding onto me as we ride the whole entire night if you're up for it. I'm just so happy. I don't want it to end."

"That sounds amazing, but do you think my car will be alright here overnight?"

"Yeah, for sure. Like I said, it's public property and there's no posted signs so they technically can't do anything about it by law."

"Then hell yeah, baby. I'm in. Let's do it."

His smile's electric, stirring those butterflies in my soul to new heights. Shoving my dress into one of the backpacks, I grab my gear from him and start the jumping motion to get the tight leather pants over my now extremely sticky skin.

"I swear I'm going to buy different ones. Especially if we stop for rendezvous more often. This is too much work to get pants on," I pant, laughing.

"As much as I would love for you to ride with no pants on tonight and lay your claim on my seat, everyone else would be able to see far too much of you, I fear."

"And it'd be unsafe?"

"Yeah, that too," he chuckles.

After what seems like an eternity, I manage to pull the rest of my gear on. He reminds me of the signals for the ride, lifts me onto the bike and gets on in front of me. He sweetly gives me a helmet kiss with his helmet before helping me clip the straps together.

The familiar vibration in the seat and roar of the engine tremble through me as soon as it comes to life. I could stay here forever with him and forget the world, I swear.

"Wait, how are we getting back to the road? I had to climb through thickets to get in here," I yell loudly over the engine.

"I made a trail over there for my bike that leads to the road," he yells back, pointing to our left.

"You couldn't have told me that when I parked so I didn't have to trek through the wilderness when I got here?"

His only response is a hard laugh that makes his shoulders shake. I smack the top of his helmet in retaliation. I'll get him later for that.

He kicks up the kickstand with his foot and we're off.

We ride and ride until the stars shine brightly and the cars on the road are few and far between. After a few hours, we stop to get gas and decide it's time to head home, shower and go to bed. Even though I have something else in mind besides sleeping as I'm sure he does too.

We hit the last intersection in town before his road, going through the green light. But out of nowhere, my body is jerked forward and the sound of scraping and loud plastic on the pavement screams in my ears before everything goes silent.

Beeps mixing with my mother's voice echo in the distance. The panic in her tone is broken in between what sounds like sobs.

What the hell? Where am I?

With great effort, I pry open my eyes, triggering pain that shoots through my eyelids and temples.

"Ah." I inhale sharply and grit my teeth. The room's bright and blurry, but there's an outline of my mother standing next to me.

"Oh, Charlotte, thank God. Thank God," she sobs, kissing my hand and pressing it to her wet cheek.

"What's going on?" I slur in a daze.

"You...You were in an accident."

Someone places a cool rag over my eyes, bringing comfort and the stinging down.

"An accident?" I reply in confusion. What the hell is she talking about?

She doesn't answer me, leaving a stark silence that my short painful breaths barely break through. After a few minutes, she removes the rag, bringing in a clearer picture. Her face is swollen from crying and furrowed brows and a painful smile greet me.

"Thanks. My eyesight was blurry for some reason, but I can see a little better now."

"Yes, they said that would happen. They put some antibiotic gel on your eyes to help with the swelling and to prevent infection."

"What happened?" I move to sit up and regret it immediately as sharp stabs riddle through my side and crack into the side of my skull.

"D-Don't move, Charlotte. Stay still."

"Why? Why am I in so much pain?" I rest back, tilting my head on the pillow to face her.

"Well, you have a couple of broken ribs, and some of the plastic vizor from the helmet was lodged into the skin on your face. Your left leg is also broken, but it's not completely shattered. Otherwise, there's nothing life-threatening, thank God."

My reality sinks in, triggering a wave of panic.

"Where's Ben?" I ask, full of dread.

She looks down and bites the inside of her cheek as a tear falls, wetting her skin further.

"Mom, where is he?" I shout before yielding to the severe ache in my rib.

With my arm bracing my side, I ask again, albeit quieter. "Please tell me he's okay. Mom. Please. Please..." Tears flow down my cheeks, mounting the severe pain in my head and eyes from the tension. A weight settles on my chest and dread wraps its cold embrace around me, taking what little air I can get away.

He has to be okay. I can't live without him. I need him. This can't be the end of our story. It's just beginning. There's so much love that hasn't been shown or experienced yet. I need him to be okay.

My silent prayers repeat, begging God to spare him from whatever I'm about to hear.

"He's alive..." she whispers quietly, still holding my hand.

"Oh, thank God," I cry harder. "Thank you, God."

My chest aches from all the pain and the agony of our situation, but a small amount of the weight lifts knowing he's alive.

"But...he's in an induced coma. It was necessary to prevent further brain damage. They were able to stop the internal bleeding but he's going to have a long road to recovery, Charlotte."

"I don't understand. How is he in such bad shape and I'm not? How did this happen? No one was even on the road! I need to see him. Take me to him. Right now."

I will my body to move, flinging the covers off and ignoring the splint on my leg and the pain that's so blinding it's about to make me pass out.

"Charlotte, you need to stay in bed! Please lay back down."

"Tell me what happened!" I yell at her, my ears now ringing loudly.

She sighs, pinching the bridge of her nose. "Only if you lay back and calm down."

Begrudgingly, I listen. I hiss through my teeth as I extend back to the pillow, keeping my splint leg bent over the edge in defiance.

"When you were found, he was covering you. They believe he pulled you up toward him in the instant before impact and shielded you by wrapping himself around you."

"Shielded me from what!" My ribs, back and chest burn from my cries, but I don't know what else to do with this mental and physical anguish, but scream. This can't be real.

"A car ran a red light and hit you."

"What the fuck? There was barely anyone on the road. Where did they even come from? I swear, I'm going to make that person pay. Did they catch them? Are they in custody? I can't believe someone would be that ignorant." I pause for a moment, trying to make sense of the situation we're in and calm down before I start hyperventilating. "Take me to Ben, mom. I need to see him," I plead.

"You *cannot* move yet. I'm sorry, but you're going to have to wait. You have to focus on *your* healing right now."

"Absolutely not," I declare as the tears streaming down my cheeks continue down my neck. I can't stand this feeling of him not being here with me. This feeling of him being in so much pain and not being able to be at his side. It's torture. Like a part of my soul is dying and there's nothing I can do to help.

"Then have someone roll me in there! I don't fucking care how you do it! Let me see him!" I'm making a scene, but I don't care. They're going to let me see him one way or another.

"Charlotte, listen to me," her voice shakes as she pleads for me to hear her out.

"What!" I snap, barely paying attention to her as I try to come up with a way to get to him.

"Your father is... missing."

"Huh? What do you mean missing?" I stop what I'm doing and look at her in confusion before glancing around the room and see that he's not here.

Rubbing her wrists together in anxiousness, she takes a deep breath and stares at the ceiling.

"He hasn't been seen since yesterday evening. We were about to go to dinner when he just up and left without saying anything. I was in the bathroom and heard the car start up but when I called him to ask him what he was doing he ignored it. I haven't been able to get ahold of him since nor find him anywhere. The police are currently out searching for him."

"Why?" I ask not wanting to hear the answer even though deep-down my gut already knows the truth.

"Charlotte, your father is the person who hit you."

The final dagger in the chest hits its mark, twisting and turning until it seems to puncture my lungs.

I can't breathe.

I can't breathe.

I grasp my chest, unable to get air in as a high-pitched noise fills my ears until it turns to crackles. The room spins as my mother's worried cries of my name become distant, the world growing ever quieter as everything goes black. The only thing able to be seen in the dark is Ben's beautiful brown eyes looking at me from the depths of my own mind and the only thing I can feel is the thinly mended pieces of my heart finally shattering, turning me numb and cold.

My muscles feel weighed down and groggy, like I just ran a million miles with no break and somehow survived. A heaviness pulls my breath down with it, only allowing shorter inhales and making me feel lightheaded.

"She's not due for another dose of morphine for six hours. I'm sorry, but we can't give her anymore," I hear a mystery woman state.

Oh, a nurse. That's right...

My nightmare isn't a dream; it's my new reality.

With glazed over eyes, I search around the room for my mother. She's biting her thumbnail, full of nervous energy talking to someone in a police uniform.

"Mom." I slur out trying to get her attention.

My body feels drunk, and my lips aren't moving right. This morphine stuff sucks.

"Mom." I try again as loud as I can even though it still sounds almost like a whisper.

This time she hears me and turns around with tears dripping steadily down her cheeks as she continues to bite her thumbnail.

"Just relax, sweetie." She strolls over and caringly strokes my arm, but her touch does nothing except repulse me.

As much as I can, I inch my arm away from her. She takes the hint and steps back.

"Take me to Ben." I groggily demand, finally becoming more aware as I awaken.

"Honey, no. You can see him when you're better. You can't move and risk injuring yourself further. I won't allow it."

I narrow my gaze, the skin scrunching as much as it possibly can. Not asking for permission again, I inhale to brace my ribs as well as wrap my arm around my side for good measure and sit up. My legs slide off the side of the bed so I'm finally sitting up. Short huffs are the only breaths able to escape as the pain restricts my chest cavity from fully inhaling.

"Charlotte Windsor, get back in bed."

I evilly glare at her once more and grab my IV cord. Lifting my arm up to expose the needle in my skin more, I get closer to it and pause right atop my skin.

"I'm seeing Ben, whether you allow it or not. So, either you help me, or I'm ripping out this fucking IV cord myself and crawling to find him. If you care about me at all, I'd like to think you wouldn't want me risking a bleed out. So, find me a *fucking* wheelchair and let's go or else." Each word is painful to get out as my muscles awaken further to restrict more from the anger tensing them up, but I push through.

Her eyebrows fold inward and her bottom lip quivers. It does nothing to me. I don't care how she feels right now. All I care about is if she's going to help me or not.

She gives a quick nod and disappears into the hallway. Soon after she arrives back in the room with a wheelchair. Her expression's troubled, but she doesn't say anything. Thank God, because I can't handle hearing her stark voice grate on my ears anymore.

"Put it right next to the bed and lift the sheet up so it acts as a hammock for me to sit into it."

"Char-" She stops her sentence at the hard expression on my face. My nostrils flare and I stare her down, daring her to continue what she was about to say.

Her head shakes in disapproval as she ties the blanket to the other side of my hospital bed and drapes it over the wheelchair. I scoot over onto it.

"Pull it taught."

Once pulled tight, I unevenly glide on it and land hard into the seat of the wheelchair. A hard, sharp sting cuts through my torso from the jolt to my rib and leg. The vomit balls up in my throat but I swallow it down, refusing to let anything else delay me from getting to Ben.

"Take me to him."

She wheels me out of the room to a few rooms over. Tears well up when she sets me in front of his door. I'm not sure if it's from relief that I'll get to see him or fear of seeing him in the state he's in. She knocks softly. Hesitantly. Like if she knocks too hard the door may explode.

Joans puffy face peeks around the now ajar door.

Now I see the real reason mom didn't want to come here.

As if I'm invisible, Joan stares her down like she's the son of Satan. It's not until I attempt to lean over to see past her to catch a glimpse of Ben and wince in pain that she notices me. Her eyes widen, mouth parting slightly, before opening the door enough to get out and closing it shut behind her.

"Charlotte." Her voice trembles as she bends down and gingerly wraps her arms around my neck.

She kisses the top of my scalp and stands back up, now directly in front of my mother.

"I'll take her to see Benjamin. *You* are not welcome to come in. I'll bring her back to her room when she's done visiting."

The angry tension crackles so much between them that if it was possible to light a match right now, I'm sure the air would burst into flames.

"I swear, I didn't have anything to do with this." Her voice quakes but she tries to hide it.

"We'll see about that," Joan says as she approaches my mom. I'm unable to turn to see what's happening behind me but I can hear their quick inhales.

Finally, I see Joan open the door enough to call Koa to hold open the door for us to go in. His face is less puffy than hers, but no less exhausted. His teary-eyed gaze watches me as she rolls me and my IV stand into the room. I don't bother looking back at my mom to see where she goes or what she's doing. I'm not sure if she had anything to do with this or not, but she's tied to my father and right now that's enough for me to want to avoid her.

Small steady beeps are the metronome that play as I finally get my first glimpse of my sweet, sweet man. Tears cloud my vision as I poorly try to control my short, sharp inhales. Pain racks my lungs and the muscles in my chest and face from holding back the cries and screams I want to let out from seeing his condition.

His head is wrapped to where you can only see his eyes, and his mouth has an intubation tube stuck out of it for breathing. His left leg is casted, and his body's encased in a metal brace for limited mobility, while the skin that is left showing on his arms is bruised black and blue with cuts all over.

Joan rolls me right up to his side so I can grab his one free hand that's almost completely taped up. It only allows a small part of skin-to-skin contact with his fingers, but it's exactly what I need. They're chilly, like he's been out working and cutting wood in the winter without gloves all day again.

The shakes overtake me as I lose control, crying to the point of near hyperventilation as high pitched squeals exit my trembling body. I bring his hand to my lips and hold it there, gently kissing what skin I can touch over and over again as I try to bring any sort of comfort I can to him and myself. Unfortunately, it does nothing to dissuade the anguish destroying my soul.

Is he going to be ok? Will he get through this? What am I going to do if he doesn't?

A comforting touch rests on my shoulder.

"He's going to be ok," Koa says reassuringly. "He's going to be ok." His voice cracks this time at the end, but his weak promise is the only thing I can cling to. It's the only thing keeping me out of the dark and falling into the pit of agony I'm dangling over.

A hand rests on my other shoulder.

"They said-," Joans voice breaks in between tears. "They said he was covered in blood but conscious when they found him. You were wrapped in his arms and all he kept saying was your name. They believe he was in shock. Once the ambulance arrived, they had to pry you out of his arms. H-He refused to let you go." Her soft sobs continue as mine finally settle down, my jaw and teeth in pain from crying so hard.

"But how is he this bad? He was wearing his gear?" I question, unconvinced this is real.

"They believe the force of the hit and how many times he tumbled on the gravel is why his gear was so destroyed. But he would have been so much worse if he hadn't had any on."

I nod, still unsatisfied with her answer.

"How long will he be like this?" I whisper.

"They took him straight to surgery when he arrived to stabilize his spine and do what they could to stop the internal bleeding. We're hoping he'll be able to come out of the coma in a couple days." She sniffles and kisses me on the top of my head again. "We're so grateful you're ok. So, so grateful."

I don't know how they can be happy I'm ok. I carry the blood of someone who tried to destroy their family. Maybe they haven't realized that part of the truth yet...

"Can you wheel me parallel to his bed so I can hold his hand and talk to you both at the same time?"

"Sure, honey."

"Thanks."

Once adjusted, I cling to his hand for strength.

"How can you not hate me? My father did this to your son. Did *this* to your family." My lips tremble as I force myself to hold it together and pray they don't kick me out of the room.

Koa squats down, resting his forearms on his thighs and pushes his neck forward.

"*None* of this is your fault, honey. What your father did..." He clutches his chin out of frustration and shakes his head. "What your father did has nothing to do with you. He hit you the same time he hit our son." He grabs my free hand and squeezes it. "We love you like our own, Charlotte. And we know how much our son loves you. You're a part of this family now and you'll always be welcome here. We will help you with whatever you need because we know you love our son as much as we do."

Gratitude and love push out the darkness just a tiny bit more, bringing solid ground beneath my toes.

"I do love your son. So, so much. I-I don't know what I'm going to do if he doesn't make it through this," I sniffle, as tears start streaming down my face again.

"He's going to get through this. We all are. I promise." His father's strength is giving me hope in a place where I'm not sure I'm allowed to have any. "We're going to leave you alone with him for a minute while we grab us something to eat. Would you like us to request a twin-sharing room?"

"You mean, you'll allow me to get care in the same room as him?"

"We'd like to keep an eye on you just as much as him. It'll be easier for us to do that with you in here. Plus, we believe it'll help with not only Ben's recovery, but yours as well."

"I can't tell you how much this means to me... but I'm not sure my mother will allow it."

"Oh, she will," Joan says, sternly.

"Can we request the move tonight?"

"Sure, honey. We'll go request it now and see what paperwork we need to fill out as well as what permissions we need from your mother."

Every time she mentions my mother, her skin scrunches like she just ate sour candy. I can resonate with her resentment. Even though my mother wasn't in the car with my father, how do I know for sure she didn't have anything to do with this? She has no backbone, so who knows if she knew the plan and didn't say anything? At this point I don't know how to start that conversation or if I ever want to take a chance at forgiveness even if she didn't do anything wrong.

"Thank you," I say, as Koa stands up and places me so I'm facing Ben again.

Then he walks out with Joan following behind him out of the room.

My voice quakes with each word but in case there's any chance he can hear me, I speak, because I have to get this out.

"Baby, I'm so, so sorry. I-I'm so sorry. Why did you risk your life for mine? Why couldn't you have protected yourself? I need you too much for this, baby. I need you to be okay. Promise you'll stay here with me, Ben. Promise me."

His fingers don't move, and there's no response. I shouldn't have hoped for anything, but I had to try. A flash of anger, like lightning striking a tree makes me fist his blanket. I lay my forehead on his hand and over the IV needle that's taped into it.

"I'm going to find my father, Ben. I don't know what I'm going to do when I find him, but I swear I'm going to find some way to make him pay for this."

I sit up too fast and hiss in pain. Did his finger just slightly squeeze mine?

"Ben? Can you hear me?"

There's no response. Maybe I'm just wanting him to show me any sign he can hear me, and the desperation made me hallucinate.

"I love you, baby. I'm not leaving you, so you better not leave me. You got that? This journey is going to be hard and long, but I'll wait for you forever. It doesn't matter what comes next, I'm going to help you through this and I'm going to make my father pay," I cry out softly.

And just like that... I can swear his finger twitches again as if he can hear my promises to him. I give him one more kiss on his hand and then rest my head down on the bed by his arm to fall asleep.

Stay tuned for the sequel

"Beyond the Helmet" Coming in

2026

REVIEWS AND ACKNOWLEDGEMENTS

Independent authors survive on reviews and the interactions with their community. If you feel so inclined, please review my book and share some posts on social media. I wouldn't be able to do this without all of your support and just know I deeply appreciate every single one of you.

To my husband: Thank you for being my emotional support human, allowing me to vent my frustrations, cry my stress and to hold me whenever I need it (and the pups too). Your encouragement and resilience keep me going and I'm forever grateful for your support and chill nature to remind me that life doesn't always have to be work. This journey wouldn't be as bearable without you.

To the internets precious YG Ressless: I never expected a simple DM request for collaboration would turn into such a fun friendship (and turn you into the Fabio of my biker romance novels). Your constant positivity, goofiness and lighthearted spirit, especially after everything you've been through, are amazing and I think your fans all can agree, we're glad to have your protective big brother energy watching over us. And lastly, thank you for allowing me to drag you into every idea and single project I come up with. I'm so excited for our future collaboration goals and to see where you go. Proud of you, always.

Roaming.Gambit: How crazy that I started following you at 600 followers and now you're in the multi-thousands. I'm so grateful you DM'd when you got scared from seeing the creepy casper head found in the basement on my story. It started a trust of communications that slowly turned you into my techy bowl of hidden horcruxes and the internet's Dark Daddy. My yapping ass appreciates the continued patience you give me when stressing or pitching my five million ideas to you. Plus, you basically were the only reason my website got up and running. I can't express my gratitude enough for that and allowing my sneak peek to launch on your own website. Your talent and written word is unique to your voice, never change your impeccable use of prose to say things without saying them directly. I'm excited for your future and I'll always be here cheering you on. (P.S. my books better be the first in your dream endeavor.)

Yamacho.r6: I will never forget the first live of yours I joined, because you were the first person who saw my author name and got so excited that I wrote romance novels and asked questions. Your excitement got me excited and encouraged me to continue on this journey. Plus, barely knowing me and allowing me to spam you with spongebob memes and review biker sex scenes to ensure their accuracy? You're the G.O.A.T. I love seeing all the hard work you're putting into your social media and am stoked that you have your new bike to ride. Keep going because your hard work will pay off.

To my reader community: I never imagined I'd have readers excited about my books and the support you've shown me is unreal. To all the encouragements, interactions, reviews and purchases, just know I care about each and every one of you, and I couldn't do this without you all.

Printed in Dunstable, United Kingdom

71363613R00245